"Just a d

Then Wyatt was taking her into his muscular arms, and she had to bite her lip to keep from moaning at the sudden, chaotic rush of emotion. It was such a consuming, overwhelming sensation, being held by a man again, and her breath caught with a sharp, audible gasp as he pulled her against the hardness and heat of his muscular body.

Trying to remember how to breathe, she placed her hands on his broad shoulders, the soft cotton of his shirt warm beneath her palms, and took a quick glance up at his face to find him watching her, his expression fierce. . .intense, and yet, somehow impossibly gentle. "I'm dizzy," she whispered.

"It's okay. I've got you," he told her, his beautiful mouth shaping the words, making them sound like something seductive and wicked.

Books by Rhyannon Byrd

Harlequin Nocturne

**Last Wolf Standing* #35
**Last Wolf Hunting* #38
**Last Wolf Watching* #39
**Dark Wolf Rising* #152
  Darkest Desire of the Vampire #161
"Wicked in Moonlight"
**Dark Wolf Running* #173

Harlequin HQN

Edge of Hunger
Edge of Danger
Edge of Desire
Touch of Seduction
Touch of Surrender
Touch of Temptation
Rush of Darkness
Rush of Pleasure
Deadly Is the Kiss

**Primal Instinct
**Bloodrunners

To browse a current listing of all Rhyannon's titles, please visit www.Harlequin.com

---

RHYANNON BYRD

is an avid longtime fan of romance and the author of more than twenty paranormal and erotic titles. She has been nominated for three *RT Book Reviews* Reviewers' Choice Awards, including best Shapeshifter Romance, and her books have been translated into nine languages. After having spent years enjoying the glorious sunshine of the American South and Southwest, Rhyannon now lives in the beautiful but often chilly county of Warwickshire in England with her husband and family. For more information on Rhyannon's books and the latest news, you can visit her website at www.rhyannonbyrd.com or find her on Facebook.

DARK WOLF
RUNNING

—

RHYANNON BYRD

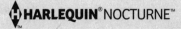

This one is for the lovely Debbie Hopkins Smart.
It's not the first book I've dedicated to you, Debs,
and it won't be the last, because there simply aren't
enough ways to say thanks for everything that you do.
You are and always will be made of awesome!!!

Recycling programs
for this product may
not exist in your area.

ISBN-13: 978-0-373-88583-1

DARK WOLF RUNNING

Copyright © 2013 by Tabitha Bird

Printed in U.S.A.

Dear Reader,

Dark Wolf Running is the fifth book in my Bloodrunners series, and I can't even begin to tell you how excited I am to be writing about this wild, wonderful world of half-breeds once again!

Sometimes going into a book, you just know the two main characters are going to make their journey anything but easy...and yet, at the same time, you know that in the end all the grief they put you through is going to be more than worth it. That's exactly how I felt with Wyatt and Elise. They've been through so much, each burdened with a painful past that was beyond their control. But once fate throws them together, they find that there's nothing they can't survive, so long as they have each other. Their darkly seductive love story is one that I hope will strike deeply at your emotions and tug at your heart, compelling you to root for them to the very end.

Up next is the mysterious Eli. . .and I can't wait to share his story with you. This bad boy Lycan mercenary might think he's seen and faced it all—but nothing in his vast experience will have prepared him for the woman who's about to show him what it truly means to fight for what you believe in...and for what you *can't* live without.

ing you all much love and happiness,

THE BLOODRUNNERS' LAW

When offspring are born of a union between human and Lycan, the resulting creations may gain acceptance within their rightful pack only by the act of Bloodrunning: the hunting and extermination of rogue Lycans who have taken a desire for human flesh. Thus they prove not only their strength, but also their willingness to kill for those they will swear to protect to the death.

The League of Elders will predetermine the Bloodrunners' required number of kills.

Once said number of kills are efficiently accomplished, only then may the Bloodrunner assume a place among their kin, complete with full rights and privileges.

THE DARK WOLF

A Dark Wolf bloodline is the purest of the Lycan race.

They are the most primal and powerful of their kind. Visceral. Predatory.

Creatures of instinct and hunger.

They are the potential for all things good and evil.

And they will forever act with furious vengeance to protect the ones they love.

Prologue

With his sharp gaze locked on the most magnificent female he'd ever set eyes on, Wyatt Pallaton did his best to choke back the deep, aggressive growl rumbling up from his chest—and for the most part, he succeeded. But then, *most* was a relative term. Several of the nearby guests glanced his way at the stifled scrape of sound, their eyes narrowed with censure, warning him not to be rude. As if he didn't already grasp the situation. He knew damn good and well that a wedding was generally considered a "no growling" affair. Even ones where the majority of those attending were a far cry from human.

Still, he didn't want to make a scene. Sending the disgruntled werewolves, or Lycans, as they preferred to be called, a tight smile, he waited until they'd turned back around in their seats before allowing his own irritation to show.

Mindful of the occasion, Wyatt was doing his best to keep a tight rein on himself—but Christ, it wasn't easy. Predatory hunger, visceral and thick and savage, poured through his veins like liquid fire, burning him from the inside out. His body was tense, muscles so rigid and tight he felt like a bloody volcano on the verge of eruption. Just another ground-shaking, life-altering, cataclysmic event in the making, putting the tension on fate's bow-string until it was ready to snap. *Twang.* Hell, it wasn't as if he and his fellow Runners hadn't had enough of those "what did I do to piss off the gods?" events lobbed in their faces recently. And here he was, balancing on the edge of a meltdown. Sweet. He was about to take the "biggest jackass of the year" award. Lucky him.

With his large hands clenched into hard, straining fists in his lap, Wyatt ground his jaw and tried like hell to keep it together. But there was only so much that a man could endure. Based on the pathetic fact that he was shaking apart inside with lust and need and too many damn confusing emotions, he could only assume that he'd finally reached his limit.

After months of biding his time, waiting for the stubborn woman to acknowledge their mutual attraction and come to him, he'd had enough. Not surprising, he supposed, since as a primal, aggressive male, waiting wasn't exactly one of his specialties. Undeniably dominant in nature, the thirty-five-year-old Bloodrunner was accustomed to going after what he wanted with single-minded intensity, not stopping until he had it—but these were unusual circumstances.

And Elise Drake was a far cry from your average female.

Considering the length of time he'd been without a

woman, he'd known tonight wouldn't be easy. He'd tried to stay calm, but the sight of Elise walking down the aisle in her bridesmaid gown, the flowing whisper of silvery-gray silk accentuating the sumptuous perfection of her figure, had damn near done him in. Now, as the sun melted into the horizon and the lavender shades of twilight darkened the sky, revealing an iridescent spattering of stars, he was forced to sit in his chair and pretend that hunger wasn't ripping him into tiny, pathetic chunks, one excruciating piece at a time.

Exhaling a slow, ragged breath, Wyatt forced his hands to relax, flexing his fingers and rubbing his palms into the black fabric of his tuxedo trousers. The monkey suit was strangling his throat, and he couldn't shake the uncomfortable sensation that he really *was* coming out of his skin.

Beside him, his Bloodrunning partner, Carla Reyes, shot him a dark look from the corner of her eye. "Stop fidgeting," she hissed under her breath.

"When is this damn thing going to end?" he grumbled, sounding like a petulant child on the verge of a tantrum. He winced, more than a little disgusted with himself.

"What's your problem tonight?" Carla demanded, arching one slim golden brow in his direction. "I thought you liked weddings."

He grunted in response and tried to force an outer look of calm togetherness. Carla was right, damn it. Unlike most men, Wyatt usually did enjoy these kinds of things. He liked the social aspect of hanging out with his friends and colleagues, the way his parents had often done when he was younger and they'd lived with his mother's family. He liked the food and the beer, the laughter and the dancing.

It was the women, though, that he'd always enjoyed the most. Like a bridesmaid banquet, there were always plenty of single ladies to choose from. He'd never been as arrogant about it as Cian Hennessey, one of his fellow Runners, but he was definitely a man who enjoyed his sexual variety.

Tonight, however, Wyatt had eyes for one woman—and one woman only.

Of course, Elise Drake was hardly just any woman. Fiery and cool, strong and yet at the same time achingly vulnerable, she was a fascinating combination of opposites that had managed to turn his entire world on its head.

"Keep staring at her like that and she's gonna notice," Carla whispered, jabbing her elbow into his arm.

"Maybe I want her to notice," he muttered, appreciating the way the twilight turned the fiery strands of Elise's hair a deep, vibrant red, her dark blue eyes the color of a storm-ravaged sky. He'd chosen his seat specifically because it afforded him a clear view of her place in the wedding party, but he hadn't anticipated how torturous it would be.

"What? Could it actually be true?" Carla gasped, pressing one delicate hand to her bountiful chest. "After months of waiting, you're finally going to get off your ass and do something about her?" She made a soft, feminine snorting sound and rolled her eyes. "Call me cynical, but I'll believe it when I see it."

Shifting in his seat, Wyatt stretched his long legs out as far as he could and tried to relax. "I've been waiting for the right time," he said tightly, wishing he'd kept his mouth shut. Sometimes he wondered why he even bothered talking to Carla. He loved her like family, but like a bratty little sister, the Runner got too big a kick out of pushing his buttons.

"Bullshit," she quietly snickered. "You've been waiting for her to make the first move. But guess what, Pall? She's never going to come panting after you like all the other ladies. Not in this lifetime."

Biting back a foul curse, he groaned instead. "Trust me, I noticed."

"Anyway, it's good to see you conquering your fear," she said brightly, patting his thigh. "I'm proud of you."

Turning his head to the side, Wyatt gave her a hard, steely look. "I'm not afraid of her."

Obviously unconvinced, Carla just smiled. *"Right,"* she drawled, her tone making it clear that she didn't believe him. Problem was…the little brat knew him too well. He'd been Bloodrunning with Carla for almost seven years now, and she no doubt understood him better than anyone. But that didn't mean he had to like it.

"Will you stop trying to pick a fight?" he muttered. "I said I'm not afraid of her and I'm not."

"Hmm. I know you're not afraid of her physically. You just don't know what to do with a woman who doesn't go all starry-eyed every time she gets near you."

Choking back another primitive growl, Wyatt drew a second round of disapproving stares from their neighbors.

"I suppose it could be that she just doesn't like you," Carla offered with a delicate shrug of her bare shoulders, after motioning with her fingers for the frowning guests to turn back around in their seats. "God knows I've seen crazier things happen."

Wyatt slanted her a mean look. "Reyes?"

"Yeah?" she asked, giving him an innocent smile.

"Shut up," he grunted, while she snuffled a quiet burst of laughter under her breath.

They listened to the ceremony for a few moments in blessed silence, until she leaned in close again, asking, "So are you on duty later tonight?"

He sighed, knowing there was no sense in lying to her. "Yeah."

"Took another shift again, huh? Now, why doesn't that surprise me?"

"Just fucking drop it," he warned, pushing his hair back from his face in another restless gesture of impatience.

"Okay, okay." Her voice softened, as if she'd decided to take pity on him. "Hey, maybe you'll even get lucky and she'll actually take you home with her. I'm sure that little scenario would be a hell of a lot more fun than watching her from the woods."

As Carla turned her attention back to the love-dazed couple exchanging vows, Wyatt leaned forward and braced his elbows on his parted knees, thinking he had about as much chance of getting invited home with Elise Drake as he did of becoming a friggin' ballerina. And the hell of it was, he wasn't even ready to go home with her. Not when he was still trying to wrap his head around how he could get everything he wanted from her without giving more than he was willing.

And, God, did that make him sound like a dick.

Yeah, there was a lot he needed to get figured out in his head. But no matter how bloody difficult it proved to be, he was done letting her pretend he didn't even exist.

Done driving himself slowly into this maddening state of frustration, with no apparent end in sight.

One way or another, he would approach her tonight—and with that firm decision finally came the merciful beginnings of peace. Leaning back in his chair, he kept his avid gaze focused on Elise as he lazily crossed his arms over his chest, the rise of anticipation in his veins like hot, thick syrup. Wyatt figured he might get his face slapped for his efforts. Hell, knowing Elise, he might even get a knee in his balls. But one way or another, things were about to change.

Come hell or high water, she was done running.

Chapter 1

Three hours later...

Elise Drake hated weddings—even ones torn straight from the pages of a fairy tale.

Not that the pure-blooded Lycan had anything personal against the institution of marriage. It was the event itself that she couldn't stand: gloms of people gathering around, smiling and incandescent with happiness, while she had to plaster on a beaming smile, doing her best to disguise the truth. To pretend that she wasn't freaking out at being in a crowd where everyone was expected to act friendly and sociable.

Brittle. On edge. About to crack at any moment, shattering like a crystal goblet slammed against a craggy surface. That was how she really felt, screaming inside her head, wanting to flee, to run, but forced to play a part, projecting an outward look of cheerful, joyful celebration. Smile, wave, laugh. And all the while thinking that she would do anything—*anything*—to escape. Twist an ankle. Fake a headache. Hell, at that point she'd have jabbed a freaking pencil in her eye if she thought it would get her out of there.

But none of those things were going to save her tonight. She was surrounded by too many who "cared"— who made it their mission in life to protect, rather than destroy. Unless, of course, the thing they were hunting deserved to be destroyed. Though years of bad blood stood between the Runners and their birth pack, the Silvercrest Lycans, the werewolves owed their survival to the half-human hunters.

After all, it was the Runners who had put an end to the gruesome events that Elise's own father, Stefan Drake, had set in motion the previous autumn. Events that had not only decimated the political structure of the pack, but which had also left the Silvercrest vulnerable to outside forces, with a new set of enemies sniffing at their borders, eager to take advantage of their weaknesses. With her brother's and the Runners' help, the Silvercrest were finally entering a new era that would modernize their archaic social structure, and hopefully lead to a day when the pack's racial injustices against the half-human Runners would become a thing of the past. But it would be a long while before they were the powerhouse they had once been.

The winter had been rough, rife with lingering animosity and grief, until the snow had finally bled away to reveal a new sense of hope that came with the spring. One not without trouble, but at least the Runners were now allowed in the pack's mountaintop home of Shadow Peak without it leading to a call for violence.

Tonight, in light of the occasion, the Runners, along with their friends and families, had agreed to put their troubles behind them—and yet, her brother's wedding or not, Elise knew they were all keeping a close eye on her, which was why she was trying so damn hard to act normal. After the craziness of the past few months— with all the murder and mayhem, the betrayal and blood-lust and strange occurrences—the protective alphas had her in their sights, waiting for the moment when they'd need to rush to her rescue.

But Elise didn't want them to save her.

All she wanted was to be left alone.

Brave words, but it's too bad they're a crock. You don't really want to be left all by your lonesome. Not really. Every chance you get, you're eating him up from the cor-ner of your eye, soaking up every detail...mooning like a pathetic love-struck puppy.

"Not going there," she muttered under her breath, frustrated at herself for even thinking about him—the one particular Runner who'd snagged her attention and whose image wouldn't leave her in peace. Tall, dark and dangerously sexy, Wyatt Pallaton was too goddamn good to be true. The first night she'd set eyes on him, last fall, Elise had decided that the fascinating hunter was a taboo subject, even within the privacy of her own mind. Being near him was impossible, and even think-ing about him made her too tense—just one more thing that she couldn't deal with right now.

No matter how badly she wished things could be dif-ferent, the mesmerizing Runner was a complication she couldn't afford, and so she'd vowed to stay clear of him.

It should have been simple, except for the frustrating fact that he showed up *everywhere*. Now that her brother Eric had become a Runner, she and Wyatt seemed to be thrown together with unbelievable frequency. Too often they were at the same dinners, celebrating the same birthdays, showing up at the same meetings. And each time she was forced to be near him, her maddening fascination grew more intense.

But that wasn't the worst of it. No, the worst was that she'd started wishing for the impossible, thinking of what could have been if she'd only met him sooner. Despite the fact they lived only miles apart from one another, Elise had never met the gorgeous Runner until a few months ago. A sad fact, but one that attested to the separation that had existed for so many years between the Silvercrest werewolf pack and the Bloodrunners, who not only handled the unsavory task of hunting down the pack's rogue wolves, but who also protected the secret of their existence from the human world.

Aside from Eric, who was as pure-blooded as a Lycan could be, the Bloodrunners were comprised of half-human, half-werewolf hunters. It was because of their human blood that they were denied the privilege of being Silvercrest members, until, according to the Bloodrunners' Law, they completed a designated number of rogue kills. Of course, that had all started to change after her father destroyed the pack's governing League of Elders. Now that the League was gone and a new era of democratic government was being chartered in, Eric had tried to have the Bloodrunners' Law abolished, but the Runners were still resisting. They had no more desire to be members of the pack than the Silvercrest wanted to share their town with them, and so while relations had marginally improved, they remained strained.

Still, some significant progress had been made, and the Runners were now in charge of securing the pack's borders. With time, Elise believed that the two sides would learn to accept one another.

Of course, that also meant that no matter how hard she tried to avoid him, the odds were strong that she and Wyatt Pallaton would be seeing more of each other.

And when that happens, you'll be going right off the deep end.

She did her best to shake off the unsettling thought and took a heavy sip of her wine, forcing her mind back to the celebration happening around her. So far, Elise had managed to avoid what seemed to be a never-ending stream of nuptials taking place in Bloodrunner Alley— a small, picturesque glade located several miles south of Shadow Peak—but there'd been no excuse that could get her out of her own brother's bliss-filled ceremony. Now that Eric had become a Runner and moved into the Alley with Chelsea, his human life mate, he'd been accepted as one of their own. The other hunters wouldn't hear of the ceremony being held anywhere but in the center of the secluded glade, surrounded by their cabins and the majestic beauty of the Maryland mountains, as was custom for the Bloodrunners.

Despite its rustic setting, everyone had done an amazing job of transforming the Alley into a flower-filled paradise worthy of any society wedding. There were white-linen-covered tables, a free-flowing bar, mouth-watering food, good music and even a gleaming parquet dance floor. It was the kind of fairy-tale wedding that Elise had once dreamed of someday having for herself, before her world had been painfully torn apart. Her body had mended, thanks to the miraculous healing powers of Jillian Burns, one of her closest friends, but the emotional wounds were still bleeding and raw, like a festering sickness in her soul.

It was all so ironic, considering her bloodline. As a Dark Wolf, the offspring of two powerful pure-blooded Lycan lines, she should have been one of the most dominant females in her pack, and instead she'd been reduced to someone spooked by her own shadow, startled by every sound, completely disconnected from those around her. She could hide behind her sarcastic mouth and attitude all she wanted, but she wasn't fooling anyone. Now that she'd spent time around the Runners, they'd slowly learned to see past her bravado and had begun treating her with…care, like something unspeakably fragile that they were afraid of bruising with their rough-edged masculinity. Even Cian Hennessey, the irreverent Irishman, was going out of his way not to be his usual arrogant, smart-ass self when around her.

There were times when it all just made her want to scream—and at others, it simply made her want to pack up her car and start driving, heading down the open highway, until she'd left it all behind her.

For the love of God, do you even hear yourself? that tired internal voice grumbled within her mind. *Can we get off the pity train already? Because in case you didn't notice, it's taking us nowhere.*

The wind picked up, blowing through the glade, bringing with it the crisp, heady scents of the spring forest, as well as the damp promise of rain. On the one hand, Elise hoped the approaching spring showers would hold off for just a little longer, enabling Eric and Chelsea to enjoy their reception. On the other, she couldn't help but think that if it rained, then the night would come to an early end…and she could finally leave.

Dressed in her sleeveless bridesmaid gown, the chill of the air quickly bled into her bones. Shivering, Elise looked out across the crowded glade, and Chelsea caught her eye from the dance floor, where Eric, looking devastatingly handsome in his tux, held his wife in a tight, possessive hold as they swayed to a sultry love song. The brunette gave her a friendly wave, accompanied by a genuinely warm smile. Radiant in an ivory gown that made her look like a princess, Chelsea's contagious happiness was almost enough to soothe Elise's brittle nerves. She managed to smile in return, angry at herself for having to force an expression of pleasure onto her face. Damn it, she liked Chelsea and couldn't have been happier that her brother had fallen in love with such a warmhearted, amazing woman. She was truly thrilled for them, and she honestly wanted their wedding to be perfect. She just…she just didn't want to have to be a part of it.

Stop whining, you big ol' baby. Just suck it up and stop acting like a pathetic bitch.

Wishing that know-it-all voice in her head would shut up and leave her the hell alone, Elise took another sip of wine while her gaze wandered over the crowd, until she came to the table where Wyatt sat. Unable to get her fill of him, she secretly watched the dark-haired Runner, same as she'd been doing all through the night. He leaned back in his chair, a cold beer in his right hand, his head tilted back as he laughed at something his Blood-running partner, Carla Reyes, was saying. The pretty, petite blonde looked like a golden little angel, but Elise knew Carla could be deadly when she needed to be, and she envied the lone female Runner that power. She'd have given anything to be like Carla, fearless and free to do as she pleased.

Wyatt rumbled something that Elise couldn't quite hear but which had everyone at his table laughing, the scene like one of those idyllic beer commercials, with close friends enjoying good times together, a harsh contrast to her own situation. It wasn't lost on her that she was the only person sitting at a table by herself. Guests had come and gone throughout the evening, trying to engage her in conversation, only to eventually move on when it became obvious she didn't really want their company.

Suddenly, someone at Wyatt's table roared with laughter, and Elise watched as Carla leaned to the side, one delicate hand pressed to her partner's firm shoulder as she nearly doubled over with giggles. In that moment, the same helpless rise of jealousy Elise had experienced each and every time he'd danced with a beautiful woman that night burned through her system, making her feel sick inside. Struggling to hide the uncomfortable emotion, she shifted her gaze back to his face, wanting to see the glitter of humor in his dark eyes, to witness the white flash of his teeth as he smiled—and almost died when she found him staring right back at her.

Oh, my God...

Panicked, Elise quickly tore her gaze away, staring anywhere and everywhere, so long as it wasn't at Wyatt. When she spotted Jillian heading her way, she nearly gasped with relief. The pack's golden-haired Spirit Walker, also known as a healer or witch, took the seat on her left, and the entire time they chatted, Elise could have sworn she could feel Wyatt's gaze lingering on her, watching...waiting for her to look back in his direction. But as Jillian's grinning, gorgeous husband finally pulled her away to the dance floor and Elise slanted another quick look toward the table where Wyatt had been sitting, he was gone.

Okay, lady. It's time to blow this joint before you make a fool of yourself.

Draining the last of her wine, Elise set down the glass, pushed back from the table and moved to her feet, already working up the lame excuse she'd give to Eric and Chelsea for bailing early. Bending down to get her purse from the neighboring chair, she'd just straightened and was starting to turn when someone walked up behind her. Caught off guard, she stiffened in alarm and dropped her purse onto the table.

"Dance with me, El."

Jesus, Joseph and Mary.

The low, husky words had been whispered just behind her ear, Wyatt's warm breath brushing against the sensitive skin bared by the upswept style of her hair, and she closed her eyes, nearly reeling as a stunning jolt of shock and lust and terror swept through her veins like a wildfire. He stood so close that she could feel his heat at her back, though he wasn't quite touching her, a whisper of air still separating their bodies.

Wondering what the hell she should do, Elise drew in a deep, shuddering breath and opened her eyes just as he placed a warm, slightly rough hand on her arm, took a step back and then turned her around so that she faced him. She was tall for a woman, and in her heels she found herself staring eye level with the bronzed skin of his strong, corded throat. It was madness, but she couldn't deny that she wanted to lean forward and press her mouth against that dark, silken skin. Wanted to feel his pulse against the tingling surface of her lips…the blistering intensity of his heat against her face.

Shivering even harder, Elise wet her lips, unable to get any words out over the choking lump of anxiety lodged against her larynx. Knowing she had to brazen this out, she slowly lifted her gaze over the square cut of his chin, then higher, over that wide, sensual mouth and strong nose, until she finally reached those dark, heavily lashed eyes. Reaching deep, she tried to find the smart-ass "I couldn't care less that you're big and bad and beautiful" attitude that she used when dealing with the other Runners—but it wasn't there. Something about Wyatt Pallaton stripped her of her hard-earned defenses, until she couldn't even fake her way through a sarcastic confrontation.

All she could do was stand there, trapped…spell-bound…transfixed, until it felt as if she were somehow falling into that deliciously dark, heavy-lidded stare. It reminded her of gazing at the midnight sky, while the glittering points of the stars dazzled her eyes. His eyes glittered in just the same way, that mesmerizing gaze fixed on her with startling, breathtaking intensity, as if she were the only thing in the entire world at that moment that had his attention. Somehow, instead of the usual panicked alarm she felt when close to a man, there was only a strange, simmering warmth, like something bubbling up from the cold, decimated depths of her soul, breaking its way through the barren layers of ice, struggling to reach the surface.

She trembled, but not from the chill of the mountain breeze. No, she was melting, burning alive, and all he'd done was say four little words to her, stroking her senses with that deep, velvet-rough voice that was so damn sexy it should have been illegal.

He stepped closer, and amazingly, she didn't flinch the way she usually did when a man invaded her personal space. But she did react. How could she not, when he was surrounding her, overwhelming her with his fierce, predatory energy, blasting it against her like some kind of freaking superpower?

"Wh-what did you say?" she stammered, stalling, wondering what in God's name she was going to do. Run? Scream? Throw herself at him...and end up making a complete fool of herself when she couldn't follow through, panicking at the mere idea of a kiss?

Poor Elise. You are so in trouble.

"Dance with me," he said again, while a slow, sensual smile lifted the corner of his mouth, and the wind blew the thick, midnight strands of his hair over his brow. Such simple little words, and yet, their effect was so utterly devastating.

No way. Never. Not in a million years. The fervent responses rushed through her mind with dizzying speed, but when she opened her mouth to tell him no, she found herself nodding instead. The music and laughter surrounding them faded to a distant blur of sound, and Elise blinked, stunned that she'd just agreed to let this man take her into his arms and slow-dance with her. Had she lost her ever-loving mind? What the hell was wrong with her?

"I was hoping you'd stop being so stubborn," Wyatt responded in a low, husky drawl, and she watched as the flames from one of the nearby fire pits cast a golden glow over the rugged angles of his face, glinting against the coal-black silk of his hair. "Took me all night to work up the nerve to ask you," he added wryly, the corners of his dark eyes crinkling as he grinned. "Imagine how crushed I'd have been if you'd turned me down."

She blinked, and his grin turned boyishly crooked, dazzling her with its beauty, making some forgotten part of her want to smile in response, though she fought against it. Elise knew he was teasing her, trying to put her at ease, and in another lifetime, words would have slipped from her lips like silk, either cutting or flirtatious in response, depending on her mood. But the woman with the ready comeback was gone.

Perhaps not an entirely bad thing, she reflected with an inward wince, seeing as how that woman had often been obsessively self-centered...and not very nice.

"Come on," he murmured, gently taking her elbow and steering her toward the dance floor. He was being careful with her, tender in his touch and manner, and it made her want to snap at him, while at the same time she couldn't help but be embarrassingly grateful.

Oh, yeah. You are so-o-o losing your mind.

Not surprising, she supposed, considering the fact he was so freaking hot her brain cells were melting by the second. She couldn't even draw in a deep enough breath, the humidity rising around them like a sultry mist as the distant rumble of storms drew closer. Despite the chill of the breeze, the air lay heavy and damp against her skin, thick with lust and anticipation and the mouthwatering scent of Wyatt Pallaton. A provocative combination of musk and salt and the wild outdoors, he smelled unbelievably delicious, and she wanted to lean closer, drawing more of that heady scent into her lungs, while at the same time she wanted to do everything she could to escape it. Trapped between the opposing urges, she somehow managed to reach the dance floor without stumbling, aware of the curious glances being sent their way from the other guests, but unable to truly focus on anything beyond the feel of his hand on her arm, his long, strong fingers hot against her skin, while that decadent scent screwed with her head.

The second her feet touched the polished surface of the parquet floor, panic slammed into her with the stunning force of a bullet. *"Wait!"* she blurted, suddenly drawing back. He stopped and turned so that he stood facing her, but she didn't dare look him in the eye, careful to keep her wild gaze focused on the snowy-white front of his shirt. He'd removed his jacket and tie earlier in the night and undone the shirt's top button, revealing just a hint of his smooth, burnished chest. "I'm sorry," she said thickly, staring at that bare glimpse of skin, "but I don't think I can do this."

"Just a dance, Elise. That's all I'm asking for." Then he was taking her into his arms, and she had to bite her lip to keep from moaning at the sudden chaotic rush of emotion. It was such a consuming, overwhelming sensation, being held by a man again, and her breath caught with a sharp, audible gasp as he pulled her against the hardness and heat of his muscular body, her head spinning as her senses went into some kind of cataclysmic meltdown.

Trying to remember how to breathe, she placed her hands on his broad shoulders, the soft cotton of his shirt warm beneath her palms, and took a quick glance up at his face to find him watching her, his expression fierce…intense…and yet, somehow impossibly gentle.

"I'm dizzy," she whispered, her pulse racing, frenzied and out of control.

"It's okay. I've got you," he told her, his beautiful mouth shaping the words, making them sound like something seductive and wicked as he spun her in a sudden turn that pulled a soft, startled burst of shaky laughter from her lips. "See, it's not so hard to have a little fun, is it?"

She blinked, dazed, too much going on inside her body and mind to focus on any one thing. "I didn't… I don't dance," she explained in a strangled whisper, when what she meant was that she didn't let men get this close to her. Ever.

"I know," he replied, and the slightly rough cadence of his words made her shiver with awareness, at the same time something thick and hot began to slip through her veins. She had the strangest suspicion that he was responding more to her unspoken thought than the one she'd voiced aloud, and an uneasy feeling swept through her as she wondered just how much he knew about her. About her past and the things that had happened to her.

He pulled her a shade closer, until his strong thighs were brushing against hers, her breasts pressed to the firm surface of his chest, and Elise could have sworn she could feel the powerful beating of his heart. Her breasts felt heavy, swollen, the rise of desire like a hothouse flower unfurling inside her body, and there was a part of her—a strange, primal, frightening part—that wanted to stretch her arms and back in a sinuous arch and melt against him, languid and soft and hungry. That wanted to hold her face up to a warm spring shower and feel it misting against her skin, wetting their clothes, until steam rose from the heat of their flesh. That wanted to rip that crisp white shirt from his lean, hard-muscled physique and press her open mouth to the pounding, urgent beat of his heart. Push her fingers through the thick strands of his silky hair and pull his mouth to hers, unleashing the primitive, predatory hunger she knew lurked inside him.

God, she just *wanted*. Wanted so badly she could have screamed.

"But you're enjoying yourself," he murmured, jarring her back to reality with the deep, rich, slightly gritty tone of his voice as they swayed to the music. "Aren't you glad you didn't tell me no?"

Surprising herself, she snuffled another soft laugh under her breath. "You're very sure of yourself, Pallaton."

"Call me Wyatt."

She shifted her gaze, staring over his left shoulder, feeling as if his dark, onyx-colored eyes could see straight into her. "I thought everyone called you Pallaton or Pall?"

"They do." From the edge of her vision, Elise watched the corner of his mouth lift in a devastatingly sexy, purely male smile. "But I want *you* to call me Wyatt."

"I'm going to call you desperate if you don't stop," she warned him, hoping like hell that her face wasn't actually as red as it felt.

"Stop what?" he asked, angling his head slightly to the side as he tried to recapture her gaze.

"All of this," she said, fully aware that she sounded like an idiot. "Trying to dazzle me with your manliness and charm."

"Oh, yeah? Is it working?" He kept his expression

carefully blank, though she could see the glitter of humor in his dark gaze.

She rolled her eyes. "Like I'd tell you if it was."

His head went back as a low, rich chuckle rumbled up from his chest, and her toes curled in her heeled sandals at the pure carnality of the sound. How did he do it, make a laugh sound like some kind of insidious new form of seduction?

Though she tried so hard to fight it, everything that he did made her feel drunk on lust, the hunger heavy in her body, like a weighty thing inside of her. The flash of his smile. The smoldering intensity in his dark eyes and the way they did that sexy crinkle thing at the corners when he grinned. She'd heard he was considered the tamest of the Runners, at times even stoic. The most easygoing of a volatile bunch. But being close to him, talking to him, Elise couldn't help but wonder if the people who held that opinion of Wyatt Pallaton knew him at all. Were they blind? Because from where she was standing, there wasn't a safe, easygoing thing about the man.

Desperate to regain control of herself and the situation, Elise asked a question that had been playing in the back of her mind for the past hour, slowly driving her crazy. "I saw you and Michaela on the dance floor earlier. Doesn't it bother Brody when you dance with his wife?"

His hands shifted, one resting against the small of her back, while the other stroked its way up her spine until it reached the edge of her bodice, his thumb brushing against her bare skin in a slow, sensual caress. Her gaze shot immediately back to his, and she watched the groove form between his dark brows as he asked, "Why should it bother him?"

Suddenly, she wished she'd just kept her big mouth shut. Thanks to her friendship with Max Doucet, Michaela's younger brother, she knew that Brody and the fiery Cajun were madly in love with one another, as did anyone who had ever met the quiet Runner and his gorgeous human life mate. Still, she couldn't help the jealousy she felt when she witnessed the closeness that Wyatt and Michaela shared. "I just thought that the two of you…that you were…"

He leaned forward, putting his silky words into the sensitive shell of her ear. "Despite what a few gossips seem to think, El, Mic and I are just friends. And that's all we've ever been. She's in love with her husband, and I… Let's just say that I don't think of her that way."

There was something there, in his words…in the tone of his voice…but she couldn't afford to look at it too closely. Not if she wanted to keep it together. Instead, she said, "Why haven't you danced with Reyes?"

She didn't know what to make of him when he lifted his head, staring down at her with a bemused expression, as if the thought of asking his beautiful partner to dance had never even occurred to him. "Carla? Hell, she'd probably stomp on my toes just to be ornery."

"But you two seem so…close. I thought…"

His dark brows lifted. "That we were also intimate?" he asked, looking as if he were trying hard not to laugh.

Before she could respond, his lips twitched with another wry smile. "We're close, yeah. But not like that. I love Carla like a sister, but she's my partner. Dancing with her would be like…like dancing with one of the guys."

"Well, there has to be some woman here who you're involved with," she practically snapped, becoming desperate. She needed a cold slap of reality in the face, some kind of sign that declared him hands-off, because if she wasn't careful, she was going to get herself in deeper water than she could handle. "Don't you have a girl-friend? Someone you're dating?"

"I'm sorry to disappoint you, honey, but no. No woman...and no girlfriend. I'm as free as a man can be."

Hell. That so wasn't what she needed to hear.

It didn't matter how badly she wanted to accept the fleeting moments of sexual pleasure he was offering her with that wicked smile and smoldering stare—she sim-ply couldn't do it—and for the second time that night, Elise wondered why she couldn't have met him when she was younger. Of course, knowing the kind of girl she'd been back then, she probably would have turned up her nose at him, believing herself too good to have a fling with a Bloodrunner. Stuck-up and snide, she'd had a mountainous chip on her shoulder, always acting as if she thought she was better than everyone around her. Disgusting, but embarrassingly true. She'd been so different then, thinking the world revolved around her and her problems, when she couldn't have been further from the truth.

It'd taken countless months of therapy after her attack to come to the understanding that she'd formed her spite-ful attitude and narcissistic self-obsession as a defense mechanism for dealing with her misogynistic father. And she'd done a damn good job of building those defenses. So much so that it'd taken a night of living hell to break her down, taking her to pieces, until there was nothing left of her to offer a man like Wyatt. The feminine part of her that longed for an emotional connection with a man, as well as a physical one, no longer worked the way that it should—and though she struggled each day to be strong, Elise knew there was nothing that could ever repair the damage. No therapeutic Band-Aid that could heal her soul.

Wyatt stared down at her with a curious look on his striking face, then quietly asked, "Are you going to keep quizzing me about the women in my life, or are we finally going to talk about it?"

"Talk about what?" she whispered, painfully aware that her panic and fear were bleeding through, loud and clear. With his heightened senses, he could probably scent her unease with every breath he took, and she fought not to cringe.

He didn't offer any inane platitudes to ease her nerves. He just smiled down at her with that slow, sensual twisting of his lips, the shape of his mouth firm, masculine and yet impossibly beautiful. There was a nick on his chin, where he'd obviously cut himself shaving, and Elise found herself wanting to lift onto her toes and press a tender kiss against the small wound. A strange compulsion, considering she hadn't kissed anyone in years—hadn't *wanted* to kiss anyone in years—but then this entire night was turning out to be one stunning dose of bizarre.

She swallowed against the lump in her throat, suddenly terrified that he wanted to talk about the way she'd been watching him throughout the night, stealing as many desperate glances as she could. Embarrassed, she looked away. She could feel the heat burning in her face, the dark, curious weight of his gaze as he stared down at her only making it worse. "Talk about what?" she asked again, unable to disguise the quiver in her words.

"About what's happening between..." His voice

trailed off as he took in her panicked expression. "You know, on second thought, I think we'll save that particular conversation for another day," he offered in a low rumble, and even though she could sense the tension in his body, she knew he'd decided not to push the issue. "But there's something I need to tell you, El. I mean to get to know you. I don't expect it to be easy, but you should know that it's something I've set my mind to."

From one breath to another, she could feel the color drain from her face, and she looked back to him, blinking against the slow rise of anger building up inside her. Hoping it wasn't true, but knowing that it was, she said, "You've asked about me, haven't you? That's why you're being so damn nice and so bloody careful, isn't it?"

His lashes lowered, shielding his gaze, and she cut him off before he could even bother denying it. "Don't lie to me," she quietly seethed, thankful he'd kept them at the far edge of the dance floor, away from the other couples. "And don't coddle me! I'm so sick and tired of everyone walking on eggshells around me, afraid I might go off the deep end. Just answer the question, Pallaton. You know about what happened to me, don't you?"

His expression was nothing short of grim. "You mean with your father?"

"No, I'm not talking about the crap that happened last year. I'm talking about before!"

For a moment, he simply watched her, the look in his eyes growing darker, deeper, and then he gave a small, nearly imperceptible nod. "Yeah, I know."

Despite the counseling she'd gone through, shame poured through her, sickening and painfully familiar, and she struggled to breathe her way through it.

"Elise, I meant what I said," he told her, his grip

firming, as if he thought she was going to pull away. It was terrifying, watching the resolve harden his features, his expression cut with stark lines of determination. "All I want right now is a chance for us to get to know each other. I'm not pushing you to do anything you're not ready for."

"You're wasting your time," she argued, flattening her palms against the solid muscles of his shirt-covered chest as she pushed against his hold. "It's not going to happen. I…I can't."

"Can't?" he quietly rasped. "Or won't even try?"

Her anger rose with her panic, and she fought to control her voice as she hissed, "I don't know who the hell you think you are, but you don't know me. You don't know my life. You don't know anything but gossip. Don't you dare judge me!"

His voice became a soft, gentle growl. "I don't want to judge you. I just want the chance to be friends with you. To deal with this thing we have going."

She blinked, wondering what on earth he was talking about. "Thing? What thing?"

They'd long since stopped dancing, though he still held her in his arms. Obviously choosing his words with care, he said, "We might not be happy about it, but there's something between us. I know you don't give most men the time of day, but I want that to change. I want you to take a chance and get to know me."

"So that I'll what? Suddenly decide to sleep with you?" she sneered, breaking away from him.

His mouth went hard, the shuttered look in his eyes narrow and sharp. "So that you can learn to trust me. Be friends with me. If that's all you want, then I'll find a way to accept it."

She lifted her chin, her arms wrapped tight around her middle, too angry to care if she was causing a scene. "You're crazy!"

He didn't reach for her again. He just stood there, looking devastatingly handsome in his tux, his shirt-sleeves rolled up to reveal his thick wrists and the corded length of his powerful forearms as he shoved his hands deep in the pockets of his slacks. The snowy-white of his shirt was startlingly bright against the dark russet tone of his skin, attesting to his Native American heritage, and she couldn't help but think that it should have been a sin creating a man who looked that good. But even more frightening than the gorgeous exterior was the man inside.

"I mean it, Wyatt. You're wasting your time."

"I know you're afraid," he told her, keeping his voice low, "but there's something you should know about me, El. I can be a patient man when I need to be."

"A patient man?" She laughed, but the brittle sound was born too much from terror and pain than actual humor. "There's no such thing!"

He leaned forward, just close enough that his lips grazed her cheekbone as he spoke. "Have heart," he murmured as the last notes of the song quietly faded away. He pressed a tender kiss to her temple, moving slowly past her right side, the solid muscles of his chest brushing against her bare arm. "Believe it or not, El, I just might surprise you."

Then he stepped away, leaving her standing alone on the edge of the dance floor, staring blankly into the dense, impenetrable darkness of the forest…wondering what in God's name had just happened to her.

Chapter 2

Forty-five minutes later, Wyatt stood with his shoulders propped against the thick trunk of an ancient pine, waiting just inside the dark line of the wooded park that bordered the back of the meticulously kept house before him. Silvery rays of rain-dampened moonlight bathed the small home in an ethereal glow, giving it a spectral appearance, like an apparition rising from the mist. The rain wasn't heavy, the trees shielding him from the pattering drops, but the rumble of thunder promised that another storm was on its way—which meant he was in for a long, wet night.

Doing his best to ignore the thick weight of sexual hunger keeping him company, Wyatt used his wolf eyes as he kept watch over the silent house, noting the personal touches that he knew were the work of the woman who lived there. The lavender trim had to have been

Elise's doing, as well as the vivid red rose bushes that climbed the white walls. Everywhere he looked, there were little sparks of her personality that set the house apart from its neighbors, much like the woman herself.

Even in a pack full of preternatural werewolves, Elise Drake stood out as something vivid and bright and unique, no matter how hard she tried to hide it.

She was shimmering and white-hot to the touch, and yet, she worked so hard to conceal herself beneath a cold, excessively controlled exterior. Struggled to cut herself off from the world, as if she needed no one to help her along the way.

On the one hand, Wyatt still savored the memory of how she'd felt in his arms, somehow better than any other woman he'd ever held before. Soft and lush, despite her nerves, with the mouthwatering scent of her body filling his head; the sensation had been richer, deeper... and impossibly sweeter than anything he'd ever experienced. Something that he knew would keep him up in the quiet hours of the night, when his body craved the feel of her curves beneath him, cushioning his heavy thrusts, welcoming him into the slick, clutching depths of her body. He loved that she wasn't a little stick-and-bones wisp of a woman. Loved her shape and her height and the way that she fit against him.

On the other hand, he couldn't ignore the frustrating fact that she deserved a man who could give her a hell of a lot more than he could. One who wasn't riddled with the guilt of his sins. Who could hold her through the night after losing himself in her beautiful body. Who could offer her *everything,* instead of something that would most likely end in a bitter nothing for both of them. But fate was a fickle bastard, and he was done arguing with himself about it. Elise wasn't someone he could ignore or forget. Staying away from her wasn't an option, and though he'd promised her patience, he wanted her *now*.

Ever since the night of Max Doucet's *Novitiate's* ceremony, Wyatt had known she was his. A rogue wolf had bitten Max because of his sister's association with the Runners, and the purpose of the ceremony had been to determine whether or not the teenager would survive his first change. In a surprising act of loyalty to the Blood-runners, Elise and her brother had sided with the half-breed hunters that night, standing against their sadistic father and his maniacal plans.

It had been a macabre, hellish scene, and yet, Wyatt hadn't been able to take his focus off the woman standing no more than a handful of feet away from him. The late-autumn winds had raged, whipping the thick, shimmering strands of her dark red hair against the perfect angles of her face, pulling her shirt tight against the womanly curves of her body. The violent gusts had surrounded him with her warm, intoxicating scent, creating a reaction in his body from which he doubted he would ever recover.

Take. Keep. Mine. Those three guttural words had echoed through his head over and over, too many times to count. Primal, raw and savagely possessive.

But while Elise Drake's scent might have told him she was meant to be *his,* body and soul, he wasn't going to allow that knowledge to rule his life. Even if his past had been…different, that wasn't something he would just accept. And he wasn't looking to make her the answer to his problems, as if saving her could save *him* from the mistakes he'd made. This wasn't a goddamn do-over. He just wanted to protect her. To hear her laugh. See her smile. And be there when she finally realized there were still things in life worth living for, rather than just existing.

She'd arrived home only a handful of minutes ago, and as she moved past one of the back windows, Wyatt couldn't help but follow the lines of her body with his gaze, appreciating the graceful, sensual way that she moved. Tension gripped him, and it took a significant force of effort to hold his position. He was debating whether or not to move in closer, when his cell phone silently vibrated in his pocket; a quick glance at the number told him it was Carla. Knowing she was going to rib him over his dance with Elise, he choked back a curse and quietly answered the phone. "What's up?"

Carla's husky laughter filled his ear. "And here I was wondering if I should be asking you the same thing."

"Cute," he muttered with a snort.

"I know, huh? But believe it or not, I had a reason to call beyond trying to get a rise out of you. A set of scouts on the south border called in saying they saw something. They tried to track it, but the rain that was coming down made it impossible. Just thought you might want to know, seeing as how your lady bird is in that vicinity."

Wyatt glanced at his watch. "When did the call come in?"

"They phoned it into the command center in Shadow Peak about an hour ago. Guess the guys on duty figured we were all too busy with the wedding to pass it along. And before you freak, a bunch of us are already on our way up to talk to them. We'll make sure they never make the same mistake again."

He grunted in response, wishing like hell that Eric

had been able to convince Elise to relocate to the Alley. The siblings had argued about it for days, after Eric had permanently moved into one of the cabins there with Chelsea. But for some reason the stubborn woman refused to leave her home, even when so many of the townspeople continued to treat her like shit simply because of what had happened with her old man.

He started to get a bad feeling in his gut. "You think someone's sneaking around on Silvercrest land again?" The last time it'd happened, they'd nearly had their asses handed to them.

"It wouldn't surprise me," Carla responded, while the guys in the vehicle with her talked in the background. "Every pack on the eastern seaboard knows we're still recovering from Daddy Drake's bullshit. They'll all come sniffing around eventually, just to test us. The Silvercrest have been dominant for too long now not to have a long list of Lycans who'd like nothing more than to see us tumble."

Lifting his free hand, he rubbed at the knots of tension in the back of his neck. "We've already tumbled."

"Yeah, but we're still on our land. Trust me, there's going to be someone who wants to try to change that fact, if for nothing more than the bragging rights. The pack that knocks out the Silvercrest, even when we're not at our best, will be one that makes others cower. After what happened between Eric and the Whiteclaw a few weeks ago, you know those bastards have to be drooling for it."

Wyatt didn't doubt that she was right. Eric had met his human wife while she was searching for her younger sister, Perry. Making a bad choice, Perry had gone chasing after the wrong guy and ended up falling in with the Whiteclaw pack who lived to the south of the Silvercrest. With the Runners' help, Eric had been able to prove that the Whiteclaw had partnered up with the Donovans, a corrupt local Lycan family, on a number of illegal activities, the most horrific being one that involved human girls. With the Donovans' support, the Whiteclaw had been drugging the girls and pimping them out for Lycan gang rapes. The drugs not only acted as an aphrodisiac on the girls, but also impaired their memories of the attacks. The Runners had managed to close down the strip club in Wesley, a human town at the foot of the mountains, that the Whiteclaw had been using to find the girls, but tensions between the two packs had never been higher. Roy Claymore, who led the Whiteclaw wolves, was thirsty for Silvercrest blood, and Wyatt knew it wouldn't be long before the Silvercrest found themselves embroiled in battle.

"Shit," he cursed under his breath, running a palm down his face to clear away the misting drops of rain. "I've got a feeling something's coming down. Soon."

There was a wry edge to Carla's worried tone. "And here I thought you'd have nothing but butterflies in your belly after that little performance on the dance floor tonight. We were all damn near riveted by the steam coming off you two smoldering little lovebirds."

Christ. Wondering how long it would be before Eric confronted him about his sister, he muttered, "I don't have time for you to mess with my head right now, Reyes. I wanna check the area, see if anything's around."

"Okay. But if you find trouble, don't be stupid," she told him, all traces of teasing gone. "We're gonna check out where the sighting took place after we're done in town, so we won't be far. Call me before you go charging in like a bull or I'll never let you live it down."

"You never let me live anything down," he grunted, ending the call before she could come back with another smart-ass remark.

Slipping his phone back into his pocket, Wyatt pushed away from the tree and began making his way through the woods, careful to keep one eye on Elise's house. He'd learned the hard way when he was younger to always trust his instincts, and right now they were shouting at him that something wasn't right. The restlessness of his inner wolf told him that the beast agreed. He drew in a series of slow, deep breaths, but the slight mist of rain made it impossible to pick up any trace of Lycan musk, the damp affecting his keen sense of smell. If there were someone out there with him, he was going to have to find him using good old-fashioned tenacity and skill.

Wyatt almost relished the thought of getting his hands on the trespasser, thinking a good knock-'em-down, claw-'em-up scuffle was exactly what he needed to work out his frustration. And if the bastard came anywhere near Elise, he was going to get more than a fight.

If he so much as set foot on her property, Wyatt was going to personally send him straight to hell.

Breathe in, breathe out. In...out. Slow and easy.

Setting her purse and car keys on her kitchen table, Elise rolled her head over her shoulders, repeating the silent mantra while wondering if her heart rate would ever return to normal. The drive back up to Shadow Peak tonight had seemed to take twice as long as it usually did, her hands damp against the steering wheel, the rhythmic slapping of the windshield wipers keeping perfect timing with the frenzied rate of her pulse.

Considering she was reeling from one innocent dance, she couldn't deny that Wyatt Pallaton certainly had a way of playing havoc with a woman's equilibrium.

By the time she'd spun around on the dance floor, ready to tell him to stay the hell away from her, he was gone. Needing to get out of there, she'd found Eric and Chelsea and told them she wasn't feeling well, then immediately headed home. Now all she wanted was to run a hot bath, put on some soothing music and soak in her tub, doing her best to forget about the man who had practically seduced her with nothing more than a smoldering look.

And the way he'd called her El had damn near made her melt.

Shivering with the decadent memory of every huskily spoken word he'd said to her, she moved to the counter and opened a cupboard, taking down a tall glass and filling it with ice-cold water from the door in her refrigerator. She tilted her head back and took a long drink, then pressed the chilled glass against her forehead, her thoughts in turmoil. Why *her,* damn it? There were no doubt dozens of single women in Shadow Peak who would have been ecstatic at the prospect of drawing his eye, regardless of his Runner status. But for some insane reason, Wyatt seemed to have singled her out, and she had no idea why. Was he one of those macho jerks who got off on a challenge? Had he been dared? Was this all just some kind of cruel, sick joke to him?

Cut it out, her conscience lectured. *He isn't like that, and you damn well know it.*

"What I know is that I'm going out of my mind,"

she grumbled into the lonely silence of the house. Hating that awful silence, she'd just lifted the glass to her lips again, when someone softly knocked on the kitchen door that opened onto her carport. Startled, she flinched, sending water sloshing over the side of the glass and onto the tiled floor. Taking a hesitant step forward, she asked, "Who is it?"

"Elise?" a deep, familiar voice called out. "It's me, Eddie."

Setting the glass down on the counter, she lifted her hands, pressing her fingertips to her temples, unable to deny the slight twinge of disappointment fluttering in her chest. Had she actually hoped that it might be Wyatt at her door? How freaking crazy was that?

"Elise? Are you okay?"

"Just a second, Eddie," she muttered, reaching for a dish towel to mop up the floor. Damn it, she was too tired for this. Too tense. Too everything to deal with her well-meaning if slightly obsessed neighbor tonight.

Several weeks ago, not long after Eric had first met Chelsea, Elise had come home from work one day and found her kitchen door slightly open, when she was always careful to lock up when she left. She'd been receiving threatening phone calls for some time and had been worried someone was inside, waiting for her. When her neighbor, Eddie Browning, had come home from work at his stepfather's garage and found her lingering on the doorstep, he'd searched the house for her to make sure no one was hiding inside, and then she'd thanked him and sent him home. But there'd been a lingering vibe in the air that had completely freaked her out. Nervous and scared, she'd tried to have someone from the pack-run security offices in town come over to take a look, but they'd refused. So she'd contacted Eric, asking him for help, but he also hadn't been able to detect an intruder's scent. Then all hell had broken loose when an angry crowd had gathered in front of her house, and a jackass named Glenn Farrow had publicly accused her of making the whole thing up in some kind of bizarre plea for attention. The crowd had joined in, and the accusations had grown ugly, bred by lingering animosity toward her father. Eric had kicked Farrow's ass, and the bastard had thankfully given her a wide berth ever since.

Shaken by the experience, Elise had made plans to have a new alarm system installed the following afternoon. Eddie, however, had proven to be even better than her security system, keeping a watchful eye on her property for what seemed like all hours of the day. The only problem was that he claimed to see someone snooping around her house on a regular basis, and now she rarely put any stock in his claims. He was a nice young man, and she knew he meant well, but she also knew he was easily confused…and she couldn't help but wish that he'd be just a little less focused on her life.

Stepping to the door, she pulled back the short curtain that covered the small panes of glass, revealing her worried-looking neighbor. With his baby-blue eyes, cherubic face and golden hair, he looked so much younger than his twenty-five years. It still surprised her that Eddie had initially been considered a suspect in her attack, since he was so childlike and sweetly naive. But he'd thankfully been cleared when his alibi for that night was confirmed.

"You need to go back home now," she told him, careful to keep her voice firm as she stepped closer to the door. He didn't frighten her, but she sure as hell didn't want to do anything to encourage him. "You don't want anyone to see you over here, remember? It's only going to cause trouble for you with the pack."

"But this is important," he argued, his blue eyes clouded with concern. "I saw someone at your house again tonight. I think he was tampering with your alarm."

"Eddie, we've already been through this," she said with a sigh. She didn't want to hurt his feelings, but it was for his own safety. Nothing good could come from his befriending her. "You have to stop watching my house."

"But I'm sure of it this time, Elise. I'm worried about you."

"I'm fi—" she started to say, only to have her words trail off as she glanced down, noticing that the latch on the door was flicked to the unlocked position. Elise was positive that she hadn't left it that way when she'd locked up before leaving for the wedding, and she'd come in through the front door when she'd gotten home. There was no way she'd missed checking the door, and familiar feelings of terror and anxiety began to work their way through her system, settling like a toxin in her muscles, making her head feel light, her stomach pitchy. Turning around, Eddie's low, fervent words faded to a buzzing whir in her head as she stepped away from the door and took a deep breath, searching for a scent, but as far as she could tell, there was nothing to cause alarm. Still, she walked across the kitchen, took one of the knives from her butcher's block and headed down the hall, flicking on every light along the way, until she reached her bedroom.

With her pulse roaring in her ears, she peered into the room, but nothing looked out of place. Then she heard the floorboards softly creak behind her, and before she could scream, a meaty palm clamped around her throat, choking off her air, while a thick, muscled arm banded her middle, pinning her arms at her sides. To her horror, she felt the knife slip from her damp fingers, clattering when it landed at her feet.

No, she thought, as tears flooded her eyes, trailing over her face. *This can't be happening!*

"Hello, cherry girl," a deep, scratchy voice whispered in her ear. "Did you miss me?"

"Who the hell are you?" she wheezed, barely able to get the strangled words out, even though he'd loosened his hold on her throat.

"Don't you remember me?" the man rasped, the crooning tone of his voice sickening her as much as it terrified.

"No," she choked out, but Elise knew it was a lie. She may not have a *conscious* memory of his voice, but something inside her screamed in fear at its familiarity. "What do you want from me?" she cried, while dread twisted through every cell of her body, holding her in an agonizing clutch of pain.

He pressed his cold, slick lips to the side of her throat, nuzzling the vulnerable stretch of skin. "Don't worry, honey. I'll refresh your memory. We *all* will." A low, husky chuckle filled her ear, making her skin crawl. "But I might have to take a quick taste before I sneak you out of here. Just for old times' sake."

Oh, God. God, no. She'd rather die!

Air finally rushed its way into her lungs as she yanked her head to the side, her fear releasing in an ear-piercing scream. Elise twisted and fought like a madwoman to break free, but it didn't matter. He was too strong, holding her tight against the front of his disgustingly aroused body as he began pulling her across the room. With sickening horror, she realized he was dragging her toward the bed. She drew in as much air as she could, screaming louder than she could ever remember doing. Screaming so hard that it hurt. Eyes watering and nose running, her throat ached as she sobbed and shouted. Then her attacker wrapped his thick arm around her throat, cutting off her air again, and her screams died to a pitiful, breathless gasp. Her vision blurred, tiny pinpricks of cold burning beneath her skin, his guttural voice feeding words she could no longer make sense of into her ear. But she knew what was coming. She was going to die. Slowly. Painfully. Cruelly.

Fight, damn it. Change!

She wished she could act on the survival instinct, but as her consciousness flickered, she knew it was too late. They'd broken her three years ago, leaving her on the verge of death in a pool of her own blood, barely breathing.

And now one of them had come back to finish the job.

Chapter 3

If the sound of those piercing screams had chilled his blood and fueled his rage, the silence that followed nearly stopped Wyatt's heart. He'd been passing along the far back corner of her property when he'd caught the faint notes of that first terrified cry, and set off running as fast as he could. Within seconds, he'd crossed her backyard, shoving past her neighbor and ordering the guy to call the Runners' security hotline, before tearing into the house through the kitchen door. He was hurrying toward Elise's scent when he plowed straight into the bastard. Snarling, they crashed to the living-room floor as they each fought for the upper hand, landing crushing blows that would have killed a human.

"You like preying on women, you sadistic piece of shit?" Wyatt roared, releasing his claws and fangs as he gripped the male's balaclava-covered head and slammed his skull against the hardwood floor. "Why don't you try taking on someone your own size?"

"You don't scare me, pretty boy," the Lycan growled, his own deadly claws extending from the tips of his fingers. "I eat half-breed assholes like you for breakfast."

They rolled across the floor, smashing into the coffee table, their booted feet knocking over furniture as they grappled, blocked and struck blows with animalistic savagery. His opponent was unnaturally strong, even for a Lycan, but Wyatt was fueled with the driving need to reach Elise and make sure she hadn't been harmed. Blocking a blow to his neck, he used his feet to toss the asshole over his head and into one of the side tables, the delicate piece of furniture splintering under the male's weight. They both twisted and lurched onto their feet, claws extended at their sides, facing off across what was left of a ruined sofa. Coarse, guttural chuffs of aggression rumbled deep in their chests, and then they exploded into action, shifting the upper halves of their bodies into the powerful shape of their beasts. With his head changed into the wolf's larger form, the Lycan's mask had dropped in pieces to the floor…but Wyatt didn't recognize the beast staring back at him. Without being able to see the male's human face, he couldn't be sure if this were someone he'd met before or not. Dodging to evade a kick to his groin, Wyatt spun with a side kick aimed at the guy's chest, slamming the bastard into one of the walls so hard he nearly went through it. Shaking his head to clear it, the Lycan lurched to his feet and maneuvered to the left, putting the broken table between them.

"Come on, asshole," Wyatt growled through his muzzled snout, his graveled tone a perfect match for his feral expression of fury. "Either fight me or admit defeat. Stop wasting my time."

"Yeah? You really think you're so smart, don't you?" the male sneered, his golden gaze glittering with something that looked strangely like humor.

What the hell did this jackass think was so funny? Wanting to finish this *now,* Wyatt's top lip curled back over his deadly fangs. "I'm smart enough to take your ass to the ground."

Snickering, the Lycan said, "And while you're wasting your precious time in here with me, your little piece of ass is getting what she deserves."

He froze, dread slithering through his system like a cold blade. Fuck, no. Had he actually made such a horrific mistake?

"What?" the Lycan taunted. "You didn't really think one of us would come alone, did you?"

"You son of a bitch!" Wyatt snarled, torn between the choice of reaching Elise or staying to fight this jerk-off to the death. But there really wasn't any choice at all. With a guttural roar, he grabbed the edges of a massive wooden bookshelf that lined an entire wall of the room and wrenched it forward, trapping the Lycan beneath the toppling case. Then he turned and raced toward the back of the house, where he knew Elise's bedroom was located. In his panic, it felt as if he'd been fighting the Lycan for hours, though he knew in reality it'd only been a matter of seconds. But they were seconds that she'd been in danger. He'd mistakenly assumed she was in her room, trying to collect herself, safe now that he'd come to her rescue. But he couldn't have gotten it more wrong. He should have known, damn it, instead of letting his bloodlust get the better of him.

Wyatt could hear the Lycan shouting from the living room, but he tuned out the words, his attention riveted on the macabre scene he found as he burst into her room. Elise was trapped beneath a second assailant on her bed, struggling to get free, while the sadistic bastard pressed his forearm across her throat, cutting off her air. The male also wore a black balaclava over his head, concealing his features. As Wyatt threw himself at her attacker, he sucked in a sharp breath, searching for the male's scent, but there wasn't one. Like a blank canvas, there wasn't a single speck of Lycan musk to pull into his lungs—a trait this one shared with his partner—and it screamed Whiteclaw. After the attack some of the Whiteclaw and Donovan wolves had made on the Runners a few weeks ago in the Alley, they knew the wolves had developed a drug that not only made them violently strong, but also camouflaged their scent. But if this were another Whiteclaw attack, why come after Elise? Because of her brother and his association with the Runners? Had it made her a target, just as Eric had feared?

Digging his claws into the male's side, Wyatt tried to bite out the Lycan's throat, but was blocked by a powerful blow to his jaw. The male was unbelievably strong—another sign that he'd been amped up with the "super drug" that blocked a wolf's scent—and Wyatt had to use every ounce of strength he possessed to pull the bastard off the bed, away from Elise, and hurl him across the room. Moving quickly back to his feet, the Lycan released his claws, looking more than ready to fight, until the sound of screeching tires on the street outside signaled the arrival of the other Runners.

"Next time you won't be so lucky," the male snarled, apparently realizing he wasn't going to win now that backup had arrived. Without another word, he turned and retreated, running down the hallway. Wyatt heard the Lycan growl something at the one he'd left in the living room. Either the guy had already gotten free or the second Lycan helped him, because there were suddenly two sets of pounding footsteps as the pair made their way outside, around the side of the house and into the wooded park. Fighting back a bloodcurdling howl, it took all of Wyatt's willpower not to run after the monsters and rip them to pieces. He wanted it so badly the need was like a festering wound in his gut—but he couldn't leave Elise. Not when she needed him. Not when she was wheezing, stammering a broken, whispered phrase under her breath that was slowly breaking his heart into tiny, irreparable pieces.

"Rather die, rather die, rather die..."

Turning toward her, Wyatt quickly shifted the upper half of his body back into his human form and retracted his bloody claws and fangs, not wanting to frighten her any more than she already was. The instant he'd pulled that asshole off of her, she'd scurried into the far corner of the room and hunched down with her arms wrapped over her head. Her eyes were glazed, her mind a million miles away. Hiding...wanting to be anywhere but here. Not that he blamed her.

Taking his phone out, he called Carla's cell, telling her that he had El but needed whoever had come with her to search the woods at the back of the property for two Lycan males. Ending the brief call, he shoved the phone back into his pocket and focused on the woman he had been more than ready to kill for.

"El?" he whispered, crouching down a few yards away from her. He tried to catch her gaze, but her vacant stare was focused inward, her head slowly shaking from side to side, body huddled into a tight ball that made her seem so fragile and small. "Baby, I need you to take a deep breath and just look at me, okay? You're safe now. No one can hurt you."

He waited, holding his position as he kept speaking to her in a soft voice, doing his best not to spook her. He was starting to think that maybe he should call Reyes inside to talk to her, when Elise finally blinked her eyes a few times and looked at him. She seemed to only just be realizing that he was there.

"W-Wyatt?" she croaked, shivering so badly that it shook her words.

"Yeah, it's me, El." He started to edge a little closer, but stopped when she made a sharp, choked sound. Before he even knew what was happening, she'd launched herself at him, nearly knocking him over, her face buried against his blood-spattered chest as she bawled in deep, wrenching sobs. He held her in a crushing grip that was too tight but seemed to be exactly what she needed. After a minute or two, her trembling began to ease, the violent crying melting into a soft wash of tears.

"Did he hurt you?" he rasped, dreading her answer.

"N-no. You got here in time."

"Thank God," he groaned, undone by the way she felt in his arms. He wanted to keep holding her, for hours on end, but his time was already running out. He sensed the exact instant she started to make her way free of the terror, her body stiffening in his arms as she pulled her head back, lifting her tearstained gaze to his worried one.

Then those soft, glistening eyes narrowed with fury, and he knew all hell was about to break loose.

* * *

"What are you doing here?" Elise yelled, trying to push away from the bare-chested Runner. But she couldn't budge free from his tight hold. "Oh, God. Are you *stalking* me?"

"Shh. Calm down," he murmured, his deep voice soft and soothing, as if he were trying to gentle a frightened child. "It's okay.… It's not like that."

She fought to control a fresh round of shivers, hating that he was a witness to her weakness, but knew she was failing. The quivering began in her bones, radiating outward, born as much from anger as it was from fear. "Then explain it. R-right now," she stammered, unable to keep her jaw from shaking.

With a rough sigh, he lowered his arms, letting her go, and a rush of cold swarmed in to replace his delicious heat. As they both moved to their feet, he said, "Your brother put you under Bloodrunner protection after what happened that day with Farrow, when you thought someone had been in your house."

Elise blinked, unable to believe she'd just heard him correctly. Bracing herself with a hand against the nearest wall, she shook her head. "What did you just say?"

He sighed again, rubbing the back of his neck. "You heard me."

Anger straightened her spine. "He had no right to do that!"

"He did it because he cares about you. And he was even more concerned about your safety after the attack at the Alley."

"So then you've all been watching me?" she choked out. "Spying on me, like I'm some pathetic little thing that gets spooked by her own shadow?"

His nostrils flared as he sucked in a sharp breath, his jaw rigid. "Those weren't shadows tonight, Elise. Those were two asshole Lycan males intent on hurting you."

"I don't care! You had no right. Not behind my back." She swiped angrily at her tears, furious that she'd so completely lost control in front of him and couldn't seem to get it back.

She flinched as he moved, then felt like an idiot when she realized he was only unknotting the sleeves of the flannel shirt that was tied around his waist. "It's okay," he told her, a husky edge to the words that touched her senses on an even deeper level than the fear—one she wasn't willing to acknowledge, not even to herself. "I'm just giving you my shirt."

"What? Why?"

Keeping those dark eyes on her face, he said, "Your dress is ripped, sweetheart."

She gasped, looking down in horror to see that the entire left side of her bodice had been torn during her struggle with the Lycan, revealing the heavy swell of her breast and the pink tip of her nipple. *"Damn it,"* she hissed, clutching the tattered fabric over her chest as she lifted her head and glared at him. "And don't call me that. I'm not your sweetheart."

He gave her a crooked smile. "Okay."

"Okay? What does *okay* mean?" she snapped, the words as brittle as autumn leaves as she grabbed the shirt out of his big, rugged hand and quickly pulled it on over her tattered dress.

"It means I'm not going to argue with you about it when you're upset," he said affably.

She lifted her brows. "But you'll…what? Argue with me about it later?"

His lips curled with the barest fraction of a smile. "Depends on whether you keep telling me not to call you *sweetheart*."

Elise tried to storm past him then, too overwhelmed to deal with his crazy brand of charm, but her stupid knees buckled with her first step and the room spun. Before she could tell him to go to hell, he had her swept up in his strong arms, clutched against his broad, muscular chest as he carried her over to the bed. But instead of setting her down and moving away, he sat down on the edge of the mattress, then carefully deposited her beside him.

"How did he get the jump on you?" he asked as she quickly scooted over, needing to put more distance between them.

"I didn't know he was behind me."

Damn it. The instant the words left her mouth, Elise realized her mistake, her heart lurching into her throat. Turning her head away from him, she tried to hide behind her hair, which had long since fallen from its twist, but he lifted his hand, pushing it behind her ear. Then he caught her chin, bringing her face back around. "They had their scents masked, but why couldn't you hear him? Or sense him?"

It took considerable effort, but she forced a smirk onto her face to hide her shame as she jerked her chin free, then met his dark gaze with her own. "That's none of your damn business, Runner."

He opened his mouth, no doubt ready to argue that point, when Jeremy's deep voice called out from the living room. "Hey, Pall, where are you guys? We let ourselves in through the kitchen door. Me and Cian need to talk to you."

The corner of his mouth twitched with a wry, fleeting grin. They both knew that Jeremy and Cian, two of the most highly trained hunters the pack had ever known, could use their acute sense of smell to pinpoint their exact location in the house. Which meant they weren't so much asking *where* they were, as they were inquiring as to whether or not they were *decent* enough for company. Idiots! She never should have danced with Wyatt at the reception. Now these jackasses were never going to let them live it down.

"We're back here!" Wyatt shouted, and Elise quickly wrapped the flannel shirt even tighter around her body. In the next moment, a rain-soaked Jeremy and Cian came into her bedroom, followed closely by Carla and Mason, who were equally waterlogged. She could only be thankful that Eric hadn't come prowling in with them because she was too on edge to deal with her brother at the moment. She hoped to God he'd stayed at the Alley, enjoying his wedding night. These four were bad enough!

Whipping her head to the side, she scowled at the gorgeous jerk sitting beside her on the bed. "Did you have to call *everyone?*" she seethed, hoping he could tell just how furious she was with him.

He gave an innocent shake of his head. "Hey, I didn't make the call. I asked that Browning guy to do it when I was rushing inside."

"Your neighbor called Mason, but we were already on our way up to check out something else," Jeremy offered as an explanation, before shooting a frowning glance at the puddle of water he was leaving on her floor.

Before she could fire off another sharp-edged remark, Cian crossed his arms over his chest, propped his broad shoulders against the wall and cut his piercing gray gaze from her to Wyatt. "So what happened?" the Irishman asked them, lifting his brows. "The neighbor was waiting out front when we got here, but he didn't know anything. Just said that he heard screams and fighting. We searched the woods back there but couldn't pick anything up to follow. And the rain is coming down hard now. It hasn't left anything on the ground to track."

Keeping it short and succinct, Wyatt gave them the rundown. "I think whoever the scouts spotted on our land tonight paid Elise a visit. I was searching the woods behind the house when I heard her scream. There were two Lycans inside her house, wearing masks that covered everything but their lips and their eyes, which were brown in their human forms. I fought them, and they took off when they heard the rest of you show up."

She could tell by the look on the Runners' faces that they knew he'd left out a portion of the story. And though she understood why he would have to fill them in later about what had happened in her room—that she'd very nearly been the victim of another sexual assault—Elise was thankful that he didn't make her sit there and listen to a recounting of the horrific event.

Looking at the others, Wyatt asked, "Can you guys give us a second?"

"Sure," Mason murmured, clapping his hand on Jeremy's damp shoulder as he steered his partner toward the door, motioning for the others to go before them. Without looking back, the handsome, rugged Runner said, "We'll take another look outside and see what we can find. Maybe we'll get lucky and pick up a scent."

"Yeah, about that," Wyatt grunted, sounding kind of shocked and embarrassed. "I forgot to mention that they had their scents masked."

A few stifled curses could be heard out in the hallway, as well as a low laugh that sounded as if it was coming from Cian, who probably thought that important lapse had something to do with *her.* Mason was at the back of the group, and he stopped and turned in the doorway with a scowl that would have scared the hell out of most people. "No scent at all—same as the ones who attacked us in the Alley?"

Wyatt nodded. "Yeah. Just like those assholes. They were also stronger than they should have been."

"Shit," Mason growled, scrubbing a hand down his face. "Did they say anything that might reveal their identity? Or what they were doing here?"

They both shook their heads, but Elise wasn't sure Mason believed her. "We'll take that look outside," he told them, "but I want you *both* at my cabin for a meeting in the morning."

She frowned as the Runner left the room. She didn't want to go to the Alley tomorrow morning. After tonight, all she wanted was to…to… *Hell,* she didn't know what she wanted.

"How long will it take you to pack?" Wyatt asked, his deep voice pulling her from her troubled thoughts as he moved to his feet.

She tilted her head back, staring up at him in confusion. "Pack what?"

"A bag. You can't stay here by yourself. You're coming home with me."

Her jaw dropped as she blinked. "Is that some kind of sick joke?"

"Naw," Carla drawled, popping her head back into the room from the hallway. She'd obviously decided to ignore Wyatt's request for privacy. "I know what Pall's joke face looks like, and that isn't it. He's dead serious."

Gritting her teeth, she said, "I'm not going anywhere with you, Pallaton."

He pushed his hands into his front pockets, his eyes hooded as he watched her stand up, grab a couple of clean towels from the basket of folded laundry that was sitting on her dresser and start laying them out over the puddles that'd been left on her floor. "Don't let pride make you stupid, El. You know this is the smartest thing you can do."

"Wow. Do you have any idea how arrogant you sound right now?" She clenched her teeth as she tossed a towel to Carla, then snapped the last one open, laying it over the water that had dripped off of Cian. "What is it with you guys always bundling up us little women and dragging us off to the Alley? Where in God's name did you all get the idea that we can't survive without you around to protect us with your big bad selves?"

He didn't say anything in his defense when she turned back to him with a blistering glare. But he didn't need to. He simply shifted his gaze to the bruise she could feel forming on her cheek, then lower, to where she was clutching the edges of his shirt over her chest, reminding her of just what he'd saved her from, and she trembled with fury as he slowly lifted that knowing gaze back to hers. "You son of a bitch," she whispered, and his expression tightened, the skin around his eyes and mouth revealing his tension and rage, though he seemed determined not to express them in front of her. For some reason, that just made her even angrier.

"We can argue as long as you want, but it isn't going to change the outcome. Either you come back with me, or

I'm planting my ass here with you. And I do mean *with* you, El. I won't be shoved out on that short-ass sofa in your living room. There's not much left of it, anyway."

"You've lost your freaking mind."

"Probably," he muttered, scrubbing the palm of his hand against the hard angle of his jaw. "But it doesn't change the fact that you need a keeper."

"I can stay with my brother!"

He arched one perfect midnight brow. "You do realize this is his wedding night, don't you?"

She flushed, wracking her brain for an alternative. "With Jillian and Jeremy, then."

"Won't work. They've already started turning their spare room into a nursery."

She blinked, stunned. "She's pregnant?"

He shook his head. "Not yet. But they're hoping she will be soon and wanted to get a head start on things."

"Oh. I...I didn't know."

As if he knew exactly what she was thinking, he said, "They only just decided this week to start on the nursery, or I'm sure she would have told you."

She chewed on the corner of her lip. "I can always sleep on their sofa."

Zoing! His right brow arched again, as if it was spring-loaded, those dark eyes starting to glitter with a spark of humor, as if he were beginning to find something funny in her belligerent desperation. "When I have a perfectly good spare bedroom? I don't think so."

She was so frustrated she wanted to scream. "Who cares what you think, you arrogant ass? I do not take orders from you! Why can't you just leave me the hell alone and stop trying to control me?"

Hmm. Maybe yelling at him again wasn't the best

idea she'd ever had. He suddenly wasn't looking as if he still found this funny, the muscle pulsing in his jaw telling her he was done with this particular argument. "I'm not interested in controlling you. I'm just trying to keep you the fuck alive. So pack your goddamn bag and start acting like an adult instead of a stubborn child. Carla and I will drive you down and she can help you get settled."

"Carla? Are you two bunking up together now?"

Carla snorted from her position in the doorway, making Elise flinch, since she'd somehow forgotten the female Runner was standing there. "You think I'm gonna live with that jackass?" The blonde laughed under her breath, blowing her bangs out of her eyes. "I'm not that crazy!"

Elise looked to Wyatt for an explanation. With a shrug, he said, "I just thought it might make you more comfortable to know that she'll be around a lot. Her cabin is right next door to mine."

"But we are *not* an item," Carla added, shuddering. "I love the guy, but I don't want you putting any sick images in my head. I'll be scarred for life."

It was dizzying, how she could go from being so pissed off one moment to wanting to bang her head against a freaking wall in the next. Glancing from one Runner to the other with a look of pure, disgruntled confusion, she said, "You two are so weird."

"Yeah, we get that a lot." Carla laughed.

At the same time, Wyatt growled, "Can we get a damn move on?"

When Elise simply remained where she was standing, he exhaled a short, exasperated breath. "Stop wasting time, El. If you don't come with me, then I'm moving in here. Which is it gonna be?"

"Fine," she snapped, making it sound like another sharp four-letter *F* word. "I'll pack a bag, *Dad*."

He ran his tongue over the front of his teeth, but didn't call her out on her snotty attitude. Instead, he simply said, "Good. And make sure you pack enough."

"Enough for what?" she asked, already walking toward her closet.

"A few weeks, at least."

Oh, hell no. "A few weeks?" she growled, spinning toward him with another furious scowl. "Are you insane?"

"Getting there," he muttered, heading for the door, the motion making all those mouthwatering muscles do interesting things under his tight, burnished skin. Even his freaking back was gorgeous, which just struck her as incredibly unfair. "If you want to argue about it, save it for the Alley," he said over his shoulder. "Right now we need to get the hell out of here."

"Why?" she whispered, his gritty words making the fear she'd been fighting down start to rise right back up. She licked her lips, struggling to stay calm, but it felt like a losing battle. "You don't think they're coming back, do you?"

"I don't know what to think, Elise. But it's better to be safe than sorry. And you'll be a hell of a lot safer there than you are here."

With her pulse pounding in her ears, Elise watched him leave the room, thinking he was probably right about her physical well-being.

She just wasn't too sure about the rest of her.

Chapter 4

After getting a still-irritated, snippy Elise settled in his spare bedroom, Wyatt grabbed a T-shirt and then walked back to the cabin's living room, where Carla waited for him in one of the leather chairs that sat across from his sofa. Too on edge to sit down, he made his way over to the empty fireplace, crossing his arms over his chest as he braced his back against the mantel.

"What?" he grunted, since his partner was staring at him with a bemused expression on her face.

"Nothing," she murmured.

Choking back a groan, he said, "I'm tired and in a shitty mood, Reyes. So, please, just spit it out."

She coughed to clear her throat, then shook her head. "I don't know. It's just that you're not usually this tense, Pall. You look ready to crack."

He shrugged, not knowing what to say.

"So what's going on with you two?" she asked, sounding genuinely concerned.

"Don't know." He rubbed his jaw as he glanced at the bottle of whiskey that sat on the sideboard against the far wall. Rolling his shoulder in a restless gesture, he kept his voice low as he said, "I want her. But I'm worried about her, too. So I'll put the other on the back burner for the time being and help her deal with whatever's going on."

"You want her how?" Carla questioned.

He arched a brow. "How do you think?" His tone was dry.

Not one to mince words, his partner asked, "You're just looking for sex?"

Wyatt scowled. "Do we really need to have this conversation? Because not to sound juvenile or anything, but it's kinda freaking me out, seeing as how you're one of the closest things to family I still have. And I sure as hell wouldn't talk about my sex life with my sister, if I had one."

"Yeah, I get that. And I'm sorry about the ick factor. You know I love you—but I like Elise, too." A notch started to form between her pale brows, just visible beneath the edge of her bangs. "I don't want to see her get hurt if you're only looking to get laid."

"I'm not going to break her heart," he muttered, shoving a hand back through his hair in a telling act of frustration. "Hell, a woman like her would never fall for a guy like me in the first place. But it doesn't mean we can't have some fun together."

The notch on her forehead got deeper. "What do you mean by 'a guy like me'? What's wrong with you?"

"Nothing," he grunted. "Just drop it."

She didn't respond right away. She just sat there staring at him from the edge of her seat, studying him, making him feel like a bug pinned down under a microscope. He didn't care for the feeling. And now he *really* wanted that damn drink. Heading over to the sideboard, he poured more than a little whiskey into a glass, then walked back and took a seat on the sofa.

"Gee, thanks for offering me one, too," she drawled wryly. "And you know what I think? I think you're full of bullshit." He started to argue, but she cut him off. "And you're blind if you don't think that Elise is interested in you. Like *really* interested. Yeah, she's skittish. She has good reason to be. But when you're not looking at her, she's watching you. She can't keep her eyes off you."

A wave of heat swept through his insides, and it didn't have a damn thing to do with the mouthful of whiskey he'd just downed.

"Whoa!" Carla pressed a hand to her chest and gaped at him, really playing up the drama. "Did you just smile so big your dimples flashed? Holy shit!"

"Lay off," he groaned, closing his eyes as he slumped down and dropped his head against the back of the sofa. But he couldn't stop his lips from twitching.

"Man, and I didn't even have my camera to document this momentous event. This is a tragedy of, like, epic proportions. I haven't seen a genuine, full-fledged smile out of you in months!"

He cracked one eye open to glare at the obnoxious little imp. "Are you going to keep giving me shit all night?"

"Probably," she admitted with a smirk.

Cursing something foul under his breath, he tossed back another hefty drink of his whiskey, clenching his teeth as it burned his throat.

"Whoa," she said again, only this time she wasn't teasing. "Easy there, Pall. It wasn't my intention to make you want to get shit-faced."

"Yeah?" He snorted as he wiped his mouth with the back of his wrist, then dropped his head back again. "Then what exactly were you going for?"

She was silent for a moment, and then she took a deep breath and said, "Look, I know the reason why this partnership between us works. Yeah, we're friends, and I would go to the line for you. But we get along so well because we don't push. I know you have shit in your past, and you know I have shit in mine, but we never hound each other for the gritty details."

Sitting up, he braced his elbows on his spread knees and stared at her over the square, rustic coffee table. "Then why are we even having this conversation?"

The look in her brown eyes was troubled. "Because for the first time since I met you, I think there's a reason to."

Swallowing the last of his whiskey, he said, "My past has nothing to do with the present, Reyes."

A crooked smile touched her lips. "Come on, Pall. You're too smart to actually believe that."

"If we're spilling blood here," he muttered, setting his empty glass on the table, "why don't you go first?"

Quietly, she said, "Because I'm not the one playing Russian roulette with a woman on the edge."

The silence stretched out, both of them refusing to back down. He blew out a rough breath and finally said, "Look, I know you're only trying to help. But stop. I don't need it." He moved to his feet. "And now it's time to call it a night."

Carla didn't argue. But she gave him a knowing look that said she had his number and wasn't letting this go.

Knowing there wasn't a chance in hell he was going to get any sleep, Wyatt locked the door behind his irritating, if well-meaning, partner, then stretched out over the long sofa and grabbed the remote. He barely noticed what was playing on the TV as he clicked it on, too busy thinking that it was the strangest damn thing, how after a lifetime of being a werewolf, it'd taken a woman to truly awaken the savage, predatory animal inside him.

Not that he hadn't already possessed a primal, predaceous side. You couldn't do the job he did without one. But that primitive, possessive, animalistic part of his nature had never bled into his sexual relationships. Being a hunter, he was one of the best, the Lycan part of his soul as skillful a predator as there could be—and he put that talent to good use. But like Carla had insinuated, his past *had* shaped the fabric of his character, and he knew he approached sex differently than his fellow male Runners. While they struggled to master their more aggressive desires, he'd never worried about losing control with a woman when he had her beneath him. He'd seen what violence could do to a female at an early age, and he wanted no part of that. Instead, his sexual relationships had been, for lack of a better word, fun. Something he could walk away from easily, and never something that made him feel as if he were coming out of his fucking skin.

At least, that was how it'd always been for him before. Now, in some kind of ironic twist of fate, the one woman Wyatt needed to treat with tender restraint had awakened a side of him he'd never even known existed. A dark, savagely dominant side that wanted to conquer and possess. That wanted to take Elise Drake beneath his fevered body, drive himself into her with all the primal ferocity of his beast and make her writhe. Make her scream and shout from the searing, relentless burn of pleasure, until her cries were hoarse and her nails were raking down his back. Until she was as wild and as out of control as he felt every time he so much as thought about her.

And now you need to cool it, you idiot, before you start howling like a sex-crazed maniac and end up scaring the hell out of her.

Cursing under his breath, Wyatt turned the volume on the TV up a little, but he still wasn't really watching the sitcom that was on, too focused on the redhead showering in his guest room. He'd heard the rattle of the pipes start while he'd been talking to Carla, and now he was in a world of hurt, thinking of Elise standing naked and wet beneath the steaming stream of water, her beautiful body slick and soft and in desperate need of comfort. A comfort he was more than willing to provide, if she would only give him the chance.

Yeah. And given how pissed she is, she'd probably rather bunk down with a bloody vampire.

Drawing in a slow, deep breath, Wyatt locked his jaw and forced his attention to the mundane TV show… knowing it was more than likely going to be the longest damn night of his life.

Elise awakened with a gasp, trying to shake off the fuzzy remnants of what had been another nightmare. She could sense the morning sunlight against her eyelids and rolled over, pressing the side of her face against the pillow. The bed was comfortable and warm, making her want to stay buried beneath the covers forever, hiding from the rest of the world. But the prickling on her skin suddenly made her realize that she wasn't alone, and she gave another soft gasp as she opened her eyes to find Wyatt sitting in a chair by the window, only a yard or so from where she lay, watching her with that dark, intense gaze that made her breath quicken.

"Bad dream?" he asked, his low voice deep and morning rough.

She pushed her hair out of her eyes, ignoring his question. She didn't want to think about what she'd been dreaming…or why. But she *did* want to know what the hell he was up to. "What are you doing in here, Wyatt?"

His sexy mouth curved in a rueful, lopsided grin as he leaned forward in the chair, resting his elbows on his knees, his legs parted. He was dressed in a pair of faded jeans…and nothing else. All those lean, corded muscles and acres of bronzed skin made her damn mouth water. "You wouldn't believe me if I told you."

"Try me," she snapped.

"All right." His lashes lowered a little, shielding the look in his eyes, his tone deliberately careful. "I was watching you sleep."

"What?" Her face flushed with embarrassment as she sat up, clutching the sheet to her chest. "Why would you do that?"

Gently, he said, "You were making these sounds earlier, like you were afraid. I came in to check on you, said your name, and it quieted you. My being here seemed to make you settle down, so I pulled up a chair and decided to let you get some more sleep."

Oh, um…*wow*. Her first instinct was to snap at him again for invading what was meant to be her personal space here in his cabin, but she knew that was only because she was self-conscious. So she choked down the knee-jerk response and somehow managed to say, "You didn't need to do that, but it was...*nice* of you. So I'll just say thanks."

He gave her a curious half smile, as if he were surprised she'd actually been civil to him for once. Noticing the dark smudges under his eyes, she shook her head and sighed. "Looks like you're going to pay for being a good guy, Wyatt. I slept and you didn't. Now you'll be dragging yourself around all day."

He lifted his broad, powerful shoulders in an uneasy shrug. "I never actually sleep much anyway."

"Why not?" she asked, unable to take her eyes off the muscular expanse of his bare chest. He scratched at the russet-toned skin with his right hand, the casual action completely mesmerizing. She wanted to look away, but she was transfixed, his sheer proximity enough to send her heart rate into overdrive.

It was crazy how he could be so gorgeous and yet so ruggedly male. A sublime specimen of both beauty and primitive, visceral masculinity. Big and broad but as lean as a racehorse, his ropy muscles packed hard and tight beneath that deliciously bronzed skin. He'd been shirtless in front of her last night, but she'd been too upset to really take in the stunning details. But wow. Just wow.

Elise didn't know how long she'd just been sitting there, staring like some sex-crazed female who'd never set eyes on a man before, but she jolted with shock when he suddenly slapped his palms against his knees and stood. "Now that you're up," he said, his voice sounding kind of tight and strange, "you should probably go ahead and get dressed. We don't have much time before we need to leave."

Color burned in her face as she tilted her head back. "Leave? Why? Where are we going?"

"Everyone's gathering for a meeting over at Mason and Torrance's cabin, remember? We need to talk about what happened last night." He paused, that wry twist back on his lips as he rubbed the back of his neck. "And your, uh, brother wants to talk to you."

"What?" she gasped, blinking up at him. "Aren't he and Chelsea already on their way to the airport?"

Golden beams of sunlight caught the blue-black strands of his hair when he shook his head. "They haven't left yet."

Crap! The newlyweds were supposed to catch a flight down to Bermuda for a short honeymoon, since they knew they were going to be needed there in the Alley when the brewing violence finally came to a head. Their trip wasn't meant to last for long, but damn it, she'd wanted them to have at least a bit of time to themselves to celebrate their marriage. And now they probably weren't even getting that! Irritated as hell at her overprotective brother, Elise forgot her embarrassment at being seen in the cotton nightgown she was wearing and quickly tossed back the covers, swinging her mostly bare legs over the side of the mattress. But she stopped almost instantly as a wave of lust slammed into her, like a hot blast of wind, her skin tingling as she sucked in a sharp, startled gasp.

Holy mother of God!

Her senses might have weakened to little better than a human's in recent months, but she didn't need to be able to pick up the gorgeous Runner's scent to know that Wyatt was aroused. A glance at his face revealed his dilated pupils, parted lips and flushed skin. Without a conscious directive from her brain, her gaze swept lower, over his broad shoulders, solid chest and chiseled abs, until she caught a glimpse of his crotch…and her shocked gaze skittered away. But what a glimpse it'd been, the well-worn denim straining over an impossibly long, thick erection that looked seriously huge—*even for a Lycan.* The knowledge that he was hard as a freaking rock made her want to get up and run every bit as much as she wanted to slug the jackass for just standing there, blasting his manliness at her, his sensual mouth curved just a fraction on one side. He no doubt expected her to lay into him for the blatant physiological sign of his interest or go scurrying back under the covers, but she wasn't going to do either of those things.

Forcing herself to be bold, Elise moved to her feet and walked over to the window, watching through the blinds as Michaela and Jillian helped to clean up from last night's wedding. Then she turned to face him with her arms crossed tight over her chest. When it seemed he wasn't capable of dragging his gaze away from her lower body anytime soon, she said, "Cut it out, Pallaton. You're staring like you've never seen a pair of legs before."

His breath sounded a little uneven, and there was a rougher edge to his deep voice that hadn't been there just a moment ago. "I haven't seen a pair like yours, that's for damn sure."

"Well, you can stop staring any second now." She slowly arched a brow. "Better yet, maybe you could just leave and let me get dressed in private."

"Yeah," he murmured, rubbing a hand over his mouth.

But instead of turning toward the door, he took a step in her direction and groaned, *"Shit."*

Elise frowned. "What now?"

"I know I shouldn't do this," he said, grabbing her by her upper arms and yanking her closer, "but you make me stupid."

"Ha! I'm sure your stupidity has nothing to do with— *Mmph!*" The rest of her words were smothered by the shocking, devastating press of Wyatt Pallaton's mouth against hers. He didn't waste any time, immediately slipping his tongue past her lips. One second they'd been standing there talking, and in the next he had her shoved up against the wall beside the window, his big hands braced against the pale gray plaster on either side of her head, while he kissed the hell out of her. And, God, what a kiss. It was lush and devouring, as if he were doing things to her mouth that were meant to make her think of *other* breathtaking, intimate things he could be doing to her body. With that clever tongue. And his impressive—

"Christ, you taste so fucking incredible," he growled, the velvet-rough timbre of his voice melting into her as he went back for an even deeper tasting that was greedy and raw, but somehow beautifully tender. She could feel her heartbeat in her throat, each drugging pulse of pleasure chasing away her fear, even as he moved closer. She should have been screaming by now, hating the feel of him, his cock a hard, thick ridge inside his jeans that he wasn't trying to hide from her as he pressed against her front. But she was too busy kissing him back, rubbing her tongue against his, unable to get enough of his taste to freak out from the stunning feel of his erection. His mouth tasted like…*God,* it tasted like sex. Hot and wet and completely addictive.

It was erotic as hell, the way his tongue hungrily rubbed and delved, seeking her secrets in the intimate flavors of her mouth, until she was half-tempted to give them to him, like an innocent girl falling under the piper's spell. She was enthralled, as if she'd slipped into a fairy ring, her arms lifting from her sides to clutch greedy handfuls of his thick, silken hair, needing him closer. Needing to trap him there with her so that he couldn't ever get away.

When she gasped his name, he responded with a low, guttural sound that was almost more animal than man, his hands suddenly on her waist, gripping her in a hold that let her feel his strength, even as he was careful not to hurt her. She moaned into the kiss, confused by how much she enjoyed his touch, his fingers clenching. Then he started moving his hands up and down, stroking her sides, the calluses on his fingers and palms snagging at the delicate fabric of her gown, each slow pass taking his touch higher, until he was skimming the sides of her breasts, while his mouth kept up that deep, evocative torture. He was melting her down—breaking her open—and she felt her nipples pull into tight, swollen points that ached for his attention. She shivered, wanting him to touch her there almost as badly as the idea unnerved her, her thoughts and body in chaos, when a loud banging noise from outside, where some of the Runners were breaking down the parquet dance floor, had them both flinching, jerking apart, panting for breath. He immediately dropped his hands and stepped back, his smoldering gaze locked hard on hers, the glowing rim of gold around the edge of each dark iris telling her just how close his beast was to the surface.

Oh, God. What the hell am I doing?

Elise had to bite her tongue to keep from begging

him to come back. She wanted him so badly. Felt desperate. Needy. *Starved.* Not for sex—just sex with *him.* Touch and taste and heat. Damp, slick skin and fractured breaths. She wanted to fling herself at him. Drape herself over that hard-muscled body and let him have at her. Beg him. Plead. Pray. But she was locked behind some kind of frustrating invisible wall, the need unable to break through into action…or even words. Instead, she made a choked gasping sound and stumbled to the side, dizzy and so freaking disappointed in herself she could have cried.

Could have?

Right. Who was she trying to fool? Her eyes were already stinging with moisture, her mouth trembling. Oh, boy. Just take a look at the emotional wreck in all her glory. At times like this she felt as pathetic as her father had always told her she was, and she wanted to lash out at the gorgeous male who'd just blown her mind almost as badly as she wanted to make him her own personal little love slave. Though *little* was probably a ridiculous choice of words, considering the guy was…well, extremely well hung.

"Please, don't panic," he rasped, holding up his hands as he took another step back, and she knew he was afraid that she'd stumbled to the side to get away from him. "I'm sorry," he added roughly, his dark gaze shadowed with concern even as he was licking his damp lower lip, as if to keep her taste in his mouth. "I tried, damn it, but I couldn't resist."

"Why are you doing this?" she hissed, her waspish tone hopefully covering the fact that she'd been enjoying his kiss *far more* than was wise, considering there wasn't a chance in hell she could follow through on where that breathtaking encounter had been heading. "Do cowards turn you on? Is that it?"

The change in his expression happened so fast she would have missed it if she'd blinked, his nostrils flaring as he clenched his jaw. "Are you calling yourself a coward?" The clipped words were hard with anger. "Because that's bullshit, El. Yeah, I want to protect you. Keep you safe. But you're fucking crazy if you believe I could ever think of you as weak. You're one of the strongest, bravest people I've ever known."

She shook her head, stunned, not knowing what to make of him.

"I mean it," he growled, pointing a finger right at her face, like putting a point on an exclamation mark. "The absolute strongest."

For some reason, his words made her furious. "Yeah," she snarled, glaring back at him. "Last night I was just the epitome of feminine *strength,* wasn't I?"

Needing to be alone, she started to storm past him, but he caught her arm, holding her in place. He didn't say anything until she finally turned her head to look at him. "If we're going to talk about last night, then there's something I want to know," he said. "Why didn't you shift? It would have given you a better chance at fighting him off."

"I..." She swallowed, then forced her response from her tight throat. "If you know anything about me at all, Pallaton, then you know I don't do that anymore."

His lashes lowered, concealing the look in his eyes. "Not even when it could save your life?"

"That's right," she said flatly, staring at his mouth. "Not even then."

A tremor moved through his powerful frame. "That's

unacceptable, Elise. You *have* to be willing to protect yourself."

A bitter laugh jerked past her lips. "Oh, I would have. I wouldn't have let them do it to me again."

He sucked in a sharp breath that lifted his bronzed chest, then slowly let it out, the hand curled around her arm shaking. "That better not mean what it sounds like."

It was strange, how shame could make you just as brittle as anger. "Why?" she snapped, actually feeling an electrical shock sizzle through her body when she lifted her gaze and locked it with his. "Does it bruise your masculine sense of honor to think of a woman killing herself? Of you not being there to protect her?"

He flinched as if she'd slapped him, her sharp words striking with painful precision. A verbal weapon that she'd used to slice him, and it'd worked. He cursed something gritty under his breath as he let go of her arm. Then he scrubbed his hands over his face a few times before lowering them to his sides, where they curled into powerful fists. "I want your promise that you won't do that, Elise."

She gave another bitter laugh that was cold and cutting, without an ounce of warmth. "You must be joking."

"Like hell I am."

"Why are you doing this? What do you want from me?"

"I told you last night." His voice got deeper...*rougher*. "I want to be your friend."

"Well, now it's my turn to call bullshit, Wyatt. You don't even know me!"

"I know more than you think," he insisted, the golden color of his wolf eyes bleeding even deeper into his piercing gaze. Streaks of glittering gold that glimmered and sparked. "I know you're hurting and that you use that little bitch-of-the-year attitude to try to cover it. I know it's all an act—one that's probably exhausting as hell. And I know, without any doubt, that the idea of you taking your own life makes me so furious I could spit nails!"

She blinked, no idea what to say in response, her pulse fluttering like a maddened butterfly trapped at the base of her throat.

"I think we've said more than enough for the moment," he muttered, rubbing one of those big hands over the grim set of his jaw. "Right now we need to get going. So be quick."

She watched with wide eyes as he turned and left the room, shutting the door behind him without even slamming it. Which, judging by the look on his face, couldn't have been easy.

God. Elise sagged down into the chair he'd been sitting in and buried her hot face in her hands, feeling as if she'd just been put through an emotional wringer. Wyatt Pallaton was freaking hell on her system, seducing her by the simple act of being, and she couldn't help but resent the way he'd taken her over so completely. Her thoughts. Her needs. Her...dreams—ones she hadn't even realized she had anymore. It was crazy and no doubt detrimental to her sanity, but she couldn't stop it, even though she knew she needed to. She'd already let one man control her life, and she wasn't about to hand over the reins to another dominant male.

Nearly everything that she'd ever done was a reflection of what her father had wanted. She sold real estate, but not because she wanted to. That had been her father's doing, his way of keeping tabs on her. After all, it wasn't as if the market was booming in Shadow Peak.

Like a good little robot, she'd done what Daddy told her to do, same as she always had. For some reason, even knowing he hated her, she'd never been able to stand up to the man. Not until the night of Max's *Novitiate's* ceremony. That had been the first time that she'd ever publicly defied her father, even though it'd scared the living hell out of her. She'd thought, for a little while after his death, that she might finally have a chance at taking control of her life, but then the feelings had started. Harrowing, frantic feelings of being watched, as if someone were stalking her, keeping a watchful eye over her. She'd been terrified she was just imagining it. Letting the townspeople's hatred and suspicion get to her. Wasting her brother's time whenever she freaked and he had to come check on her.

But as she remembered what her attacker had said last night, Elise knew that she hadn't been imagining things. Oh, God. She *hadn't*.

Looking around Wyatt's spare bedroom, she supposed she could chalk up her current circumstance to letting another man push her around. But to be fair, it didn't feel like that. She might be irritated with him, but Wyatt's insistence that she stay with him hadn't been a chauvinistic need to belittle her. He was truly worried about her. Since she didn't know quite what to do with that at the moment, she tucked it away in her mind and focused on what needed to be done. Another hot shower was what she needed more than anything, to help calm her nerves. And how lovely that she wouldn't have to keep constantly checking the other side of the curtain, terrified some monster was going to creep up on her and tear her life to pieces all over again.

Shower time when you'd been living in terror for

years was not something that could be called relaxing or enjoyable. But she'd enjoyed the hell out of the one she'd taken here last night. Making her way into the soothing gray-and-white-tiled bathroom, Elise turned on the water, slipped out of her gown and wondered if her heart rate would ever return to normal. Strangely, it wasn't last night's attack that had left her so shaken. Oh, she was sick with fear about what had happened, and she didn't see that changing anytime soon. But it was Wyatt who had really played a number on her equilibrium.

And the way he'd kissed her had damn near fried her on the spot, leaving her wet and aching and wracked with confusion.

Whatever was going on between the two of them, it was going to lead to trouble. And yet, even knowing it, she was incredibly tempted to stay and see just what other surprises fate felt like throwing at her before it was done.

Elise just hoped, in the end, it didn't throw her to the wolves.

Chapter 5

Stepping out onto Wyatt's front porch, Elise shielded her eyes from the bright glare of sunlight and looked out over the place the Runners called home. The Alley was actually nothing like its namesake. Instead of being dark and grungy, the Runners made their home in a secluded, sloping glade surrounded by the wild, natural beauty of the forest, housing only the Runners' individual cabins, along with a few that were currently empty. Eric and Chelsea had taken one and now lived here permanently. And, God, did that sound wonderful.

Elise knew she didn't belong in this idyllic place, but she couldn't deny that there was an incredible feeling of safety here. Yes, the Runners were vigilant about defense, especially since the attack that had been waged over Chelsea and her sister—but she thought the feeling had more to do with the fact that those living here were a family in the truest sense of the word. They loved each other, and were willing to die for each other, in a way that the Silvercrest had lost at some point. Or maybe the mountaintop Lycans had simply never had it, stubborn bastards that they were.

Eric believed it was the pack's pride that made them so obstinate in their refusal to fully accept the Runners, and Elise couldn't help but agree. Without the Bloodrunners, those who had survived her father's maniacal bid for power would have been forced to live under the rule of a sadistic madman, and their lives ultimately destroyed. After the way the townspeople had treated the Runners for so many years, the fact that the Runners had saved them was a difficult pill to swallow for many in the pack, and they reacted with wariness or anger because they didn't know how else *to* react.

God forbid they just suck it up and be grateful for the help they'd been given.

Wyatt came out onto the porch, closing the front door behind him, and she frowned, the similarity in the situations not escaping her. This man had put his life on the line to protect her. Had brought her into his home without asking for anything in return. And how was she repaying him? By acting like the biggest bitch this side of the Mississippi. God, why was he even bothering with her?

"Let's go," he said, coming up beside her. "Now that they've gotten the dance floor broken down, everyone will be waiting over at Mason's."

As they started across the sun-dappled glade, she tugged on the hem of the thin, slouchy gray sweater she'd pulled on with a tank top, jeans and sandals, unsure of what to expect at the meeting. Despite Eric's status as a Bloodrunner, she wasn't a part of this close-knit group, which meant she didn't belong here. She knew they were an incredible bunch, but come on. How much could she honestly expect them to care about her problems? Were they going to be pissed that Wyatt had brought her here, when she could be putting them in danger? She didn't know if it were simply coincidence that the Lycan who'd attacked her last night in her bedroom was one of the ones who'd raped her three years ago or if he had purposefully sought her out. Had she been targeted because of her brother's connection to the Runners? Because of her father? Or simply because of what had happened to her?

And how were the Runners going to react if they learned that the Lycan from last night was almost certainly one of her rapists? Did she have the guts to tell them, when she could barely think about it in the privacy of her own mind?

Her internal stream of doubts and questions was cut off the instant she spotted her brother walking out the front door of his cabin with his new wife right beside him. Eric's dark gaze instantly locked with hers, and though he had his wife's hand clasped securely in his, he did *not* look like a man simply enjoying his first day of married life. God, Chelsea must be furious with her for screwing this up for them. Instead of getting wrapped up in the excitement of their honeymoon, her idiot brother was letting what had happened last night work him into one of his pissed off "I'm the male, which means I know how to protect you" moods. She loved him more than anything, and while he was as far from their father as a man could be, there were times when Eric was just a little too freaking alpha for her tastes.

Marching toward him as he came down the front steps of his cabin with Chelsea, Elise scowled and said, "This is ridiculous, Eric! Either you go on your honeymoon or I'm leaving and going back up to Shadow Peak!"

Her brother's silver gaze was hard and sharp. "This isn't the time for a tantrum, Elise."

"Bullshit!" she snapped. "I am not a child and I am not *your* responsibility."

Letting go of his wife's hand so that he could wrap his arm around Chelsea's waist instead and pull her into his side, Eric slid a hooded look toward Wyatt, who'd decided to join them, rather than heading on over to Mason's on his own. "We'll lay low here for a week or two," Eric said, the look in his eyes a little sharper as he finally looked away from Wyatt's deliberately neutral expression, and locked his gaze with hers again. "Once we know you're okay and that everything's settled, then we'll take the trip to Bermuda."

"Eric, that's—"

"That's final, Elise. I'm not going to argue with you about it. No way in hell am I leaving when you might need me. That's not what family does."

"He's right," Chelsea added, giving her a small smile. "You can't ask us to leave when this is where we need to be."

"Fine." She fisted her hands at her sides and narrowed her eyes, her nostrils flaring as she pulled in a deep breath. "But I'm not staying with you, so don't even ask."

She could tell that Chelsea was trying to bite back another smile, while Eric just scowled. But he didn't argue against Elise's statement, obviously wanting some privacy with his wife when they were at home. Of course, he also obviously wasn't done acting like a total meat-head. "I don't care if you stay at Wyatt's," he told her, his jaw hard. "I trust *him* to do what it takes to keep you alive when I'm not with you. But I want your house on the market by tomorrow."

Elise gaped, unable to believe she'd just heard him correctly. "What? Why would I—"

He cut her off with a frustrated snarl that reminded her of Eli, their older brother, and her chest ached with familiar pain. "It's time you stop acting like a stubborn little brat and move your ass to the Alley permanently. We all want you here."

"That's absurd!" she railed, so angry she started to tremble. "I'm not a Runner!"

Eric snorted as he cut another look toward Wyatt and then brought his hooded gaze back to her. "Like anyone who lives here gives a shit."

"The others are all inside waiting for us," Chelsea murmured, moving forward a little and tugging on Eric's waist. "Come on. You two can finish this argument later, when you've both had some time to cool down."

Gritting her teeth, Elise waited until the couple had walked away, then pulled in another deep, shuddering breath. She was grateful for Wyatt's silence, though she could feel the warm force of his gaze as he stared at her profile. She didn't know what to say, so she said nothing. Exhaling in a low, audible rush, she finally turned her head and locked her gaze with the dark, smoldering heat of his. She didn't know if he was still turned on from the kiss they'd shared that morning or if something else had gotten under his skin, but she didn't have the strength to deal with it now. Not when she was heading into God only knew what at this meeting. "I guess we might as well get this over with," she muttered, relieved when he simply nodded and fell into step beside her as they made their way over to the cabin.

Less than a minute later, Elise found herself packed into a warm, vanilla-scented kitchen with everyone who lived there in the Alley, along with an older couple sitting at the table who she knew were Mason's parents, Robert and Olivia Dillinger. Wyatt took a seat beside her at the table, along with Carla, Cian, Brody and his wife, Michaela. The others either sat on chairs that had been carried in from the living room or propped themselves up against the kitchen counters, their ankles crossed in front of them. Steaming mugs of aromatic coffee were passed around, and then they got down to business. Mason asked Wyatt to explain about the attack that had taken place at her house the night before, since not all of them had been there, and there was a collective air of tension when he shared the Lycans' lack of scent.

"So it was most likely two Whiteclaw males," Brody said in a low, strained voice, his scarred face set in a worried expression. "But the question is who? We have to assume that they all have equal access to the drugs. Which means it could have been anyone from the pack."

"Then we're essentially back at square one," Cian murmured.

"Exactly," Brody muttered. "And who knows where they've sold that shit in the region? It could have easily spread beyond the Whiteclaw by now."

"Now, hold up there a minute," Mason's father argued. "We can't just start looking at *everyone* as our enemy. That's the kind of thing that starts wars."

Jeremy crossed his arms over his chest and scowled.

"Open your eyes, Robert. We're surrounded by enemies. War is inevitable. The only variables are *who* and *when*."

The older Lycan slapped his palm against the top of the table, making several of the women jump, including herself. "It's that kind of attitude that's going to get us all killed!"

"Can we save the bickering for later and get back to the subject?" Mason snapped, sounding like a father who was getting ready to separate his bickering kids. Which was kind of funny, considering one of the males arguing *was* his father.

Cian leaned forward in his chair, braced his elbows on his parted knees and looked at Mason. "How did the meeting you had this morning with the Youngbloods go?" The Youngbloods were a small pack to the west of the Silvercrest, and they had strong connections to the Donovan family, who were working with the Whiteclaw. Elise knew that neither of her brothers had ever trusted the Youngblood pack, and she was curious to hear what Mason had to say about them.

Setting down his coffee mug, the Runner scowled as he answered Cian's question. "They were tight-assed and close-lipped. I'd say Claymore has definitely dug his blackmailing claws into more than a few high-ranking members in the pack."

After an unlikely ally had saved Eric's life when a dozen of the Whiteclaw and Donovans had attacked the Runners in the Alley the previous month, they'd learned that Roy Claymore was using blackmail—in the form of taped recordings of Lycans participating in gang rapes on drugged human girls—to gain control not only within his own pack, but also among the others that surrounded the Silvercrest. For the Whiteclaw, the rapes were about more than evil, deviant appetites. They were about power. Like a chess master setting up his game, Roy Claymore was plotting the destruction of the Silvercrest clan, one sadistic move at a time.

Her face unusually pale, Carla said, "Are you saying that you think he's hit the leaders in the Youngblood pack?"

A dark lock of hair fell over Mason's brow as he nodded.

"Oh, God. That's insane. Are there really that many evil assholes out there just waiting for the opportunity to abuse a woman?" Chelsea asked, her voice cracking with emotion. Eric reached over and grabbed her hand, giving it a comforting squeeze, while a brutal look of rage hardened his face. After the Whiteclaw attack on the Alley, Elise knew that her brother had spent days going to the pack's borders and demanding that Roy face him in a Challenge Fight to the death. But the Lycan had never accepted Eric's challenges. Instead, he hid behind his "super soldiers," refusing to defend his honor because it was clear he didn't have any.

"Unfortunately," Mason added, "Roy probably knew exactly who to target." His scowl deepened. "I wouldn't be surprised to learn that there are a few in Shadow Peak he has under his thumb, as well."

Michaela's soft, husky voice entered the conversation. "So then, depending on what the Greywolf to the north of us decide to do, it looks like we might very well be on our own."

A grim smile touched Cian's mouth as he shifted his gaze toward the stunning brunette. "That's nothing new for this group, lass," he offered drily. With a smirk on his sensual lips, he looked at his fellow Runners. "We're used to it by now."

While the others nodded their agreement, Mason looked at his dad. "Can you start putting the word out for anyone up in town who might have combat experience?"

Elise knew exactly what the Runner was thinking. It was time to start training the pack for all-out war, and while the Silvercrest knew how to hunt, the majority had never gone claw-to-claw with another Lycan or had any sort of weapons training. If it came down to it, they probably wouldn't know the first thing about fighting in a full-scale battle situation. But if they wanted to survive, it looked as if they were going to have to learn.

Mason and his father discussed setting up several training camps in town, once Robert had found some others who could work with the Runners, and then they took a moment to pass around a fresh, steaming pot of coffee.

"We know what's coming," Brody grunted after taking a drink from his mug. "And that means we know what we have to do. I like the idea of these training camps, but we need to do more. It's time we took some action to get ready, instead of just protecting our borders."

Nodding his head in agreement, Wyatt said, "We need to broaden our scope. Make contact with packs that don't border our land. There's the Blackstone to the north of the Greywolf. And the Claxton pack to the southwest of the Whiteclaw. They're both worth approaching for a possible alliance."

As everyone was offering their approval, Eric cleared his throat, and in a raised voice, he said, "I'm thinking it's also time to bring Eli home."

Wyatt heard Elise's soft gasp of surprise as every head in the kitchen turned toward the newest Runner. Eli Drake was Eric and Elise's older brother, and a banished member of the Silvercrest pack, though Wyatt knew the banishment order had been total bullshit. Knowing her father, he didn't doubt that Stefan Drake had probably been behind the League's decision to banish Eli for killing one of the males who'd raped Elise without their permission. The Lycan should have been made a damn hero, but he'd been forced from his home instead. Wyatt had learned, from talking to Eric, that neither Eric nor Elise had seen Eli since he'd left.

Judging by the determined look on his face, Wyatt could tell that Eric had thought he might have a fight on his hands at the idea of bringing home the man who now traveled the world fighting as part of a nonhuman group of mercenaries who were rumored to be as dangerous as they were good. But as he watched Eric look around the room, meeting the gaze of every man and woman there, it was clear that the Runner had been wrong.

"Long past time, if you ask me," Jeremy finally offered, leaning over so that he could give Eric a slap on his shoulder.

"I agree." Setting his mug on the table, Cian threaded his fingers behind his head and leaned back in his chair. "And that group he works with could be damn useful right about now," he added with a sharp smile.

"I've put in some calls to try to find him," Eric told them, throwing his arm around his wife's shoulders as she leaned into his side, her expression one of obvious relief. "So far, he hasn't called me back. But I'll keep trying."

"Good," Mason said, looking around the room. "That

should be it for now, but I'll call another meeting once we've got more information. In the meantime, let's keep our eyes and ears open, and stay sharp."

The group disbursed, setting off to get things done. Carla's chair nearly crashed into the wall as she shot to her feet and hurried out, but then she was sometimes like that. Wyatt moved to his feet at a slower pace, wanting a word with Jeremy about the patrols they—along with the help of a few scouts from the Runners' security team—were running around the Alley on a twenty-four-hour basis. But before he could get Jeremy's attention, Eric's deep voice came from just behind him. "We need to talk."

Elise was in the middle of a conversation with Jillian and Torrance, so he slipped into the hallway with Eric. Crossing his arms over his chest, he turned to face the newest member of their group. "Shoot," he said, wanting Eric to say whatever he needed to as quickly as possible, so that he could get back to Elise.

"I didn't want to do this in front of my sister, because God knows I'm thankful that you were able to get her here. But why did you take her home with you? What the fuck is that about?" Eric demanded, looking at the moment like a seriously ticked-off bruiser, with his bulging muscles, tats and angry scowl.

Keeping his expression neutral, Wyatt said, "What do you think it's about? She needs protection, but she refuses to let you do it. I'm not giving her a choice."

Eric's silver gaze was piercing. "Then what *are* you planning on giving her?"

Wyatt knew the guy was just trying to be a good brother, but now he was starting to piss him off. "I'm not going to force myself on her, Eric. I just want to help."

Eric scrubbed a hand down his face, then shook his head. "Just be careful with her," he muttered in a low voice. "She puts on a tough-ass bitch routine most of the time, but it's not who she is. She's still hurting and scared and entirely too vulnerable. The last thing she needs is more grief in her life. And she sure as hell doesn't need a man like you—one who doesn't know the first thing about sticking around for the long haul—messing with her."

Lowering his arms, Wyatt shoved his hands into his pockets and thought that if there were ever a good time for a poker face, it was now. "I get that you're her family, Eric, but Elise is a grown woman."

The Lycan slowly arched a brow. "Meaning what, exactly?"

"Meaning it's none of your goddamn business if she needs or doesn't need a man *like me.* That's her choice, not yours."

Eric didn't say anything right away. Just studied him with those hooded eyes that were shadowed with worry. Then, after what felt like forever, the Runner finally blew out a rough breath and muttered, "If you hurt her, you die. You understand what I'm saying?"

"I won't. But if it happened, I would expect nothing less from you."

Eric nodded, then gave him a sharp smile and smacked him on the back. "Hell, you screw up, Chelsea's so protective of Elise, there probably wouldn't be anything left of you for me to finish off."

For some reason, the idea of having to face the little human's wrath was even more unsettling than having Eric Drake gunning for his throat. He frowned, stifling a shudder, and Eric laughed, the look on his face saying he knew *exactly* what Wyatt was thinking.

With a knowing smirk, Eric turned and walked back into the kitchen, leaving Wyatt alone in the hallway. He propped his shoulders against the wall, dropped his head back and took a deep breath.

Did he know what he was doing?

Shit, did he even care if he didn't?

Whatever the answer, it didn't matter. She was in trouble, in danger, and he *needed* to be the one looking out for her. It wasn't a case of want, though that was part of it. And it wasn't about responsibility, either, though as a dominant male, he certainly felt responsible for her. It was simply a case of…need. Of necessity. He needed to protect her like he needed to breathe and drink and eat. It was something that vital. That real.

No matter what it took, he wasn't going to lose her.

Chapter 6

Despite the increasingly violent, chilled winds whipping through the forest as the sun began to set, Wyatt's skin was heating as if he'd been on a long, grueling run. Just from the thought of seeing her again. After the meeting that morning, he'd spent the rest of the day on patrol with Cian, leaving Elise to spend the afternoon with Jillian and the others. He should have been as focused as a laser, but his concentration was shit. No matter how hard he tried, he couldn't get that goddamn kiss they'd shared out of his head.

Stay alert, you jackass. Don't let your dick screw this up.

He took a deep breath and continued making the last pass on the eastern side of the Alley, nearly a half mile from the cabins. Cian was mirroring him on the western side, and when they met up it would be time to head back and let Mason and Jeremy take the next shift.

When both he and Cian had reached the northern point of the patrol route, they started making their way home and ran into Mase and Jeremy a few minutes later. "We heard from my dad before we headed out," Mason told them. "He already has ten names who are willing to help train the others."

"Any backlash from the pack?" Wyatt asked.

"Sounds like Glenn Farrow is foaming at the mouth over the idea," Jeremy replied, "but Robert said he would deal with him."

Running his tongue over his front teeth, Wyatt made a private decision to pay Glenn Farrow a personal visit as soon as possible, making it clear to the asshole that he had better keep his distance from Elise. The Lycan wasn't to be trusted, and Wyatt wanted to make sure he made the fact that she was now under Bloodrunner protection—and more important, *his* protection—crystal clear to the jackass.

Recalling the other issue they'd been waiting for an update on, he asked, "Has Carla learned anything about whether or not someone tampered with Elise's alarm?" His partner had traveled to Shadow Peak late that morning to speak with an employee she knew at the security company that had installed Elise's system. They'd decided the inquiry was better done in person than over the phone, since they didn't know if the company's calls were being monitored. They suspected someone might have tried to gain illegal access to Elise's account, learning a way to bypass her system, and needed Carla's contact to look into it for them.

Mason shook his head. "Not yet. But she said it might take a few days to get the information we're looking for."

They let the guys get on with their patrol and resumed their walk back to the Alley. After making their way in silence for a few minutes, Cian said, "Why doesn't that partner of yours ever date?"

Wyatt gave an uneasy shrug. "Don't know. Why?" He knew Carla was a grown woman, free to make her own choices. But that didn't mean he was going to stand by and let her get her heart broken by a notorious, unapologetic womanizer like Hennessey.

"I was just curious," Cian was saying, pulling out a cigarette. "I mean, have you taken a good look at our little group lately? We're not so little anymore. Half of us have mated and married since last autumn, and now we have Eric and Chelsea. You, me and Reyes are the lone singles of the group, which got me thinking. You would think the one female Runner would have mated before the males."

"Well, I don't know what Carla's story is when it comes to men," he muttered, his nose tingling from the sharp scent of tobacco as Cian lit his smoke. "I prefer to think of her as… *Hell,* I don't know. I just prefer not to think of her that way."

"Yeah, I get that. I think we all see her as a kind of sister, you even more than the rest of us." Cian took a long drag on the cigarette, held the smoke in his lungs and then slowly let it out. "Which means that if there's something keeping her from getting out there and having a good time, we should know what it is."

Wyatt laughed. "Oh, yeah? And have you shared all your secrets with the rest of us?"

The Irishman frowned. "It's not the same. We're males."

"I would love to see you say that to her face," he offered drily. "Something tells me you wouldn't have all your teeth for very long."

"Hmm. You may be onto something there," Cian murmured. "She is a ferocious little thing. Probably scares the crap out of most of the guys she comes into contact with. Maybe that's the problem right there."

With the conversation about his partner at an end, Wyatt had expected to get grilled about Elise as well, but the Irishman wasn't pushing the issue at the moment, and he was silently grateful. Last thing he wanted to be doing was dodging questions about what was going on between them.

"Did you hear that?" Cian asked, cocking his head toward the direction of the Alley as they got closer.

Wyatt started to ask what he was talking about, when he heard what sounded like a feminine, high-pitched scream, quickly followed by another. "What the fuck?" he growled, and they immediately took off running, jumping over fallen limbs, his boots almost slipping on a thick patch of moss as they raced to reach the glade. Fear churned through his veins like an acid, his head pounding as he worried about what might be happening. Had one of the Whiteclaw Lycans managed to get past them? Were they being attacked? But when he and Cian burst through the trees, slamming to a stop at the edge of the Alley, they stared in amazement, struggling to figure out what was going on.

"What in God's name are they doing?" Cian muttered.

"Beats the hell out of me," he replied, wondering why Elise, Michaela, Carla, Chelsea and Torrance were all standing on the hood of Brody's poor truck, clinging to each other, squealing at the top of their lungs. Brody and Eric stood on Eric's front porch, bent over at the waist as they roared with laughter, while Jillian tried to get them to shut up. Sayre Murphy, Jillian's beautiful eighteen-year-old sister and a powerful witch in her own right, stood a few feet away from them, on the porch steps, wringing her hands with worry as she called for the women to calm down. Sayre didn't live in the Alley, but she was often there, visiting with her sister.

Wyatt was getting ready to shout over the racket and demand an explanation, when Chelsea started pointing at the ground on the side of the truck and screamed, "Oh, my God, there are *three!*"

"Three what?" Cian muttered, sounding as confused as he was.

Narrowing his eyes, Wyatt scanned the ground and caught sight of three massive rattlesnakes slithering out from the far side of Brody's truck, toward the center of the clearing. "It's snakes," he said, pointing toward the reptiles. "Three of them."

"All this racket over some snakes?" Cian gave a husky laugh as he eyed the screaming women. "They look bloody ridiculous up there."

Wyatt kept his mouth shut, biting back the denial burning on his tongue. Personally, he thought Elise looked hot as hell, even when she was jumping up and down and squealing like a girl. It was pretty fucking adorable, if you asked him.

"What is it about lasses and snakes?" he murmured, which made Cian laugh again.

"You do know that you could just eat the damn things, right?" Cian called out to Carla, who looked ready to hyperventilate as she watched the snakes slither through the recently cut blades of grass, the late-afternoon sunlight glittering against their brown scales.

"Eat them?" Carla choked out, turning an interesting shade of green. "I'd rather eat a skunk! Snakes are repulsive!"

"Are you blind? They're beautiful!" Sayre argued, looking thoroughly insulted as she glared up at Wyatt's partner.

"Eric, stop laughing and kill the damn things!" Chelsea screamed, shooting a furious look at her husband while she continued to cling to the other women.

"No! No one is killing anything! They're not going to hurt you," Sayre snapped, coming down the steps, which made the women shout for her to stay back. The young witch shook her head in exasperation. "Seriously, they're more frightened of you than you are of them. You're damn near scaring the poor things to death."

Wyatt choked back a laugh and scratched his chin. "Uh, is she, like, channeling the snakes' feelings or something?" he asked Cian.

The Irishman grunted, "God only knows with that one."

As they watched, Sayre's eyes began to glow with a fiery light as she held her hands out toward the snakes, her fingers extended. The wind blew her strawberry blond curls around her delicate face, whipping the fabric of her sundress against her slender form. The snakes came to a stop, lifting their wide heads and looking toward her, almost as if they were listening to her speak to them in some strange, wordless language. It seemed as if Sayre were actually communicating with the reptiles, and the scene sent an eerie shiver down Wyatt's nape. He'd known, from talking to Jeremy, that Sayre was talented—but the young witch's powers appeared to be growing beyond anything they had expected. After several tense moments had passed, the snakes flicked their tongues from between their jaws, seemed to give Sayre a regal nod and then quickly slithered across the clearing as they made their way back into the woods on the far side of the Alley.

With a wry look on her face, Sayre lowered her arms and turned back toward the slack-jawed group of women. "You can come down now."

Wyatt glanced at Cian, who stood beside him with a cigarette hanging precariously from the corner of his mouth, his narrowed gaze still focused intently on Sayre Murphy. "Whatever you're thinking, don't," he muttered under his breath. "She's too young for you, man."

At his quiet words, Cian seemed to shake himself out of his daze, his lips twisting in a cocky smile. "Trust me, boyo. I know better than to mess with little girls."

Wyatt smirked. "If you don't, Jillian will no doubt make sure you wished that you did."

"Make sure he wished that he did what?"

They both looked ahead to see Jillian coming toward them, a pink-faced Michaela at her side. Cian gave a low laugh. "You know how Pall is," he murmured with his lilting accent. "He's just giving me a hard time."

While Wyatt looked over the women's heads, watching Elise and Chelsea lay into Eric for laughing at them, Michaela said, "Instead of standing over here snickering, you two could have helped!"

"And risk getting bitch-slapped by Jilly's little sister?" Cian drawled. "Not in this lifetime. I'm—"

"Before you two start bickering, I came over because

I have something important to say," Jillian murmured, cutting the Runner off. Then she looked at Wyatt. "I've been thinking about Elise," she explained, lowering her voice. "About what happened to her three years ago. And I think there could be a connection between her attack and what we learned about the Whiteclaw's rape drugs when Chelsea was searching for her sister."

His gaze instantly sharpened, while his insides twisted with fury, same as they did each time he thought about what Elise had been through. "What do you mean?"

"When we were talking about the drugs the Whiteclaw use to mask their scent this morning, it started me thinking about the other drugs they're manufacturing that affect the girls' memories when they're attacked." Jillian took a quick breath, then added, "Elise can't completely remember hers, either. Maybe there's a connection."

"It could have been the trauma that makes her unable to remember what happened that night," he pointed out, his voice raw. "Hell, if it'd been me, I wouldn't have wanted to remember it, either."

"But what if it wasn't?" Michaela asked, her beautiful face pinched with concern. "What if it has some connection to what's happening now?"

Swallowing against the blistering lump of rage burning in his throat, Wyatt had to choke back a deep, guttural growl. "You think they used one of the early versions of the drug on her?"

Sunlight glinted against Jillian's blond hair as she nodded. "I think it's definitely possible. And maybe it was more than the rain that night that made it impossible to track the males' scents. They could have used their drugs for that, as well."

"If that's true," Cian said, lighting up another cigarette, "and we assume that this recent attack on Elise is related more to what happened to her before than it is to the coming war, then why wait all this time to start messing with her? It's been three bloody years."

The four of them shared a few heavy, thoughtful moments of silence as they worked the problem over in their heads, and then Michaela said, "Maybe the question we should really be asking ourselves is who's here who wasn't here before?"

Cian's dark brows lifted with interest. "Are you talking about Roy's nephews, the Claymore brothers? About Sebastian and Harris?"

At the mention of Harris Claymore's name, Wyatt's heart started to beat in slow, painful lurches, a muscle pulsing just beneath his left eye, while his hands slowly curled into fists at his sides. "I don't really know them," he growled. "But from the things I've heard about Harris Claymore, he's nothing more than a thug. And we know they were only recently called back home by their uncle."

Cian exhaled a sharp stream of smoke and nodded. "I'll talk to Mason about setting up some kind of surveillance on him. It won't be easy, if he's staying with Roy. But we should be able to pick him up the moment he sets foot out of Hawkley."

Wyatt looked at Jillian and tried to gentle his tone. "This is good, Jilly. It could be the break we're looking for."

She gave him a sad smile. "I just want her to be okay, Wyatt. I appreciate you looking out for her."

He didn't know what to say to those heartfelt words,

so he looked at Mic and asked, "Have you been able to get any kind of read on her? Is she...okay?"

Though human, Michaela possessed the remarkable ability to read the emotions in those she was in close physical proximity to, giving her a rare insight into their feelings. At the moment, Wyatt imagined the worried look on her face was a result of the seething rage she could no doubt sense coiling through his insides, demanding he hunt down Harris Claymore right then and there. The only thing that kept him grounded was the fact that Elise needed protection, and he was going to be damned before he let one of the other Runners provide it for her.

"I've been able to pick up a few bits and pieces," Michaela told him while he struggled to calm down. "She's worried, but she feels at ease here. I think today is the safest she's felt in a long time. Carla told us about the argument the two of you had last night, but you did the right thing to force her down here, Wyatt."

He nodded, wanting to ask her more, but not wanting Elise's secrets blurted out in front of Cian. He liked Hennessey, but the more distance the womanizing Runner kept from Elise, the better.

"We've bought some stuff to make pizzas for dinner tonight," Jillian told them, offering an appreciated change of subject. "You guys coming?"

Thinking Elise would probably feel more comfortable hanging out with the group, rather than eating alone with him in his cabin, he said, "Yeah, we'll be there. I just need to get cleaned up."

"Same here," Cian said, and they all parted ways.

To Wyatt's surprise, Elise made her way over to him as he headed toward his cabin, asking him how the patrol had gone as she followed him inside. He teased her a little about the snake incident, which had her laughing, then told her to make herself at home while he grabbed a quick shower. He wasn't quite sure if there had actually been a spark of heat in those beautiful jewel-toned eyes when he turned to go or if it'd just been wishful thinking on his part, but he ended up taking the first deliberately cold shower of his life. And it sucked as badly as he'd thought it would.

An hour later, they were all gathered in Jeremy and Jillian's cabin, except for Eric and Chelsea, who had decided to have a quiet dinner at home, and Jeremy and Mason, who were still out on patrol. The open windows let in the cool evening breeze, the air filled with the mouthwatering scents of freshly baked pizzas, crisp Caesar salad and ice-cold beer and wine. Even Max Doucet, Michaela's younger brother, and his friend Elliot Connors came down to join them, after taking care of a private project for Wyatt, and they fit in as easily as they always did. Wyatt had remained by Elise's side ever since they'd arrived, and though she was quiet, he knew she was having a good time. He could tell by the relaxed look on her face that she was comfortable here. For a woman who'd been raised on daily doses of hatred and racism, she was nothing at all like her father.

The group was spread out across the living room, sitting on sofas and chairs, while some just sat on the floor. The pizzas were consumed over a lot of laughing and talking, as well as a hefty amount of good-natured ribbing. When Carla asked if there was any more salad, after already eating two platefuls, Wyatt watched as Cian smirked at her. "Jesus, Reyes, you eat like a horse," the Irishman drawled, which had Michaela jabbing him in the side with her elbow. "Ouch, damn it!" He turned to glare at Mic. "What the hell was that for?"

"Be nice," she hissed.

"Or what?" Cian asked, arching one of his dark brows.

Michaela gave him a sharp smile. "Or my husband will kick your ass. Right, babe?"

Brody's thick auburn hair was pulled back from his scarred face with a band, his green eyes burning with emotion as he grinned at his wife. "Anything you want, beautiful."

Mic looked at Cian. "See? And now you should get up off your sarcastic backside and get the woman her salad."

Carla laughed. "No thanks. He'd probably just spit in it."

Elise smothered a giggle behind her hand, and Wyatt couldn't help but grin at the infectious sound. Had he ever heard her laugh before? Not with sarcasm, but just a real, honest-to-God laugh? He didn't think so, and it made him want to rub the center of his chest, where there was a sharp, strange burn that had nothing to do with his dinner and *everything* to do with the woman.

"I'll get your damn salad," Cian muttered as he stood up from his seat, reaching for Carla's plate. "And it'll even be spit-free," he added drily.

Carla eyed him suspiciously, holding her plate just out of his reach. "You promise you won't do anything gross to it?"

The look of insult on Hennessey's face was completely priceless. "Christ, woman. Am I five?"

Carla just gave him that "I'm waiting" look that women did so well, until Cian finally growled, "Fine, I *promise*. Scout's honor, too, though I was never a bloody scout. Now give me the damn plate!"

"Only you could manage to give Cian a conscience," Mason's wife, Torrance, said to Michaela when Cian had walked into the kitchen.

"That was fun to watch," Brody murmured, winking at his wife.

Michaela opened her mouth to respond, when a booming crash suddenly came from the kitchen. "What the hell was that?" she whispered.

A laughing Max quickly came into the living room. "You guys aren't gonna believe this, but Sayre just threw her plate at Cian's head!"

Jillian looked worried. "What? Why?"

"From what I caught," the soon-to-be Runner told them, "he was making fun of some guy she has a date with next week. Guess she took exception."

"That's understandable," Michaela offered with a frown that matched Jillian's. "But she's normally so mellow. It isn't like her to be riled so easily."

Brody snorted. "This is Cian we're talking about, Mic. The guy could make a saint want to kick him in the balls."

"Yeah, I guess you're right," she agreed, a look of surprise flickering across her face when Cian stalked out of the kitchen just ahead of Sayre, his dark brows drawn into a deep crease over the bridge of his nose. Wyatt wondered if Michaela was using her "gift" at that moment to get a read on the Irishman and, if so, what she was learning. Because Cian looked like a man ready to commit murder with his bare hands.

Wyatt didn't know what to make of Cian and Sayre, but it didn't matter. Even if he'd wanted to figure out their strange little drama, he wouldn't have had the time. He was too busy watching Elise, hanging on to her every murmured word and expression like a pathetic, lovesick fool. God, he wanted so badly to make her smile at him the way he'd caught her doing several times tonight with the others. Wanted to find a way to break through her shields. To give her things he didn't even have it in him to give. But he'd go as far as he could. Claim her body. Drench her in pleasure. Make her laugh. Make her smile. Not with one of those pained smirks, but an honest-to-God "so happy she couldn't hold it inside" kind of smile. The kind that would light her up from the inside out and make him feel like the luckiest man alive.

She started to get up with their dishes, but he told her to relax and took them into the now vacated kitchen himself, determined to show her that he wasn't one of those chauvinistic assholes who expected a woman to wait on him hand and foot. His mother, God bless her, had taught him from an early age how to treat a woman right. And while he usually kept his relationships so brief there wasn't much of a chance to put what he'd learned to use, he was for damn sure going to use it now.

Grabbing himself a fresh beer, he started to head back, when Carla came through the archway, setting her empty wineglass by the sink.

Catching a glimpse of his partner's expression, Wyatt knew exactly why she'd followed him into the kitchen. "Wow, is it already time for another lecture?" he drawled. "And here I thought you were starting to slack."

She grimaced, then sent him a contrite, kinda crooked smile. "I deserved that," she murmured. "But I'm worried about you."

Taking a long swallow of his beer, he wiped the back of his wrist over his mouth. "Why?"

She leaned against one of the counters and crossed her arms, then spoke in a quiet, troubled tone. "When a woman goes through something like what happened to Elise three years ago, it…sometimes breaks them, Pall. I know Elise is tough. Just be careful. If she doesn't want to move on, to try to move past what happened, you can't make her."

Voice so hard it was brittle, he said, "I would never do that. I'm not a fucking bully, Reyes."

Shaking her head, she said, "I know that, Pall. That's not what I'm saying. You're golden, okay? Just don't let her break your heart, hoping for something that might never come."

He cut his gaze to the far side of the kitchen, his chest rising with a sharp breath as he gripped his beer bottle even tighter. "I'm not in love with her, Carla. I just want to help her."

Quietly, she asked, "You sure about that?"

"You know me," he muttered, bringing his shuttered gaze back to her worried one. "You know what I'm like. I care about her, but it's nothing more than that."

Her head tilted a bit to the side as she studied him. "Because you won't let it be?"

"Because that's the way it is," he explained through his gritted teeth. "So drop it."

"Wyatt," she murmured, "is there something you're not telling me?"

"Like what?" he asked, feeling hunted, as if she were determined to pull things out of him he was nowhere near ready to admit to. Forcing a bored look onto his face, he took another casual drink of his beer.

"Is she your life-ma—"

"Don't," he snapped, cutting her off with a snarl that sounded as far from casual as you could get. "We're not having that conversation."

Holding up her hands in a "take it easy" gesture, she said, "Okay. I get it. Just…promise me that you'll take my advice and be careful. It's hell to be in love with someone who can't love you back."

He frowned, wondering if it were possible she was speaking from experience. Then a horrible thought slammed into him and he blanched.

"Oh, God," she said with a laugh, frantically waving her hands between them. "Just stop! I'm not talking about *you*, Pall. I swear! That's just… Seriously, I love you, but *not* like that. Yuck!"

"Then who?" he demanded, ready to kick the bastard's ass for her.

Patting his arm, she said, "It's none of the guys, okay? So you don't have to worry about killing anyone right this second."

"Carla…"

"Come on," she said, waggling her brows as she pulled on his arm. "Let's get back in there before we miss more of the crazy Cian and Sayre show. I swear that shit is hilarious."

He thought about arguing, then let it go, not wanting to push. And, hell, it wasn't as if that was the kind of conversation he wanted to have with his partner anyway. Realizing she'd already ditched him and he was now standing in the kitchen by himself, Wyatt went back into the living room and took his seat beside Elise on one of the leather sofas. They hung around for coffee and brownies, listening to Torrance and Michaela tell a funny story about one of the customers at the mystical shop that Michaela still owned down in the human town of Covington, before everyone eventually agreed to call it a night. He and Elise said their goodbyes, then made their way out into the moonlit darkness. They stayed silent as they walked back to his cabin.

"So, it, um, looks like I'm staying for a while," she murmured as he locked the front door behind them.

"I'm glad you've decided that, because I wasn't letting you go."

She gave him a tight, nervous smile as she stood beside the end table where a lamp was spilling out a soft, muted glow of light, then took a deep breath and said, "There's something I need to tell you."

Chapter 7

"Okay." Wyatt pushed his hands in his front pockets, hoping the casual gesture would help put her at ease. "I'm listening, El."

She licked her lips, then whispered, "What happened last night, it wasn't just because of the war. Or the tensions in town. It was…personal."

"Because of your old man?"

She shook her head, thick waves of auburn hair that his fingers itched to touch spilling over her shoulders with effortless sensuality. "No. Because of *me*."

He took a step toward her, his muscles bunching with tension. "What aren't you telling me?"

Her breath released on a soft shudder, and she blinked up at him. "He… The one you found in my room. He told me…"

As her words trailed off, it took everything Wyatt had

to keep his voice soft while his inner beast chuffed with frustration. The dark, dangerous, visceral kind. "You can trust me, El. I won't tell anyone else what that son of a bitch said unless you want me to."

"Not even Eric?" she whispered, the trembling of her jaw making him want to take her into his arms and crush her against his chest. "Because I've already lost one brother to this nightmare, Wyatt. I know Eli is still alive, but he's gone. I never see him. Never hear from him. I don't want Eric to do something in anger and end up losing him, too."

"I know," he rasped, fucking hating that she was upset. "I get it, sweetheart. I know what you're saying."

She moved to the window, and he turned, watching her profile as she stared out into the darkness. She took a deep, shaky breath, then finally told him what the Lycan had said to her. How he'd claimed to be one of the monsters who'd raped her. Though Wyatt had suspected as much, especially after the conversation he'd had with Jillian and Michaela, it still twisted his gut with rage. With his hands fisted in his pockets and his pulse roaring in his ears, Wyatt listened until Elise's husky voice trailed off again. Then he crossed the space between them and stood at her side. When he spoke, his own voice was rough with emotion, and it took every damn thing he had not to reach for her. Not to grab hold of her fragile form and pull her into his arms, where he could keep her safe.

"We can talk about this more tomorrow," he told her, reaching up and tucking a gleaming strand of hair behind the tender shell of her ear, where a tiny diamond earring sparkled in the light. "Right now you're tired and you need to sleep, El. Why don't you get in bed and I'll bring you in something to drink? Okay?"

She turned her head to look at him, her eyes glassy but the tilt of her chin proud. She was such a hard-ass at times, but he knew that was her go-to defense mechanism. The way she held herself together, when so many things had tried to tear her apart. Her father. The attack. Eli's banishment. And now this new nightmare bearing down on her. So that meant that for the moment, he sucked up his own wants and needs and did right by her. Which was why he was sending her sweet little ass to bed instead of doing everything he could to make sure he ended up there with her.

She didn't say anything in response to his quiet words. Just watched him with those beautiful blue eyes, gave a little nod, then turned and headed toward the hallway. Wyatt scrubbed his hands down his face and sucked in a deep breath, giving himself a moment to get his shit together. To fight down the lust and primitive sense of possession that was riding him hard, so that he could do the decent thing and be a friend when she needed one.

Christ, there were times when he fucking *hated* being decent.

With a muttered curse, he headed into the kitchen, pouring them both shots of Jack Daniel's. Her eyes went a little wide when he carried the drinks into the spare bedroom, and he forced a lazy grin onto his lips. "I don't expect you to toss it back, El. You can sip it, and it'll help you relax."

She murmured a quiet thanks as he handed her the heavy shot glass, knocking his own drink back as he watched her take a cautious sip of the amber-colored liquor. She winced a bit, her nostrils flaring as she swallowed, then gave a little cough. "Wow. That's strong. Good, but strong."

"Just make sure you finish it," he told her, turning and heading back for the door, every second he had to stand there and see her lying in that bed, propped up against the pillows, with the sheet drawn up under her arms, playing absolute hell on his system. He'd nearly reached the door when her softly spoken question stopped him.

"Why now?"

Elise watched as Wyatt's left hand tightened around his empty shot glass, and then he slowly turned back around to face her.

"What do you mean?" he asked, the grittiness of his voice making her shiver.

"Why now? It's been three years. So why come after me *now?*"

The muted glow of light from the lamp on her bedside table made his hair look midnight-black, the dark locks gleaming as he shook his head. "I don't know, babe. Maybe the fact that your father was killed not that long ago. Maybe that we're vulnerable. Maybe all the pieces just fit together. Maybe they've been biding their time all these years, just waiting." He paused, then shoved his free hand back through his hair, looking as if he were having some kind of internal debate with himself. After several heavy moments of silence, he spoke again in a low, gruff tone. "There's something we're going to check out, but I don't know if it will actually lead to anything."

"What is it?" she gasped, jerking up into a sitting position. Despite her surprise, she was careful to keep the sheet pressed against her chest, since she wasn't wearing a bra with her tank top.

"What do you know about the Claymore brothers from the Whiteclaw pack? You ever meet them?"

"No," she told him, feeling as if her heart were trying to climb its way into her throat. "Why?"

"You sure about that?"

Her eyes went wide. "Yes. *Why?* What's going on?"

"They're Roy Claymore's nephews. I don't like the older brother, Harris. Only met him a few times, but he's a thug, like his uncle. The younger one, Sebastian, is a little different. Not sure what to make of him, to be honest."

"Wyatt, what aren't you telling me?"

Rubbing his hand along the hard edge of his jaw, he said, "Jillian started wondering today if maybe there's a connection between your, um, memory lapse of your attack and the drug the Whiteclaw are using on the human girls."

She swallowed against her rising panic and felt all the blood drain from her face, her thoughts spinning. "Oh, my God."

"It got us thinking about why someone would start messing with you now, and we thought of the Claymore brothers. Their old man sent them both out west three years ago, where they remained until Roy took control of the pack and called them home."

"And you think…" She had to stop and clear her throat before she could go on. "You think what happened to me might have had something to do with them being sent away?"

"I don't know, El. I don't have a shred of proof. But after what you've told me that bastard said to you last night, my gut tells me it's something worth looking into."

"What do we do?" she asked, biting her lip.

"We stay smart and we don't assume anything until we have some solid answers. I'll also try to track down some photos of the Claymores online to see if their faces are at all familiar to you. You might have met them at some point and not even realize it. And we sure as hell don't let down our guard just because we might have an idea of who came after you."

"All right. I appreciate you telling me."

"Yeah, well, I can imagine how frustrating this situation is for you, and I don't want you worrying that we know things we're not sharing with you. I will *always* be honest with you about what's going on. I won't bullshit you."

"Good." She lifted her chin, dredging up every pitiful ounce of strength she possessed in order to put her brave face on. "Because I'm tired of everyone thinking I'm going to crack."

"That's not gonna happen, El. You're strong. Stronger than you even realize."

A bitter, humorless laugh jerked from her throat, making him frown. "Not strong enough, Wyatt. I'll probably end up spending half the night reading again, just so I don't have to keep having nightmares."

"Like the ones you had last night?" he asked, his frown deepening as he stepped closer to the bed.

She swallowed again, forcing the words from her tight throat. "Um, yeah. I think pieces from that night three years ago are starting to come back to me. Not any vital information that helps me identify them. Just fragments. Voices. Things they called me. I guess it's a good thing, because I hated relying on Jillian to know what happened. But it's—" She broke off as a tight smile twisted her mouth. "It just makes it impossible to sleep."

He didn't mock her or make her feel like an idiot. Instead, he simply cocked his head a bit to the side, watching her with those beautifully dark eyes, and asked, "Would it help if I read to you?"

Her heart gave a little jolt in her chest. "Seriously?"

"Sure." He flashed her one of those sexy, crooked smiles that always quickened her pulse. "What are you reading?"

She bit her lip again, trying not to laugh. "Um, just something that I borrowed from Torrance," she murmured, taking out the book she'd left under her pillow and handing it to him as he came closer to the bed. She expected him to balk when he realized it was a romance, but he simply lifted a brow at the somewhat racy cover, flashed her a devastating grin and settled back in the chair she'd found him sitting in that morning. Then he set down the shot glass, flipped to the page she'd earmarked and started reading in that deliciously deep, velvet-rough voice that sounded like sin. Before she knew it, nearly two hours had gone by, and he was reading the last line of the book.

"I've never read one of these, but it was good," he told her, setting the trade-size novel on her bedside table. At her look of surprise, he said, "I'm serious. But I thought the guy was a pussy to run from her. He should have manned up and just been honest with her from the start. Would have saved them both from having to go through all that bullshit."

The grin on her lips started to slip. "Yeah, well, it's not always that easy."

He sat back in the chair, looking as if he were working some kind of problem out in his head. The silence stretched out, becoming awkward and heavy, until he finally said, "But if he trusted her, he would have told her."

"Trust is a complicated thing, though, isn't it?"

Rubbing the back of his neck, he said, "Yeah, I guess it is."

Needing to change the subject, she gave him a teasing smile. "Well, the good news is that you have an incredible voice. If you ever give up Bloodrunning, you could always make audiobooks. Women all over the world would be in heaven listening to you."

He blinked, looking a little warm under his skin. "Uh, thanks."

With a soft laugh, she said, "Wow, you're pretty cute when you're blushing, Wyatt."

He snorted, giving her a mock glare. "And you're a little brat for trying to embarrass me."

Elise fluttered her lashes. "I was just being honest."

"Uh-huh," he murmured, rolling his eyes. "And Bambi isn't the saddest frigging movie that was ever made."

She laughed again, liking the way it made him smile as he stood up from the chair. The air practically crackled with sexual tension as he stood there by the side of the bed, just staring down at her, the hooded, hungry look on his face sending her heart rate tripping. Her giggles faded as she held her breath, waiting for him to go ahead and tell her to stop wasting his time and lose the damn clothes, then spread her legs and let him have his mind-shattering way with her. But even though she would have sworn to every deity she'd ever heard of that that was what he wanted, in the end he simply cleared his throat and muttered, "I'll just, uh, let you get some sleep now."

Elise stared in stunned amazement as he turned and made his way across the room. He'd just reached the doorway when she blurted, "You're not even going to try to kiss me good-night?"

He gripped the door frame with clenched fingers, the muscles in his arms ropy and hard, thick veins pressing beneath his dark skin. It had to be one of the sexiest, most masculine poses Elise had ever seen, turning her blood molten, her pulse rushing with a low roar in her ears. She was scared that he wouldn't turn around—and equally frightened that he would. But in the end, he made a rough, primitive sound deep in his chest and kept his back to her as he said, "If I stay, I'll want to do a hell of a lot more than kiss you, El. And you're not ready for it."

"But—"

"Come get me if you need anything," he rasped, cutting her off. Then he walked out and closed the door behind him, leaving her with nothing but her churning thoughts and terrifying desire for company.

Chapter 8

Elise had never imagined she would be walking into her house with Wyatt Pallaton at her side, but that was exactly the situation she found herself in the following day. After waking up early and sharing coffee and croissants with Jillian—Jeremy and Wyatt had driven down into Wesley for some supplies for the Alley—she'd spent the rest of the morning familiarizing herself with Wyatt's cabin while she waited for him to return. She liked his rugged, minimalistic style of decorating, with comfortable leather sofas and chairs, rustic wooden tables and plush pewter-colored rugs over hardwood floors that gleamed. The walls were covered in crowded bookshelves and austere but beautiful black-and-white nature scenes.

It was fun to look around at his things, as if they were little clues to questions she hadn't even realized she had.

His reading preferences ran toward military thrillers, but there were also titles from authors like Vonnegut, Kerouac and Koontz. From his bookshelves she moved onto his DVD collection, laughing when she saw a copy of *Elf,* which she considered the greatest Christmas movie ever made. But she was surprised by the fact that such a masculine, purely alpha guy like Wyatt enjoyed it, too, and she couldn't help but wonder what he was like at the holidays. Christmas with the Bloodrunners was no doubt a festive, cheerful occasion, and she was thrilled that Eric would now be a part of it. Her brother might drive her crazy at times, but he truly deserved every bit of happiness he could find here.

When Wyatt finally made it back from his trip with Jeremy, they'd made some sandwiches for lunch and sat at the kitchen table to eat. Wyatt showed her a few photographs he had found online of Sebastian and Harris Claymore, but neither Lycan looked familiar to her. Elise hadn't known whether she should be relieved she didn't recognize the brothers…or disappointed. She'd told Wyatt that she didn't like the look of either of the males but knew she probably would have felt that way about anyone the Runners suspected might have some kind of connection to her attack.

As soon as they'd finished eating, Elise had mentioned that she needed to pick up a few things from her house that she'd forgotten, like her laptop and also some of her files from work. While her office would remain closed while she was gone, she figured she could use her time at the Alley to get caught up on things, as well as work on some of the writing projects she'd been fiddling with in private. She'd known the trip was going to be a test of her willpower where Wyatt was concerned, considering her growing fascination with the Runner, but was determined to keep her cool and refrain from throwing herself at him. Her emotions, however, couldn't be so easily controlled. They were like a giant boulder tumbling down the side of a mountain, taking on mass and speed, barreling toward an uncertain target that they would, without doubt, obliterate upon impact.

And yet, even knowing that disaster loomed, she still couldn't stop herself from wanting to spend time with him, and so she'd simply asked him if he wanted to take her up to Shadow Peak...or if he'd rather she ask her brother. It'd been obvious from the look on his gorgeous face that being her first choice had surprised him. He'd probably thought she would be embarrassed to be seen with him in town, which was as far from the truth as you could get. The old Elise...who knew? That woman had been a stuck-up bitch much of the time, acting snide toward others as a way to cover how awful her father had made her feel about herself. But the person she was now felt nothing but pride at the idea of walking down a Silvercrest street with this man at her side.

As they'd neared her home—the one she *never* had any intention of selling, no matter what her brother said, because she'd put so much of her heart and soul into it— she'd picked up on a slight tension in Wyatt's posture, unsure what it was about until they walked through her entryway and into her living room. Her clean, *completely* refurnished living room! It looked like something right out of a Pottery Barn catalog, the style similar to what she'd had but obviously better quality. She knew, without even asking, that this was Wyatt's doing. It must have cost him a freaking fortune, and she couldn't manage to close her mouth, her jaw hanging open in stunned surprise.

Finally shaking herself out of her stupor, she turned and found him looking out the front window, his hands shoved deep into his pockets, his broad shoulders tight with tension. Voice little more than a shivering rasp, she said, "I don't understand, Wyatt. Where did this all come from?"

"It's not that big a deal," he murmured, hitching his shoulders. "I just went online the other night, made a few calls and was able to have it delivered yesterday afternoon. Eric gave me the code to your alarm and I passed it on to Max and Elliot. They came over and had some of the scouts clear out the old stuff, then made sure that everything was put in the right place after delivery."

"Why would you do that?" she whispered, so shocked she could barely manage to put two words together. Not even Eric had ever done anything like this for her, and she knew her brother loved her like crazy.

Looking over his shoulder, he said, "Your things got broken during the fight."

"But that wasn't *your* fault," she told him, unable to resist running her hand over the back of the espresso-colored sofa, the ultrasoft leather making her sigh with pleasure.

"It wasn't yours, either," he pointed out in a low voice, turning around to face her. He watched her stroking her hand across the leather for a moment, his jaw tight. Then he slowly lifted his enigmatic gaze back to hers. "Like hell was I going to let you pay to replace furniture that asshole broke."

She bit her lip, wishing his expression could be easier to read. "I don't know what to say, Wyatt. This is one of the sweetest, kindest things anyone has ever done for me."

"You don't have to say anything, El." She could have sworn his eyes were getting darker, his gaze hooded. "I did it because I wanted to. Not because I expect anything from you."

"I know." She swallowed, wanting to say so much that she didn't know how to put into words, but was saved by a knock on her front door. Wyatt instantly shifted into protective mode, giving her a sharp look as she started out of the room. "It's probably just my neighbor wanting to check on me," she said over her shoulder. "He's off early sometimes."

"Check before you open the door, Elise."

"Yes, sir," she drawled, though she was secretly pleased by his concern. No one but her brothers had ever worried about her safety before and it was a heady, comforting feeling. She knew that some women might have felt smothered, but Wyatt wasn't an overbearing ass about it. He just…cared, which was really the most stunning part of all.

It *was* Eddie at her door, his blue eyes nervous as he caught sight of Wyatt somewhere behind her. It took nearly ten minutes to convince her well-intentioned neighbor that she was fine and there was nothing he could do to help. His devotion to her was always going to be a source of worry because she knew where it was going to lead: to the young Lycan being blacklisted by the town and given a hard time by those who hated her and her family.

Closing the door after their brief chat, she turned and found Wyatt standing in the archway that led into the living room, his powerful arms crossed over his broad chest, the pale green of his shirt looking incredible with his bronzed complexion. "What?" she asked when she saw the odd look on his face.

"What's wrong with him?"

She winced, knowing Wyatt wasn't going to like this particular story. Fiddling with one of the oversize buttons on the gray cardigan she was wearing over a white tank top, she related what she knew. "Eddie's biological father took a baseball bat to his head when he was only a kid. Jillian's mom, who was the pack's Spirit Walker at the time, wasn't allowed to visit him, so it never healed correctly."

A frown wove its way between his brows. "Jesus."

"I know. The Lycan ordered Eddie to make a kill on a young deer, and he refused. He'd become friends with the animal, caring for it when it was injured."

"So the bastard beat him?" he growled. "That's effed up."

"I know," she murmured again, wrapping her arms around herself. "We're a brutal species, aren't we? Too many times we try to kill kindness, thinking it makes us weak."

Shoving his hands back into his front pockets, he propped his shoulder against the archway. "It's because the Lycans fear it will change them." His deep voice was soft but rough. "That it will make them more human."

A sad smile twisted the corner of her mouth. "The more time I spend around Michaela, Torrance and Chelsea, I no longer think that's a bad thing. We could learn so much from them. How to be there for each other. How to nurture and love, instead of just…" She shook her head with frustration. "I don't know *what* it is that we do. Whatever it is, too many of us are broken inside. Scarred. Cracked into pieces that no longer even make a whole."

Pushing away from the archway, he came toward her, his dark gaze burning with heat...and something that was too breathtakingly intense for her to even name. "You're not broken, Elise. You're beautiful."

She swallowed so hard that it hurt. "I'm not, Wyatt."

"The hell you aren't."

Trying hard not to shatter, she twisted her lips with a smirk. "Careful, Runner. You're going to be bad for my ego."

"Good." He lifted one of those big, strong hands to the side of her face, his thumb stroking the apple of her cheek so tenderly it made her gasp. "There's nothing wrong with knowing you're beautiful," he told her in a low, husky rumble. "And there's sure as hell nothing wrong with knowing you're wanted."

Oh...God.

She couldn't do anything but shiver as he reached down with his other hand and grasped her wrist, lifting it to his face. He nipped the tender flesh just above the base of her palm, making her heart stumble and trip, while her pulse rocketed. Then he let go of her wrist, wrapped his fingers around her upper arms and buried his face in her hair, breathing in her scent as if he couldn't get enough of it. His mouth found the sensitive spot beneath her ear, and he trailed kisses down the side of her throat, breathing warm puffs of air against her chilled skin. But she wasn't cold for long, a fever building in her blood, melting her down. She was suddenly on fire, burning with need. Molten. Slippery. So freaking desperate for him she couldn't stand it, even though there was a part of her still nervous as hell. A part that was completely freaking out, wondering if she'd lost her mind.

"Wyatt," she whispered, swallowing thickly. "What are we doing?"

He cursed something hot and sexy in response that was more of a sound than an actual word, just before he shoved her against the entryway wall and his mouth found hers, his wickedly talented tongue damn near making her eyes roll back in her head. He was *that* good. That incredible. And she was in so much freaking trouble.

"Oh, God, Wyatt. *More.*"

Hearing that husky plea on Elise's soft pink lips was going to be the death of him. And her taste—*Jesus,* she tasted too damn sweet for words. She could have asked any of the Runners to come with her today, but she'd chosen *him,* and Wyatt couldn't help but feel a sense of triumph in that. But that satisfaction paled in comparison to what he felt in this moment, kissing her so hard and deep he was practically fucking her mouth. And what a mouth it was. Lush…tender…exquisite and rich and fine.

He needed more, damn it. And he needed it now.

Reaching down, he grasped her behind one jean-clad knee, lifted and moved against her, letting her feel how hard she'd made him. She gave a sharp cry, pulling back from the kiss to gasp for air. But she didn't push him away. She gripped his shoulders as she arched her back, rubbing herself against him, and it took every ounce of his control not to rip those damn jeans out of his way, rending the denim with his claws, until he had smooth, slick skin beneath his fingertips. He wanted to touch her so badly it was a physical need in his bones, grinding through him, coloring every thought and action with his lust.

Still holding her knee to his hip, he skimmed his free hand over the front of her body, touching her through her clothes. He shaped and kneaded the lush swell of her breast, stroking one tight, plump nipple with his thumb before trailing his hand down to the curve of her hip, then pushing between her thighs and cupping her mound. The crotch of her jeans was already damp, his jaw clenching as he rubbed and felt the slick slide of moisture against her folds. Voice rough and breath tight, he said, "You're soaking wet down here, El. Tell me why."

She kept her heavy-lidded gaze on his chin as she blushed. "Why are you—"

"Because I want to hear you say it," he rasped, squeezing her with his palm, the heady scent of her arousal making him want to howl with excitement. "*Now,* Elise."

"Um…you," she breathed out, closing her eyes as she tilted her head back, grinding it against the wall. "It's because of *you.*"

"You want me?" he growled, feeling his beast start to prowl beneath his skin, desperate to get its hands on the woman it already considered its perfect match.

"Yes, damn it. Yes! I wanted you last night and I want you now!"

Using every ounce of strength he possessed to keep his wolf under control, Wyatt scraped his teeth along the delicate edge of her jaw. "I want you, too, sweetheart. I want to put my fingers in you," he confessed, licking the side of her throat. "I want it so bad I can taste it. Want to feel you pulse and clutch at them. Feel you from the inside out as you come, drenching my hand."

She moaned, arching her neck to give him better access as he licked and nipped at her soft, pale skin. He gripped her harder between her legs, rubbing against the tight little bundle of nerves that was so screamingly sensitive. He was so hard he hurt, but he couldn't make himself let her go, more caught up in the erotic moment than he'd ever been caught up in anything in his entire life.

Lips moving against the tender shell of her ear, he said, "And when you're finally done, your swollen sex all soft and slick and spent, I'll pull my fingers out and put them in my mouth, El. Lick your taste off my skin with my tongue. Suck on them, so that I can get every drop of your hot, sweet—" He broke off with a shudder, growling low and deep in his chest. Shaking. Trembling. Feeling as if he was falling the hell apart, and all because he was driving himself insane with his own goddamn words.

"Wyatt?" she whispered. "Why did you stop?"

"Because you make me crazy." He winced, his voice so graveled he barely recognized it. Letting go of her knee, he gripped her hips and muttered, "Fucking crazy."

She stiffened against him, her hands moving to the front of his shoulders, as if she were going to push him away. "Did I do something wrong? What did I—"

"You didn't do anything. Everything you do is perfect. It's just that you make me…you make me want to—" *Shit,* he was rambling like an idiot. Taking a deep breath, he forced himself to lift his head, look her in the eye and tell her the truth. "You make me want to fuck, El. More than anyone else ever has. You understand what I'm saying?"

She blinked, face pink, blue eyes glistening and bright with need. "I affect you?"

"Yeah." A harsh sigh slipped past his lips. "In a big way."

Instead of flinching or telling him to get lost, like he'd feared, she simply gave him a smile that was slow and sweet and painfully beautiful. "Good. I'm glad. Because you affect me, too."

"As much as I love the sound of that," he groaned, a gritty laugh rumbling up from his chest, "I don't think we're talking about the same thing, honey."

Enjoying herself, Elise slowly arched an eyebrow. "Just because I can't throw you down and screw your brains out doesn't mean the idea doesn't appeal to me, Wyatt."

He looked surprised by her words, and then a sexy, lopsided grin lifted the corner of his mouth. "Who says you can't?"

"Oh. Well, you're bigger than I am. Not to mention stronger." And then there was the fact that she was... Well, she didn't exactly know *what* she was. *Afraid* was no longer the right word when it came to Wyatt and the way he made her feel. Hopefully cautious?

Lifting a hand to the side of her face, he brushed his thumb against the corner of her mouth. "It doesn't matter if I'm bigger or stronger than you," he said in a husky, devastating rasp. "You ever get that urge, El, you let me know. I'll let you do whatever the hell you want to me."

She wanted to smile and tease him but found herself hit by a sudden rush of sadness instead. "Maybe now you would," she offered softly. "But one day you'll have a wife and a family, Wyatt. And having my way with you will no longer be an option."

"No, I won't." She opened her mouth to argue that

surprising denial, but he cut her off, saying, "I'm not the marrying kind, El."

"Are you kidding me? You'd be an incredible husband."

He shook his head, his fingers clenching on her hip. "I won't. Just trust me. That's not gonna happen."

She went silent, studying him. There was a story there in those roughly spoken words, but it was clear from the look on his face that it wasn't one he wanted to share. And she couldn't push. She wasn't that big of a hypocrite. What right did she have to go snooping after his secrets when she held so tightly to so many of her own? So instead, she simply said, "That's too bad."

A pained expression flashed across his face, and the next thing she knew he was kissing the hell out of her again, ravaging her mouth, his tongue moving against hers in ways that could only be described as wicked and wild. She shoved her fingers into his thick hair and held him to her, kissing him back just as hungrily, loving the way he tasted. Honeyed warmth and sexy male with a touch of coffee. She felt a hard shudder go through his powerful frame, and his hands moved behind her, gripping her ass as he jerked her against him, possessive and rough, his mouthwatering body giving off a feverish heat.

And then, as quickly as it'd began, it was over.

"Damn it," he growled, suddenly ripping his mouth from hers and pushing her away with his hands on her shoulders. "We have to stop."

"Stop?" She blinked up at him, trying to bring him into focus through the fog of lust still clouding her gaze. "Why?"

With his nostrils flaring and his jaw clenched, he

said, "I can't lose my focus here. It's not safe. I will *not* put you in danger, no matter how badly I want you. You understand?"

She nodded, relief sweeping through her system in a sweet, stunning rush. He hadn't been rejecting her. He was simply worried about the location, which made perfect sense.

But instead of moving away, he just stood there, staring down at her as if he wanted to eat her alive, until she finally forced out a tight laugh and gave him a push. "Stop trying to melt my circuits with that hungry look in your eyes. We're leaving, remember?"

"Right," he grunted, looking very much as if he wanted to take her down to the floor and do things that would make her forget not only her name but also the name of every person she'd ever known. Then he jerked his chin toward the door and said, "Okay. Let's go."

It took Elise only a moment to grab some of the things she wanted from the house, like her laptop, throw them into a backpack and slip it onto her shoulder. Then she set the alarm and locked the front door behind them as they left. She knew he wanted to drive his Jeep into the town center but suggested they walk instead. She wanted to show him that she was proud to have him by her side, to hell with what everyone else thought.

But that didn't mean she wasn't still reeling.

Jesus, Joseph and Mary...

Now that she'd calmed down a bit, her heart rate returning to something closer to normal, she was stunned by what had almost happened between them. By the way she'd reacted to his touch and taste. Her thoughts were in chaos, same as her emotions, and she knew he could sense that she was pulling back in a way, trying to regroup. She also knew, by the hard set of his jaw, that he wasn't happy about how she was feeling. Striving to ease the growing tension between them as they headed into the town center on foot, toward her office, she said, "Jillian's house is just around the corner from here. Do you think she and Jeremy will ever spend any time there?"

He kept his dark gaze focused ahead of them as he replied, "They intended to, before all hell started breaking loose. I like to think that when we weather this storm, the town will be a place they feel comfortable spending time in. Because Mase and the others are right. If the Silvercrest don't learn to live without hate, then they won't have to worry about bastards like the Whiteclaw. They'll end up destroying themselves from the inside out. And as much as I don't like it here, I would hate to see that happen."

She murmured her agreement, knowing he was right. And that her father had been responsible for so much of that hatred. He'd poisoned minds, and now it would take time to undo the mess he'd created.

Curious about what kind of family Wyatt had come from, considering how messed up her own mother and father had been, she said, "You never talk about your parents. Where are they?"

They turned left at the next corner, nearing the street where her office was located. Nearly a minute had passed since she'd asked her question, and she'd thought he just wasn't going to answer, when he finally pulled in a deep breath and said, "My maternal grandmother was Sioux.

gether for my sake, and he did. When I became a Runner, he stayed near her family. But I visit him a few times a year and we're still close."

"That's why I never saw you, isn't it? Because you didn't grow up here."

He glanced over at her with one of his ridiculously sexy, crooked smirks. "Even if I had, our paths wouldn't have crossed. I sure as hell wouldn't have been part of the social structure here in town."

She looked away, biting her lower lip. "Still, it's odd, isn't it? The way we never met until the night of Max's ceremony."

"I never have been one for town," he murmured, then gave a quiet laugh. "Which is a serious understatement. The times I was here before becoming a Runner, I laid low, hanging at my parents' cabin that sat on the outskirts of town. I spent my time with guys like Mason and Jeremy, swimming in the local lake and hanging out down in places like Wesley, along with a few of the other human towns. But Shadow Peak never held any appeal to me. Hell, I don't know how Carla and most of the guys stomached it for as long as they did."

"Maybe it's a good thing," she admitted, tucking her windblown hair behind her ear. "If we *had* met, you would have hated me."

He turned his head toward her, his expression making it clear that he didn't like what she'd said.

"Don't scowl. It's true. If you think I'm a bitch now,

"Yeah, well, I like to think I'd have been smart enough to see through the act."

Surprised, she lifted her brows. "What makes you think it was an act?"

"Despite what you keep telling me, I *do* know you, El. You've had a shit life, thanks to things that were beyond your control, and you haven't always handled it well. But you have a good heart. You're a good person."

Oh, my God. She didn't have any idea how to respond, his unexpected words hitting her low in her body, filling her with warmth. She wanted to tell him that he was amazing. That he was too good for someone like her. That even though she didn't deserve it, she wanted to take a chance and—

"Wyatt!" she suddenly screamed, reeling with pain as she clutched the side of her head and staggered into him.

"Fuck!" he growled, his strong arms wrapping around her as he quickly pulled her between two buildings. "Jesus Christ, El. Are you okay?"

"I don't know," she whispered, tilting her throbbing head back to look up at him. "What happened?"

"Some bastard threw a goddamn rock at you and then took off running," he said through his gritted teeth, gently inspecting the side of her head. When she asked how it looked, he told her that there was a small knot swelling up, as well as blood oozing from a shallow but painful-looking cut.

"Oh. Well, considering he threw the rock at me and not at you, I guess we can say that the Lycans here are definitely more accepting of the Runners now. At least more than they are of me." She forced a grin onto her lips, trying to lighten his mood. "You probably shouldn't be seen here with me, Wyatt. Want to put a bag over my head?"

"Don't." His voice was rough and guttural, with more of the beast in it than she'd ever heard before. "This isn't the time for fucking jokes. That scared the hell out of me."

"Sorry. But I'm fine. Really. You don't have to look so worried."

He gave a sharp nod, his nostrils flaring as he slowly released his breath. "We're only a few doors down from your office," he told her, a cold, deadly rage burning in his eyes. "I'll cover you when we hit the street and walk you down. Then I want you to go inside and lock the door, okay?"

Frowning, she asked, "Why? Where are you going to be?"

Glaring at her bleeding scalp, he said, "I need to find the stupid asshole who did this to you and teach him a lesson."

"Wyatt, no!" she argued, clutching the hard bulge of his biceps. "I don't want you to leave me. And I don't want you wasting your time on some idiot." Forcing a smile, she added, "If you found him and tried to kill him, he'd probably just whine about it."

"I'm not gonna kill him, El." A muscle pulsed in the hard edge of his jaw, and his voice got lower. "But I wouldn't mind making him sorry he was ever born."

"Well, considering he's probably one of Farrow's goons, I'm sure he's already sorry. So let's just get out of here. I...I want out of this place. I want to go home."

"Home?" he repeated, an arrested expression on his face that told her just how deeply her words had affected him.

"I want to be back in the Alley, where I feel safe," she whispered. "Will you take me?"

He nodded, keeping a close eye on her as they quickly grabbed what she needed from her office, then made their way back to the Jeep. They didn't say much at first as he drove out of town, both lost in their thoughts... and she wondered if they were thinking about the same thing....

Trying to figure out precisely when she'd started to think of the Alley as her *home*.

Chapter 9

They eventually struck up a conversation about music and movies, of all things, as they made the drive back to the Alley. Wyatt was friendly and funny, as well as a good listener. Elise always got the sense that he was taking in everything that she said, no matter how trivial, unlike so many of the other men she'd known. Her brothers had never been dismissive toward her like that, but her father had. And then there were the chauvinistic jerks she encountered at work and in the local business groups. But she had Wyatt's complete focus, and she'd have been lying through her teeth if she'd said it wasn't sexy as hell. And yet, despite the camaraderie between them, he showed the unmistakable signs of tension and fatigue.

She could tell by the dark circles under his eyes that he hadn't been sleeping well, and couldn't help but wonder what secrets he was hiding. Considering how many she was holding close to her chest, Elise recognized the signs, and she wanted to know what haunted him. Had someone hurt him? It took her by surprise, the anger that spilled through her system when she thought of someone causing him pain, be it physical or emotional. She wanted to ask but knew better than to push. Knew that by doing so she could very well end up shoving him away, when there were too many parts of her at the moment that simply wanted to pull him a little closer.

That night, they stayed in and ate dinner in his cabin, just the two of them, since she'd had to take some pain meds for her head. He cooked, which surprised the hell out of her—and even more surprising was the fact that he was damn good at it. But she should have realized he would be. Wyatt Pallaton was the kind of man who excelled at anything he put his mind to, whether it was Bloodrunning, cooking fettuccine Alfredo, or making her open her eyes and start looking at the world again, rather than avoiding it.

And he was the man who'd somehow made her start thinking about sex again, when she hadn't thought it would ever happen.

She hadn't been a virgin when her world had fallen apart three years ago. There had been a few before that night. Not many, contrary to what most in the pack probably believed. She'd had attitude, and they'd assumed she liked to sleep around. But the truth was that it'd never been all that easy for her to trust a man enough to enjoy herself with him. Sadly, the few times she'd engaged in sex, it'd been more about rebelling against her father than it'd been about finding pleasure. And to be honest, finding pleasure had never been all that important to her. Not when every day of her life was a constant battle to feel worthy and useful.

But it was important to her now. To the woman she was becoming. And she'd finally admitted to herself today who she wanted to help her find it. Even knowing there wasn't a chance in hell she could keep him, she still wanted to seize this moment and have it. Own it. As many of these moments as she could get, until it was too late and her secrets stood between them, keeping them apart.

They'd finished dinner over an hour ago, just sitting and talking at the table until well after the sun had finally slipped beneath the horizon. Then they'd loaded the dishwasher together, she'd gone to take a shower, and Wyatt had headed to his bedroom. With her hair still damp and her body clad in nothing more than a skimpy bra-and-panties set, tank top and cropped pair of sweats, she walked to his closed bedroom door. She counted out ten heavy, painful heartbeats, then reached down and twisted the doorknob, walking into the room without even knocking. He looked over from where he was sprawled across a massive king-size bed in nothing but his jeans, watching a ball game on the TV. Elise could tell by the look on his face that she'd shocked the hell out of him by coming in here, and she quickly blurted, "I can't sleep."

He muted the TV, and she watched his abs ripple as he sat up in the middle of the bed, the mouthwatering sight making her feel a little light-headed. "Nightmares?"

When she finally forced her gaze back up to his face, she shook her head. "No. I, um, I haven't actually *tried* to sleep yet. But I know I won't be able to."

His hooded gaze did a swift pass down her body, lingering for a moment on her breasts, her nipples thick against the thin veils of lace and cotton, and then he seemed to shake himself a little, before lifting those dark eyes back to her face. His expression was etched with concern. "Why? Is it because of what happened in town today?"

"No." Determined not to panic and run, she forced herself to take a step toward the bed. "I just… I want to feel safe tonight."

"You feel safe with me?" he asked, and it was clear from his husky tone that she'd surprised him once again.

She bit her lip. "Yes," she said a little breathlessly. "I don't…I don't know why, but I do. And please don't ask me to explain. I just want to be close to you."

Lying back down against the pillows, he shifted onto his side and said, "Then come here and I'll hold you. Just hold you. Okay?"

She nodded with a profound surge of relief, then swiftly went into his arms, her back to his front as she cuddled against him on the bed. She should have been terrified, choked with fear, the same way she'd been every time she'd thought about being this close to a man in the past three years. But she wasn't. She didn't. Instead, she felt as if she were exactly where she was meant to be. And, God, was that a mistake, considering everything that stood between them. Everything that would keep them apart.

"I have to be honest with you," she whispered into the heavy silence, feeling like an idiot but needing to make at least this one confession. "I didn't come in here because I'm scared. I came in here because I wanted to feel like this with you. Breathless…*excited.* But I don't know if I can go to the end with it, and that isn't fair. Not to you. I'm just…just using you."

"Like hell you are," he grunted, holding her a little tighter, his heart pounding hard and fast against her spine. "If you want pleasure, El, I'm more than happy to give you some. Or a lot. Do *not* feel bad about that or second-guess it. Just go with what feels right. We get to the point you want to stop, then we stop. No argument. You get me?"

She nodded but didn't say anything. Minutes ticked by slowly, and though she was enjoying the hell out of being in his arms, wrapped up in his intoxicating warmth, she couldn't hold back the words that had started building inside her. Clutching his forearms, she said, "Wyatt, you're hot as sin and a nice guy. You could choose *any* woman you wanted and she would be thrilled to go out with you."

He laughed quietly just above her ear, and she could hear the smile in his voice as he said, "But not you?"

Instead of answering, she asked, "So why aren't you out with one of them?" She rolled over so that she could see his face, her gaze remaining locked with his as he shifted to his back. When he raised one of his muscular arms and tucked his open hand behind his head, it was so freaking sexy she nearly forgot what she'd been saying. Voice a little huskier than before, she licked her lips, lifted up onto an elbow and finally managed to demand, "Why are you doing this? What the hell are you trying to achieve? Because you can't fix me. And it's not even your place to try."

His lashes lowered over the smoldering heat in his eyes, his chest rising with a deep, almost aggressive-sounding breath. "Whose place is it?"

"No one's, other than my own. And I'm fine with the way things are."

"Bullshit," he muttered. "You can spout that 'I'm a tough bitch and don't need anyone' crap to everyone else, but I'm not buying it, El. You're lonely and you're scared and you deserve a hell of a lot more than life has thrown at you."

She closed her eyes and bit her lip again, letting those harsh but incredible words wash through her, making her shiver. The old El would have gotten pissed and mouthed off—but he was right. At least about the lonely-and-scared part. When she lifted her lashes, she sat up and forced herself to say, "When you kissed me today, I felt... I didn't think I would *ever* feel like that again. And I don't know that I could ever have more than that now. I also know it isn't fair...I mean, I don't want you to think that I'm a tease. I just..."

"You just want another kiss."

It wasn't a question, but she answered him anyway. "Yeah."

His abs bunched beneath his tight skin as he sat up, moving the hand he'd had behind his head to her face and rubbing his thumb against the side of her mouth. "Christ, you are so beautiful."

"I'm not. I'm scarred, Wyatt. Inside and out." His gaze flickered with irritation, but she cut him off before he could argue with her. "It's the truth."

"I call bullshit again, El. Because you *are* beautiful. Gorgeous. The most perfect thing I've ever seen. But I *will* control myself. I want you, but I won't push you into anything. I'm willing to wait for you to be ready, so don't waste time worrying about what you think is fair and what isn't."

Wrapping her hands around his wrist, she said, "Just tell me why, Wyatt. Why would you do this? I meant what I said. You're… You could have any woman you wanted. Why *me?*"

He leaned toward her and answered with the electrifying heat of his mouth, rubbing his lips against hers. Then he deepened the kiss, tongue to tongue, his rough hand gently cupping the side of her face. She got lost in the velvety dark heat of his mouth, the kiss flavored with the whiskey he'd drank after dinner. It was slow and sensual and heated, asking nothing of her except that she give in to the pleasure and not fight it. That she let it flow through her veins like a fine wine, the heavy beating of her heart telling her exactly how much her body liked the feeling.

When he finally broke the kiss and lifted his head, he stared down at her through the thick weight of his ink-colored lashes. They were so decadent and long they left shadows just above his sharp cheekbones. "I can be patient because I think you're worth waiting for," he told her in that low, smoky voice that seemed to melt into her. "So don't, for one second, think I don't want you, because I do. I'm hard and hurting, but I can wait. I *will* wait."

She shook her head, no idea what to make of him. He seemed too freaking good to be true. "You're… I don't understand you."

"Trust me," he muttered, pressing his lips to her forehead. "I don't understand me, either. If I had any brains at all, I'd be doing everything I could to talk you into wanting more right this second so that I could strip you out of those little sweats and bury myself so deep you could feel me here," he growled, pressing his big hand over her belly.

Clenching her teeth, Elise tried to deal with the need twisting through her that was unlike anything she'd ever known. Tried to beat it down into something that she could swallow and hide. That she could ignore, pretending it didn't exist, since she wasn't ready for what he wanted. But it was impossible. Damn it, she *needed* him. Needed him to make it right!

"Wyatt, p-please." Her voice quivered, face tingly and hot. "I'm not ready for that, but please give me… something. *Anything.* Don't make me leave your bed feeling like this."

"Christ, El. I couldn't ever make you leave my bed," he admitted in a guttural rasp, kissing his way down the side of her face as he moved the hand on her belly in firm, soothing circles. "I want you here too badly."

Oh, God. In that moment, she was nothing but sensation, pulsing in tender, sensitive places—her eyelids, throat, the insides of her wrists, behind her knees. The pleasure of his touch had invaded every part of her, coursing through her system like an addictive force, overtaking her, overwhelming her.

"Tell me what else you want," she whispered, digging her nails into his powerful shoulders, undone by the feel of his tight skin stretched over heavy muscle. By his power. His heat. "I love the sound of your voice."

Nuzzling her ear with his nose, he said, "You want to hear what I want to do to you?"

Her answer came on a soft, shivering moan. *"Yes."*

"All right. But I get to touch you while I'm talking. Okay?"

She nodded, so excited she couldn't stay still, her body thrumming with need.

He lifted his head, locking her in a gaze that was so heated she felt burned. "I need the words, El."

"Yes. Okay," she breathed out, trying hard to keep her voice from shaking. "You c-can touch me."

"Thank God," he muttered, nipping her chin. He kissed his way down the front of her trembling throat as he pushed her to her back, then braced himself over her on his hands and knees. Lying against the Wyatt-scented bedding, she shivered as his lips coasted over her collarbone, traveling lower, until he took the neck-line of her tank top in his teeth. Then he tugged it down, shifting his hold, until he'd managed to get it caught under her breasts.

"Jesus. You're so damn beautiful," he growled, star-ing down at her bra-covered breasts as if he wanted to eat her alive. Her bra was pale cream lace, almost the same color as her skin, the pink of her nipples easy to see through the intricate pattern—but thankfully not her scars. She blinked, panting, as she watched him lower his dark head and flick his tongue against one lace-covered tip, licking it four more times before moving to the other one. She watched, transfixed, wanting to see him lick that nipple, too. But he flicked his sharp, searing gaze up to hers as he took the sensitive peak in his mouth in-stead. She gasped at the wet, delicious heat of his mouth surrounding her—then cried out as he started to suck on her...*hard.* Intense, piercing shards of pleasure spread out from the tip of her breast, coursing through her sys-tem, making her moan and writhe. He growled low in his throat, moving back to the nipple he'd first licked and sucked at it even harder, and she could feel that rough animal sound vibrating against her, her cries ratcheting up a notch, throaty and raw.

"That's it, El." His breathing was hard and loud, each ragged pant blowing against her tingling nipple. "Let me hear you, sweetheart. Let me know how much you like it."

"I love it!" she practically shouted, lifting her hands and shoving her fingers into his silky hair, holding him to her tighter as she arched up, pressing her breast against his gorgeous face. "Love it, love it, love it," she chanted. "God, Wyatt, I am so freaking in love with your mouth!"

She could feel him smile against her breast but was feeling too incredible to be embarrassed. "That's good, baby. Because I want every part of you in it. These sweet little nipples—they're like pieces of candy on my tongue. I can't get enough of them." He went back to her other breast, sucking and licking through the lace, nipping at the softly pulsing peak, then rested his forehead between the quivering mounds, his breathing jagged as he gripped her sides in his big hands, his thumbs stroking against her ribs.

"Wyatt?" she whispered, when a hard shudder wracked his powerful frame. "You okay?"

He lifted his head, and for the first time since she'd met him, she could see the primal hunger of his wolf in his eyes, burning in that glittering midnight-black. He ran his tongue over his lower lip and said, "I mean it, El. Every part of you. In. My. Mouth."

Her eyes went wide, then even wider when she heard herself ask, "What part do you want the most?"

She could feel the tremor that moved through him as she gripped his broad, muscular shoulders, her own body shaking with sweet, shivering chills as he skimmed his lips along the edge of her jaw. "I want that sweet little cove between your thighs, El. I want to lick it. Lap at it like a cat. Suck on your clit until you can't do anything but hold on to me and scream from the pleasure."

She trembled even harder as his husky, erotic words curled against her skin, same as they had earlier that day, at her house. Lowering his head, he pressed his lips between her breasts, then to the hollow of her throat, where her pulse was rushing madly, and finally back to her lips, his tongue raking her mouth with melting, destructive skill.

"I want to put my tongue inside you, just like this," he whispered, thrusting his tongue into the tender depths of her mouth. "Want to put my lips around your delicate little opening and drink from you. Take those slick juices into my mouth and swallow them down."

"Oh, God," she gasped, moaning his name.

"You want me to give you more, sweetheart?"

She caught her lip in her teeth, loving how it made him groan almost as much as she loved the way he called her *sweetheart*. "Y-yes. But I'm… I don't know if I can…"

He muttered something against her hair, his breath warm against her scalp, sending another delicious shiver racing over her skin. Then he pulled back and braced himself on his straight arms, his thick hair falling around his face like a silken wave of darkness. "Do you trust me?" he asked her. His voice was rough and low but soft, a tender look of hunger burning in the glittering depths of his eyes. It made her feel molten, restless, as if she was getting ready to come out of her skin. "Answer the question, El."

"Y-yes," she answered with all honesty, stunned to realize that it was true. "I trust you."

The next thing she knew, she was sitting up on the bed alone, watching him cross the room to his dresser. He opened a drawer, rummaged around in it, then turned and came back to the bed, a dark blue tie clutched in one powerful fist.

Whoa. What the hell?

"I'm not letting you tie me up, Wyatt." *Not in this lifetime!*

He smirked as he came onto the bed on his knees. "It's not for you, El."

"Huh?"

Tossing the tie to her, he laid down on his back and stretched his long arms over his head, gripping one of the slats in the headboard. Her gaze pinged from the impressive bulge at his crotch to the dark, masculine tufts of hair under his arms, then settled onto his breathtaking gaze. "Now what?" she asked through tingling lips.

"Now *you* tie *me* up."

Her jaw dropped. "Are you serious? You'd let me do that?"

"Sure. I trust you," he murmured with a sexy, playful wink. "I'd let you do anything you wanted to me."

She shivered again and had no doubt he could see just how aroused she was by the look on her face and in her eyes, her body practically steaming she was so turned on. It took her a few tries, with the way her fingers were shaking, but she finally managed to get the silky tie secured around his strong wrists, binding them to the headboard.

"Done," she whispered as she sat back on her heels, impressed with her handiwork.

He gave a little experimental tug, then jerked his chin at her. "Now get your gorgeous little ass over here and ride me."

"Through your jeans?"

"Yeah, sweetheart." His voice was raw, every mouth-watering muscle in his long body coiled tight with need. "Right through my jeans."

Biting her lip, she straddled his waist, then scooted back, until she could feel the hard ridge of his erection pressing against her core. He was long and hard and impossibly thick, but instead of freaking her out, her body responded with a melting rush of heat that was probably soaking through her panties and right through her sweats.

"Now take control of me, El. Use me. I'm all yours. Just be gentle," he said with another sexy smirk, staring up at her from beneath the thick weight of his lashes. She knew he was trying to tease her, to ease her through her fears, and she couldn't help but smile, completely charmed. He was wonderfully hard, everywhere, his arms and torso corded with muscle and sinew, powerful thighs tensed and ready—and yet, he held himself completely still for her, giving himself over to her in a way that she never would have imagined a man as dominant as Wyatt could do.

"Christ, El. You are so beautiful," he rasped, the quiet words rough with lust. He was always saying things like that to her, and she knew she would never get tired of hearing it.

"Wyatt," she breathed out, leaning over him and gripping his round biceps, loving how they flexed beneath her hands.

"Move," he forced out through his gritted teeth. "Now, El. Fucking ride me."

Biting her lip again, she gave a tentative roll of her hips, her breath catching at how incredible it felt to rub that most sensitive part of her body against his denim-covered erection. He was unbelievably huge and so freaking hard it made her insides clench when she thought of how mind-shattering it would be to have all those long, stiff inches buried deep inside her.

His head dug into the pillow as he stared up at her, a feral look in his eyes. She moved a little harder against him, increasing her speed, and watched those dark eyes nearly roll back in his head. His throat worked on a hard swallow, voice little more than a guttural, savage animal sound as he said, "You feel so damn good."

"You, too," she whispered, breathless, thinking that friction was great. Friction was her freaking new best friend. Forget chocolate and ice cream and hazelnut lattes. Her and friction were going to be inseparable from now on, so long as Wyatt Pallaton was willing to lend her a hand. Or his body.

"You gonna come, El?"

"Yes," she hissed, moving her hips faster, her fingers clenching against his hard biceps as she felt her body flush with heat, the roots of her hair damp with sweat. "Can you?"

"Can I what?" he asked, his eyes gleaming with a wicked, predatory spark within his outrageously beautiful face. He was the most gorgeous thing she'd ever set eyes on, and yet, he was 100 percent male. Rough and rugged and deliciously masculine, from his woodsy scent to his incredibly ripped physique. Even his forearms were sexy as hell, muscle and sinew and thick veins bulging beneath his bronzed skin as he gripped the headboard tighter, until the wood started to groan.

"Can you come this way?" she gasped, so wet now she knew she was probably leaving a damp spot on the front of his jeans.

"You want me to?" he growled, his nostrils flaring as she watched him from beneath her lashes, both of them breathing as if they were nearing the finish line of a marathon.

She nodded as she licked her lips, not trusting her voice if she tried to speak.

"Then touch yourself." The rough words were sharp with command. "Put your hand inside your underwear and get your fingers wet for me."

"Why?" she asked, curious about where he was going with this.

"Because if I'm going to come in my pants like a goddamn horny teenager," he explained, lifting his hips against her, "then I at least want your taste in my mouth when I do it."

Oh. Well, when he put it like that…how could she argue? And why would she even want to? Color burned in her face, but she didn't let embarrassment hold her back. Damn it, she wasn't a virgin, and she didn't plan on acting like one. So with that private little pep talk ringing through her head, she took a deep breath and slipped her fingers under the waistband of the sweats, inside her panties and down between her legs, where she was slippery and slick, melting into a liquid rush of heat.

"Fuck, yes," he hissed a moment later, when she pulled her glistening fingers from the top of her sweats. "Now put them in my mouth, El. Let me suck on your juices while you're rubbing me out."

Gripping his hard shoulder with her other hand, she lifted her wet fingers, thinking she'd simply place them against his parted lips. But as soon as they were close enough, he lifted his head and covered her fingers with his mouth. She gasped, the sight of him sucking so hungrily on her taste almost as sexy as the primal, animalistic sounds he was making.

"So goddamn sweet," he snarled when he finally pulled back, his rough tongue still licking her fingers clean, as if he were greedy for every drop of her flavor.

"Wyatt, I'm c-close," she stammered, her voice rising.

His jaw tightened and she felt his legs shift, then realized he'd been bracing his feet against the bed when he suddenly shoved his hips up harder against her, his cock like a brand against her sensitive folds even with the layers of clothing between them. "Do it *now*," he ordered, the guttural tone of the wolf nearly drowning out the voice of the man. "I want to come with you, El. So do it the fuck now!"

She flung her head back and screamed as the orgasm tore through her, her body reacting to his raw, erotic command as if she'd been put under his spell. And maybe she had. This certainly didn't seem like her, because she could never remember being this wild with her pleasure, her arms folded over her head as she ground her pulsing sex against him so hard she could feel the instant he started to ejaculate. His back arched, tendons straining, as the most visceral, guttural roar she'd ever heard surged up from his chest, the powerful feel of his own release pumping through him only making her come even harder. Her orgasm was lush and strong and bone-meltingly good, and after what seemed like a long, endless forever, she finally collapsed against his hot, sweaty chest, his mouthwatering scent filling her nose as she struggled to remember how to pull air into her aching lungs.

The sound of his rough voice telling her to untie him was the only thing that could have compelled her to move. Still a little too shaken to look him in the eye, she kept her gaze focused on her task as she leaned over him and undid the knot, freeing his wrists. Before she could even lean back or move to his side, he sat up and wrapped those strong arms around her, clutching her against him. One hand found its way into the back of her hair, fisting the heavy strands, the other moving low across her back as he kissed her, letting her taste herself on his lips and his tongue. When she groaned, liking the taste, he took her mouth even harder, deeper, eating at her as if he needed her to breathe. She hoped she would one day be able to capture this kind of need in her writing, but knew she still hadn't come anywhere close. How could she have, when she'd never experienced it for herself until now?

"You're fucking incredible, you know that?" he growled against her lips.

"You're pretty incredible yourself," she whispered.

When he finally stopped ravaging her mouth, he rubbed his nose against hers, the tender gesture making her breath catch. Then he carefully twisted and laid her down against the bed so that her head was on his pillow, and reached for the blanket at the foot of the mattress to cover her up. "Sleep tight, beautiful."

Uh...what on earth?

"Wyatt?" she murmured, sitting up as he slipped off the bed and back to his feet. With a start, she realized he was already hard again, his cock rigid behind the damp fly of his jeans, his gorgeous eyes still heavy with lust. But if he was still aroused, then why was he leaving her? "Where are you going?"

"To take a shower. The colder the better," he told her, a wry grin on his sensual lips as he backed away from the bed. He moved slowly, almost as if he didn't want to go but was forcing himself to. "We're talking arctic, because it's the only way I'm going to be able to keep my hands off you until you're ready for more." His gaze swept over her face, taking in her kiss-swollen lips and the hot flush of pleasure on her cheeks, and he winked at her just before he turned and walked through the doorway. "And you'd better not be laughing at me, woman, because that ain't cool after you got me in this state!" he called out from behind the closed bathroom door, the teasing note in his voice making the grin that had suddenly started to curl her lips turn downright sappy.

Flopping back onto the bed, Elise buried her face in his pillow and muffled the laughter she couldn't stop, wondering if she'd lost her mind. It was either that or her heart. She was screwed, either way. But at the moment she was just too damn happy to care.

She might not have made love to Wyatt, but she'd brought him pleasure. Had made him curse and moan and come. It was something she'd never thought she would have—but now that she'd gotten it, she wanted more. If she wasn't careful, she was going to want every single freaking thing he could give her.

Even though she knew they could never be hers.

Chapter 10

Three days later, Elise closed down her laptop and moved it to the end of the kitchen table, where she'd been working for the evening. Wyatt was out on patrol again, which meant she had the cabin to herself. But aside from the times when he was guarding the Alley, they'd spent nearly every waking moment together. Moments that she'd enjoyed so much more than she'd ever expected. Hell, they were so good she was craving him in his absence. Not just his incredible looks or his sexy, lopsided grins. She missed everything about him. The way he made her feel. The way he made her smile in a way that she never remembered doing, even before the attack that had changed her life. The kind of smiles that bloomed from deep inside, in the place where hopes and dreams and wishes were stored. She'd thought that place had been killed in her a long time ago. But she'd been wrong. And she had Wyatt to thank for showing her that.

Actually, she had Wyatt to thank for a lot of things—but she wanted more. Only problem was, he wasn't giving them to her. Not since the day he'd taken her up to Shadow Peak. It was a little surprising at first, but she should have known he would be different. With any other guy, she'd have expected him to keep trying to get in her pants, whether it was what she wanted or not. But Wyatt wasn't just any other guy. There was so much more to him than that Y chromosome, and she was falling hard because of it.

He was, quite simply, too good to be true. Funny. Charming. Patient.

And yeah, there were also times when he could be quiet and self-contained. But she had a feeling those moods were a learned behavior for him. A way of coping. There was pain somewhere in his past, though she was no closer to learning what had caused it. But she knew it was there. Like a shadow that always followed him, it flavored his moods, shaping his expressions and the things he said. The way he reacted to certain situations…and to people, as well. Like her. Did everyone else see it? Or did they simply buy his sometimes-stoic act and think it was just a part of who he was? Yeah, he laughed and joked around and used his sharp sense of humor like a whip, but it was so obvious to her that there was a part of him always under lockdown. That was something she didn't have any problem understanding. Hell, she'd spent most of her life with some of her soul locked up tight inside her, where she could keep it safe.

She'd spent the night they'd made out in his bed, but only the one. He hadn't kissed her again, and she hadn't asked him to. But the looks he gave her were still as heated and intense.

Elise didn't know why he hadn't slept beside her, considering she'd been in *his* bed, but tried not to worry about it. She knew she could always ask, but that seemed kind of desperate, and she didn't want him to think she was obsessing about him. Even though she *was,* which was embarrassing and probably pathetic. But, God, if a woman were going to obsess about a guy, Wyatt Pallaton was the *perfect* choice.

Though she felt safe and at ease in the Alley, her nightmares were becoming more frequent, and the worst had been just that morning, at daybreak. She'd dreamed she was running through a forest, being chased by a bloodthirsty pack of wolves intent on destroying her, body and soul. She'd woken up screaming, only to find a protective-looking, bare-chested Wyatt rushing into the spare bedroom where she slept. Once he'd realized what was wrong, he'd climbed onto the bed, braced his back against the headboard, pulled her across his lap and tucked her head under his chin. Then he'd wrapped his strong arms around her trembling body, lowered his head and softly sung a Native American lullaby to her that he'd said his mother had often sung to him when he was a boy. It had been haunting and beautiful, his deep voice lulling her back to sleep within minutes. When she'd awakened later in the morning, she'd been alone, and he hadn't mentioned what had happened when she'd briefly seen him for breakfast. Actually, she hadn't seen him much during the daylight hours at all today, since he'd been busy with the other Runners, and she'd been wrangled into helping Jillian with painting the nursery. Then they'd shared dinner with everyone at Carla's cabin, and Wyatt had left to go out on patrol. *Again*.

As she glanced at the clock on the wall, seeing that it was fast approaching midnight, she couldn't help but frown. She knew Wyatt wasn't purposefully avoiding her during the days, considering how much time they'd spent together…but she was beginning to suspect that the nights were a different matter. Though the patrols were meant to be spread evenly among the Runners— with the exception of Eric, who was being given time to spend with his new wife—Wyatt had been on patrol for the past three nights.

Or at least he'd claimed to be.

That thought brought another frown to her lips, just as she heard him come in through the front door.

"Where do you go every night?" she heard herself ask, the moment his tall, ripped body appeared in the archway that led from the living room into the kitchen.

His dark eyes narrowed at her tone. "What do you mean? You know I've been out on patrol."

"But I've seen the schedule at Torrance and Mason's. You're not scheduled *every* night. No one is."

He propped his shoulder against the archway, thumbs hooked in his front pockets, blasting a dose of visceral, primal sexuality at her without even trying. No other man in the world came close to making boots, jeans and a loose flannel shirt look so impossibly sexy. "What are you getting at, El?"

She wet her lips, forcing herself to ask the question. "Do you…do you have a woman that you go to? Is *that* what you've been doing?"

He blinked, looking a little stunned. Then he shoved a hand back through his hair and made a low, kind of husky sound that was a little too raw to be a laugh. "You mean am I running off to screw some other woman? What? You think I'm crazy?"

Elise frowned. "I don't understand."

The look in his eyes as he stepped toward her made something in her body give an excited little flip, while her breath quickened. "El, why would I go after something I don't even want, when what I *do* want is right under my own roof?"

Confusion bled through her tone. "Then where are you going? I know you're not spending every moment of the time you're gone out on patrol. You have to be doing something."

He reached up and rubbed at the back of his neck, his gaze sliding a little to the left of her. "Sometimes I can't... I just need to get away for a while. That's all."

Her brows lifted and she slumped back in the chair, a sense of defeat settling low in her belly. "You mean you need to get away from me? Why?"

"I don't want to tell you," he admitted with a low, jerky laugh, his lips curling in a lopsided smile that was almost a grimace.

"Why not?" she asked, hating that he still wasn't looking at her.

He pinched the bridge of his nose, then lowered his hand and finally looked her right in the eye. "Because the last thing I want is for you to be afraid of me." Exhaling a rough breath, he struggled to make her understand. "I tried to explain it to you before, at your house. About the way that you... The way that I... *Shit.* What I'm trying to say is that you make me want things in ways I've never wanted them before."

Her brows actually arched a little higher, her frustration and disappointment melting into a warm, exciting glow that she wasn't quite sure what to do with. Not yet. "Are you talking about sex?"

His eyes were so dark now they looked black. Black and dark and smoldering. "Yeah, I am," he murmured, raking his hand back through his hair again. "The others…they've always had to work hard for control. Me, it was fun. Not always sweet…but a good time. But with you…let's just say you've drawn the interest of both the man *and* the wolf."

She licked her lips. "I see."

He came a little closer. "But that doesn't mean I can't control it, El."

"I know. I…I trust you, Wyatt. I wouldn't be here if I didn't."

"Good," he said, pinning her in place with the blistering intensity of his gaze. "Because as much as I want to help protect you, I want to spend more time with you, too."

Oh, wow. Her stomach was definitely flipping now, her pulse so frantic she was probably close to a heart attack. "Are you saying that you want to get involved with me? For us to be a couple?"

He didn't actually flinch at her breathless rush of words, but it was close enough. The slight stiffening of his facial muscles, the tightening of his jaw, widening of his eyes. Oh, my God! Her stomach clenched, breath sucking in on a sharp, embarrassed gasp. She was so freaking stupid! He hadn't been talking about a relationship. He wanted to fuck her. To be the guy who thawed her out. She should have been insulted, but she was too… God, she didn't know what she was. Mortified, yes. But more than that. She suddenly felt deflated, like a shell. The spark that had been heating her from the inside out only moments before had just dwindled like a flame doused in water. Guttered out. *Gone*. Now she was cold and silent and stark beneath her skin. She moved to her feet and started walking around him, heading for the hallway, needing to be by herself.

"Elise. Damn it, don't walk away from me. It's not… I'm not—"

"Just leave me alone, Pallaton. I'm tired. I'm going to bed now."

He grabbed her shoulder but didn't try to spin her around. Just kept her in place, his hand warm and hard, though his touch was careful not to bruise. "The problem is *me,* not you." Her head whipped to the side and he scowled when he saw the look on her face. "Shit, I know that sounds stupid, but it's true. I'm not a—"

"No, there is no problem," she snapped, shrugging out of his hold as she jerked away from him. Anger was quickly taking hold of her, melting the ice, fueling her actions. "We are *nothing* to each other, so how could there be a problem?"

He easily closed the distance between them with a single step, getting right in her face. "That's bullshit and you know it. I want you. And you want me, too."

She curled her lip as she sneered. "Conceited much?"

"It's not conceit when it's the truth. I don't expect it, like it's my goddam due. But I'm not a fool," Wyatt growled, reaching up and digging his fingers into her hair, gripping the silken strands at her nape. "It's there, and I'm glad as fuck that it is. And you're crazy if you think I'm going to let you ignore it. You've ignored your life for long enough. Wake the hell up and start living again!"

She ripped herself out of his hold, lifted her arm and

slapped him, the flat of her hand striking him so hard that it jerked his face to the side. "What do you know about my life?" she choked out, her voice rising.

Bringing his narrow gaze slowly back to hers, Wyatt started to argue, but the words wouldn't come. Fuck, she was right. Who the hell was he to lecture her on living and throwing off the past? He wore his own like a miserable hair shirt, never letting it out of his sight, keeping it close and tight to his skin so that he'd always feel that keen, bitter edge of guilt.

There were no words for what he wanted to say, but it didn't matter. Words weren't going to get them where they needed to be. He spoke better with his body anyway, and they were nowhere near done with this conversation. Digging his fingers into the rich auburn silk of her hair again, he pulled her toward him and slammed his lips down on hers, taking her outraged gasp into his mouth. She bit his lip, and he laughed, thrusting his tongue inside, nearly howling with satisfaction when she snarled and started kissing him back. It was hard and angry and rough, and he loved it, because it was Elise, she tasted incredible, and it was *real*. Real emotion. Real anger and lust and need. Boiling over. Burning them both. They might be left in a pile of ash when it was done, but he'd have died happy.

And more complete than he'd ever been.

"Wyatt," Elise groaned, trying to think as he wrapped his arms around her body, molding her to him. But it was impossible. The moment the heat of his mouth had touched hers, it shook her apart inside. Melted her down.

Yeah, his words had broken something in her chest that felt an awful lot like her heart, but that didn't mean she had to stop. The rules she had laid down for herself with him no longer applied now. What did it matter if she took what she wanted from him without full disclosure? If she used him for her pleasure? He was using her, too, wasn't he?

Kissing him back with everything that she had, Elise pushed her fingers into his thick hair and went up on her tiptoes. He gave a hard shudder against her, his arms banding around her even tighter, while a low animal sound rumbled up from his chest. She loved the sounds that he made when he was aroused. The way he growled her name into her mouth, feeding it to her. For a wolf, he could purr in the most delicious ways, that dark, luscious voice the most intoxicating thing she'd ever heard. And his tongue. *God.* The way he claimed the inside of her mouth was more wicked than sex.

Breaking her mouth from his, she lowered her hands to his broad shoulders and forced a bit of space between their bodies, both of them breathing hard. "I'm not ready to try to sleep with you. I might *never* be ready." Not now, when she knew the score. Knew what he was in this for. "But I want something."

His fingers flexed against her back. "What do you want?"

"You. I want to touch you, Wyatt." She lowered her gaze to the stunning bulge at the front of his jeans, then slowly lifted it back to his face. Licking her lower lip, she said, "I want to *do* things to you. Things I've been thinking about doing for what feels like forever."

A notch formed between his dark brows, and his breathing got a little rougher. "Are you talking about my dick, El? Is this some kind of game? Are you messing with me?"

She shook her head, and said, "No. I just want to make you feel good."

"Why?" That single word was low and clipped.

Squeezing his shoulders, she admitted, "Because it will make me feel good, too."

His eyes narrowed to the point that his thick lashes were tangled together at the edges, but she could still see the blast of need she had a feeling he was trying hard to hide. She could even feel the rise in his temperature and knew if she had her heightened senses she would be able to detect the hot, primal scent of his hunger. She didn't know which way he was going to go—*yes or no?*—until he crushed her against his chest and lifted her off her feet. With his face close to hers, their smoldering gazes locked hard and tight, he carried her through his cabin and back to the guest room. Then he set her down on her bare feet in the middle of the room, walked away and sat down on the side of the bed. After taking off his boots and socks, he swung his legs up, then scooted back until he was propped up against the pillows. His biceps bulged as he lifted his long arms, locking his hands behind his dark head, his expression that of a man who wasn't sure the next few minutes were going to go the way he wanted them to or not.

Oh, wow, she thought, unable to keep the smile off her face as she realized what he was doing. Surrendering himself to her. Giving her what she'd asked him for. Freely, even though he wasn't sure she wasn't going to screw him over in the process.

Caught between exhilarating extremes of excitement and lingering hurt, Elise climbed onto the bed, threw a leg over his hips and straddled him, almost losing her breath at the feel of his erection pressed against her core.

Against that tender part of her body where she was warm and wet, aching for relief. But this moment wasn't about her—it was about Wyatt. About what she needed from him. About indulging her senses and getting as much of him as she could while she still had the chance.

Gathering herself, she reached down with trembling fingers and unbuttoned his shirt, her breath quickening as she caught sight of his bronzed, muscular chest. She leaned forward, pressing a kiss between his small brown nipples, and could have sworn she could feel the pounding of his heart against her lips. If her Lycan senses had been at full strength, she was sure she'd have been able to hear that heavy, sexy beat resonating through her head. It sucked that she couldn't, but she shoved the depressing thought from her mind, more than ready to lose herself in the beautiful male bounty that was stretched out beneath her.

And, God, was he beautiful.

Scooting back, she licked the tight skin just above his waistband, loving the low groan that vibrated in his throat. Moving lower, she ran her teeth down the hard, thick ridge straining against his jeans, and that low groan became a primal, visceral growl. The aggressive animal sound should have scared the hell out of her, after what she'd been through, but it didn't. Not from Wyatt. It made her hot, the tender folds between her legs swelling, heating. And she was getting wetter. God, she was melting into hot liquid, slippery with craving, too far gone now to let her pesky emotions hold her back. If she couldn't have his heart, she at least needed this. As much of this—of *him*—as she could get.

Desperate to get on with it, she slipped the button free at the top of his fly, then carefully lowered the zipper over his straining erection. He lifted up for her as she tugged his jeans and tight black boxers over his hips, nearly dying when he sprang up in all his hard, mouth-watering, masculine glory.

Okay. Um, wow. Total...freaking...wow!

He was beautiful and also incredibly well hung. Even more so than she'd imagined, and she'd been imagining a hell of a lot.

A quick glance up at his face showed him with his head raised, lips parted, dark eyes kind of dazed and heavy as he watched her. She could tell by that intense, wild look on his face that he liked the way she'd been looking at him...studying his cock. The bead of moisture gathering on the broad, slick, bruise-colored head told her that he liked it *a lot.*

Her heart started to beat a little harder.

"Fuck," he growled, his hips bucking when she suddenly gripped the long, vein-ridged shaft in her hand. He was so thick she could barely fit her fingers around him.

"Honestly, Wyatt. Huge much?" she teased with a crooked, playful smirk. "I mean, talk about excessive."

"Oh, shit," he wheezed, digging the heels of his hands into his eyes. "Don't. Don't make me laugh."

"Why not? Isn't this meant to be fun?"

He lowered his hands and glared, his chest rising and falling with his hard breaths. "You've got me strung so tight I don't know what the hell I'm doing. My goddamn eyes are wet. Laughing. Crying. Losing my fucking control. You are *wrecking* me, El. Piece by bloody piece."

"In a good way?"

"I don't know," he groaned, still sounding as if he was having trouble getting enough air. "I just know that I'd do *anything* to have these moments with you."

At his incredible words, heat spilled through her insides in a decadent, completely addictive pleasure rush, like an emotion orgasm for her soul. For her heart. Which was freaking unfair as hell, seeing as how he didn't want it. Needing a distraction before she started sobbing and clinging to him like a child—begging him to care about her when she was so not the kind of woman to believe in happily-ever-after—she leaned down until her mouth hovered no more than an inch above that heavy, glistening head. She felt him shudder as she breathed on him, and looked up at him through her lashes to find him watching her again. "Do you mind?" she whispered, wanting the feel of him against her tongue so badly she could taste it.

Raw, predatory hunger burned in his gaze. "You take my dick in your mouth, El, and I'm going to come in it," he growled in warning. "I won't be able to stop myself."

"I'm good with that," she said with a smile, already lowering her head. She gasped at the first brush of him against her lips, his skin hot to the touch, as if he were burning with fever. Her lips felt sensitive and full, loving the velvety feel of his flesh, her hand squeezing him tighter as he jumped in her grip.

"Fuck!" he shouted, when she flicked her tongue against him, taking a tentative taste that made her moan. Mmm…she hadn't expected that. Hadn't expected him to taste as incredible as he looked, but he did. Warm and salty and deliciously male. So good that she had to lick him from root to tip, tasting every inch of him while his back arched and he shoved his fingers into her hair, gripping her head. Then she took the thick shaft into her mouth and started to lick and suck, unable to get enough of his taste, he was *that* addictive. With his harsh breaths

and hoarse groans playing in her ears, she used her saliva to get him nice and wet, then drew in a deep breath and took him even deeper, his graveled shout telling her that she was definitely doing something right. So she just kept doing it, using her hand on the wide inches she couldn't fit between her lips, licking and sucking on the ones that she could, determined to make this the best oral sex he'd ever been given.

She moaned around his beautiful cock when he started lifting his hips, rubbing himself against her tongue, and a coarse, chuffing sound vibrated in the back of his throat. "You're killing me, you know that?" he snarled.

"Good," she panted against the slick head as she let him slip from her mouth, her lips pressed to the blunt tip. That was what she wanted. To make him as desperate as she felt. Make him crave her. Get him so addicted he didn't know up from down anymore, then show him what it was like to get cut down to size. To have something you didn't even really understand how badly you wanted ripped away from you before you even had it. This was going to be Queen Bitch Elise at her finest, and she was going to—

No! Oh, God, what was she even thinking? She didn't want to hurt him. She just…she just wanted…

Shit! She didn't know what she wanted. Except for this. His pleasure. The feel of his strong, magnificent body trembling as she took him to the edge and shoved him over.

"I'm gonna come," he growled, warning her.

Like hell am I pulling back. She only sucked on him harder, taking him deeper, until she could feel him bumping against the back of her throat, her hands busy stroking and squeezing the rest of him. He made a raw, guttural sound, and his hips punched up, pushing him even deeper, and she loved it. Loved feeling him lose control. Loved knowing that she was the one making him do it.

Then he started ejaculating, his release on the cusp of being violent, and it was the most provocative, exciting, erotic thing she'd ever experienced. He wasn't gentle, his hips pumping him in and out of her mouth as he gripped her head with both hands now, but she didn't give a damn. Like the animal he was, he took his pleasure in a way that was rough and hard and powerful, and she couldn't get enough of it. Of feeling him lose control, shattering, as she took everything he had to give. It was so sweet and intimate, despite being so explicitly raw. Or maybe because of it. She'd given him something, a part of her that she hadn't wanted to give any man in years. Had battered down his shields so that she could get under his skin, and in doing so, she'd let him…

Oh, no. Lifting her head, she wiped her lips with the back of her wrist as she met the sharp, piercing intensity of his dark gaze, and reeled.

Oh, God, backfire. Total backfire!

Her lips felt tingly and full, her body heavy, weighted with desire, her need now like a wet, slick warmth in her veins, coursing through her limbs, invading every part of her. Even though she wasn't the one who'd climaxed, she felt as if her shields had just been blasted to hell and back, and knew she'd made a massive error. God, she'd been so wrong. She couldn't go through with this and use him. Not without it coming back and slapping her in the face. If she did, he was going to know her. Truly *know* her. All of it. Everything. Each and every one of the secrets and scars she hid on the inside, where no one could see them. It was going to happen because blasting him to pieces had blasted her right along with him, on a level that was so much deeper than emotion. One that resided down in her blood and bones, and her very soul. She hadn't been expecting it, because it had never happened to her before. But then, nothing with Wyatt was like the things she'd known in her past.

Damn it, she had to go. *Now.* The only way she might have been able to trust him with those secrets was if he loved her—but he'd already made it clear that he wasn't looking to fall in love. Which meant she needed to pull back, no matter how badly it sucked. It was either that or risk full disclosure and the shitty reality that would follow. He would eventually spill to everyone, claiming it was for her own good, and they would all know. Then she'd be smothered with looks that turned her stomach. Stares of pity, revulsion and disappointment. Thanks, but no thanks.

"What's wrong?" he asked, seeing the look that crashed over her face as she scrambled back from him. She didn't stop until she'd reached the far side of the bed.

Panting, she said, "I…I need to go."

His worried expression instantly shifted to surprise. "What?"

"You don't do relationships, and I don't do casual sex," she explained huskily, shaking her head. "Not anymore. I don't know how to explain it. I just… I need more than that if I'm going to put myself out there."

He sat up and shook his head, too, as if he were trying to clear it. "You're fucking serious?"

"Um, yeah," she whispered.

She could tell he wanted to argue her decision. But

what could he say? He didn't want to make her promises. He just wanted sex. And no matter how badly she ached to be that close to him, she knew it would be a mistake for her.

"Fine. But you stay. This is your room now. I'll go," he muttered, scrubbing his hands over his face as he swung his legs over the side of the bed. He hitched his boxers and jeans over his hips as he moved to his feet, then turned and looked back at her over his shoulder. Their gazes locked, and she knew he didn't know what the hell to do with her. *About* her. She caught the movement of his throat as he swallowed, before looking away and heading toward the door that led to the bathroom. It slammed behind him, and she flinched when she heard what sounded like a fist connecting with one of the bathroom walls, followed by the sound of the shower turning on, water rattling through the pipes.

When she heard the TV turn on in his bedroom across the hallway, she realized he must have exited the bathroom through the other door, no doubt wanting to avoid her. Not that she blamed him. She should have been smart. Should have kept her distance. Should have goddamn known better!

And Elise didn't think she was ever going to forgive herself for being such a fool.

Chapter 11

As a crack of thunder rumbled in the distance, Wyatt lifted his hand to wipe the rain from his face. He was out on patrol again with Jeremy, and they'd gotten caught in another rolling series of storms. Jeremy was unusually quiet tonight, which left him with nothing but time to think about what had happened with Elise the night before.

If there were prizes for colossal male fuckups, he definitely deserved one. It made him sick every time he thought about the look on her face when he'd told her he didn't want a relationship. It'd been like watching the light go out in something beautiful. And he'd done that. Crushed the trust that had been growing between them because he was a goddamn guilt-riddled coward. He was going to die old and alone, watching her fall in love with some other Lycan and build a beautiful life, seething with cancerous jealousy, and have no one to blame but himself.

Shoving the maudlin thoughts aside, since they were playing hell on his stomach, Wyatt focused on the surrounding forest. The fresh moss was springy beneath his feet, verdant and lush, the air crisp from the constant fall of the rain. They were getting soaked and wouldn't be able to track shit in this weather, but they kept on with it, knowing damn well that Roy was just waiting to make his move against them. The bastard was lying too low, being too quiet, not to make them suspicious. And despite having scouts from Shadow Peak watching the roads out of Hawkley, there hadn't been any sign of Harris Claymore.

"Dude, this sucks out loud," Jeremy muttered, glaring up at the dark, cloud-swollen skies. It didn't look as if it was going to stop raining anytime soon.

"What sucks is you calling me *dude.*"

The Runner snickered, slapping him on his shoulder. "It's okay. You've just forgotten how to be hip."

"I was never hip," he muttered derisively. "And I don't think *hip* even means the same thing anymore. You're dating yourself, idiot."

Jeremy scowled. "We need to spend more time with Elliot and Max."

Rolling his eyes, Wyatt said, "Face it, man. You're a grown-up now. Hanging out with the boys isn't going to change that."

"I don't want to change it," Jeremy drawled, laughing under his breath. "I *wouldn't* change it. Not for anything in the world."

The guy hadn't come right out and said it, but Wyatt knew he was thinking about his wife when he spoke with such conviction. And that made him think of Jillian's friendship with Elise. "Has Jillian ever told you anything about Elise's attack?" he asked, before he could talk himself out of it.

Jeremy didn't respond at first. But after a couple of moments, his friend finally muttered, "Yeah. But I don't think you want to hear it, Pall."

"You're right. I don't," he grunted, feeling the familiar anger, which came whenever he thought about the attack, pulse inside him. He felt it everywhere. Not just fury, but a raw, eviscerating rage. It swept through him like embers, curling into places where it could settle and seethe. "But I need to. I need to know as much as I can about what happened to her."

Jeremy blew out a heavy breath, as if bracing himself for the story. "You know how Jilly's healing abilities work. When someone has endured a lot of…trauma, she has to go in deep and that usually opens up their minds to her."

At the mention of trauma, his fangs had almost slipped from his gums. "And that's what happened when she healed Elise?" he asked, practically grinding the words out.

Jeremy rubbed his jaw and nodded. "Yeah."

"Just tell me what you know, man. I need to hear it."

"Jilly doesn't like to talk about it," Jeremy rasped while they continued making their way through the misty forest. "Not that I blame her. But she told me a bit when we were working together, investigating Elise's crazy father. From the things she saw in Elise's mind, Jillian learned that she'd been attacked while she was out on a walk one night by at least three males in their Lycan forms. She was conscious during the attack, and they did shit to her that was as twisted as it was cruel. Not only hurt her, but did their best to terrify her. It... it was nothing but pure evil, Pall. I wish to hell we'd known at the time so that we could try to find them, even though the rain that night made it impossible to track their scents. But Stefan did everything he could to keep the Runners from knowing the truth."

Christ, no wonder Elise didn't like to shift. He hadn't known that they'd been in their wolf forms during the attack. Considering the rogues he'd had to hunt over his years as a Runner, Wyatt knew damn well how much damage a fully shifted Lycan male could inflict on a woman. Even one from a Dark Wolf bloodline like Elise's. Especially when she was in her human form.

"It kills her that she can't remember what happened," he muttered, wanting nothing more at that moment than to take her in his arms and hold her. But they still had nearly thirty minutes left on their patrol, and he wasn't done questioning Jeremy. "Do you think it has something to do with the drugs the Whiteclaw have been manufacturing?"

"I think it's definitely possible," Jeremy replied. "Like I said, Jillian was able to tell that Elise was conscious during the attack, but there's nothing in her memories to help identify who they were. It's like part of her brain was just wiped clean. The things Jillian learned were buried deep in her subconscious."

"Which is why she dreams them," he murmured.

"Shit," Jeremy cursed. "That sucks."

He jerked his chin in silent agreement, hating that there was nothing he could do to make it better. Goddamn story of his life. He couldn't help but think that if he and the others hadn't been so damn stubborn about staying out of Shadow Peak, then he might have met Elise sooner. If he'd known her before the attack, would he have recognized her as his own and gone after her? Been there to protect her that night, letting his wolf rip those sons of bitches to pieces?

"You know, I've always wondered how Eli found the one that he killed," Jeremy said, cutting into his dark thoughts. "I mean, if there wasn't a scent trail to follow, either because of the rain or some drug the bastard might have taken, how did he know the guy was one of the attackers?"

"I've wondered the same thing," he muttered, scrubbing a hand down his face. "But I guess we'll never know until he comes back and tells us."

"Yeah, I guess you're right." Moonlight glinted off Jeremy's blond hair as he lowered his head to check his watch. "We should be heading back soon. It's almost time for a shift change."

They hadn't taken more than ten steps when Wyatt threw his arm out to the side, stopping Jeremy in his tracks. The Runner cut him a sharp look, and Wyatt hitched his chin ahead of them. The forest had gone unusually quiet, and they both sensed that there was something out there, no doubt waiting to ambush them. There was no scent, but they knew better than to rely on their sense of smell. While the rogues who'd learned the art of day-shifting—thanks to Stefan Drake—had been accompanied by an acrid aroma, the Whitelaw's "super soldier" drug simply removed any trace of scent altogether.

Jeremy was motioning for Wyatt to take the right while he took the left, when the bastard came right at them. Wyatt caught a flash of movement at the corner of his eye, and then the fully shifted Lycan was on him, going for his throat with his deadly jaws. Shifting the top half of his body, Wyatt went to knock him aside, when the Lycan landed a punishing knee strike to his ribs, the strength behind the blow making it clear that the male was hyped up on the drug. Jeremy immediately joined in, exchanging blows with the Lycan, claws striking against claws with an eerie hiss as the forest filled with their guttural snarls. When Jeremy tripped over a thick root, Wyatt lunged to protect him and ended up getting struck, his shoulder burning as his flesh was clawed open. Ready to end this bullshit, he went on an aggressive charge, blood spraying in a wide arc as Wyatt slashed the Lycan's chest with his lethal claws. As messed up as it was, he was enjoying the violence of the fight, pouring all his anger and frustration over the way he'd handled things with Elise into teaching this asshole why it was a mistake to get near the people he cared about.

"What the fuck are you doing here?" he demanded, once he had the blood-soaked Lycan slammed up against the moss-laden trunk of a massive pine tree.

"What do you think?" the male snarled, his voice roughened by the muzzled shape of his ebony snout. "I was told to watch her."

He knew damn well the bastard was talking about Elise.

"Why?" When the jackass simply glared at him, Wyatt put one claw-tipped hand around his neck, letting his thumb claw dig into the base of the Lycan's throat. "I asked you a question. *Why?*"

"Because he wants her!"

"Who wants her?" he growled through his own muzzled snout, while Jeremy came up beside him. "Who the hell are you talking about?"

The male's bright green eyes went wide. "You don't know? Oh, fuck, that's priceless," he wheezed with a gritty laugh.

Letting his claw dig a little deeper into the Lycan's throat, Wyatt muttered, "Your time's ticking, asshole. You really gonna waste it laugh—" *Bam!* One second the Lycan was glaring back at him, and in the next the guy's head simply exploded, bits of brain and skull flying everywhere, splattering across both him and Jeremy.

"What the fuck?" Jeremy shouted, which pretty much summed up exactly what Wyatt was thinking.

"Get down!" he snarled, but Jeremy was already dropping beside him. They lay on the forest floor on their bellies, braced on their elbows, sniffing the air as they listened to the wind howling through the trees, trying to determine where the danger was coming from. Someone was out there armed with a high-powered assault rifle, and they weren't going to stand around making easy targets of themselves. Bullet wounds were something a Lycan could usually survive, especially with the help of a healer like Jillian—but when the shot blew a Lycan's head into pulp, there wasn't any coming back from it.

"You scent anything?" he asked Jeremy, careful to keep his voice as quiet as possible.

Jeremy shook his head. But as it turned out, they didn't have to search for the shooter. The shooter came to them.

"It's all right. You can get up now," a voice called out from the darkness. "He was the target, not you. I shot him to protect you, since he no doubt had orders to assassinate you both."

"Who's there?" Wyatt grunted, searching the tree-shrouded shadows as he and Jeremy both moved to their feet. Whoever it was, he'd taken the same drug as the dead man lying at their feet, his scent completely disguised.

"It's Sebastian Claymore," the male said, coming into view as he stepped through the pines. He was small for a Lycan, maybe five-eight and nowhere near two hundred pounds, but he was fast. And he was clever. A hell of a lot cleverer than the rest of his clan.

"You're trespassing," Jeremy snarled, his long, sinister fangs gleaming white in the milky moonlight. "What the hell are you doing here?"

Gesturing toward the rifle hooked over his shoulder, Sebastian said, "I would think that's obvious. I was saving your lives."

"You murder your own people now?" Wyatt growled, the guttural words rough with pain. Blood oozed from a nasty cut on his cheek and slipped down the side of his face. But it was his shoulder that was really screwed. The Lycan had caught him deep with his claws, tearing into the muscle and striking bone. It would heal, but the process was going to be painful as fuck.

"Trust me when I say he was a necessary kill," Sebastian murmured in response to his question, before a crooked smile lifted the corner of his mouth. "And before you ask about the gun, let me just say that, given my size, it was either learn to shoot or be killed. The White-claw aren't known for being the most gentle of packs."

"Then why did you come back to them?" Wyatt asked, his breath hissing through his teeth as he retook his human shape, the change making his injured shoulder burn with a fresh wave of pain.

Sebastian's response was simple. "Because I was needed."

"For what?" Jeremy grunted. The Runner had retaken his human shape as well and was now standing with his arms crossed over his bare chest, his steely gaze narrowed suspiciously on Sebastian.

"That's why I'm here. I need to talk to you."

"Then talk, and make it fast," Wyatt snapped. "I want to know what you're doing on our land."

Hitching the rifle strap just a bit higher on his shoulder, the Lycan said, "I'm here because I don't want what's coming. I don't want the war. I would have called to warn you, but I can't guarantee that my calls aren't being monitored. Coming here to talk to you in person was my only choice." He glanced at the fallen body of his pack mate, then returned his gaze to Wyatt. "Luckily for you, I came when I did."

Ignoring that statement, he asked, "Warn us about what?"

His low voice rough with emotion, Sebastian said, "There's something not...*right* with my brother. With Harris." He started to pace, rubbing one hand against his lean jaw, his eyes worried behind the round lenses of his glasses. "Don't get me wrong. I'm not a traitor. I love my brother, but he and Roy are going to destroy the Whiteclaw and I can't let that happen. We might not be the most upstanding pack around, but there are women and children with us who need a home."

Jeremy made a rude sound in the back of his throat. "You really concerned about women? What about the ones being drugged and gang-raped in your hometown?"

The Lycan's mouth tightened. "You think I'm not disgusted by that filth?"

"If that's true," Wyatt muttered, "then what are you doing about it?"

Stopping his pacing, Sebastian stood with his hands shoved in his pockets and met their belligerent glares with a frustrated one. "There are those of us in the pack who hate what Roy's trying to do. But we have few resources. He controls everything."

"Tell us about Harris," Wyatt prompted, wanting to get the hell out of there and back to Elise so that he could see with his own eyes that she was safe and secure.

Sebastian lifted his shoulders in a weary shrug. "I don't know. He's just… I have a bad feeling. His interest in the Silvercrest…it isn't healthy."

"What kind of interest?" he growled. "Did that bastard break into Elise Drake's house the other night?"

Sebastian's brows lifted. "Someone broke into her home?"

Wyatt locked his jaw and kept quiet, choking back his words. He didn't want to tell Seb anything about Elise's life—he just wanted to know what was going on with the guy's brother. But after Sebastian failed to answer the rest of their questions, it became clear that the Lycan either didn't know anything more…or was simply unwilling to share. He claimed he didn't even know who the Lycan he'd killed had been sent to the Alley to watch or who exactly had sent him. Dissatisfied with the lack of answers, Wyatt called in the two scouts who were taking over the patrol for them. After briefing the scouts on what had happened, he told them to escort Sebastian off their land and to make sure that the Lycan took the body of his pack mate with him. Then he turned his attention back to Sebastian and said, "If you learn anything that can actually help us, then find whoever's on patrol, like you did tonight. They'll know to be on the lookout for you."

With that, he and Jeremy headed back to the Alley, neither of them comfortable with what had happened... or with the things Sebastian Claymore had told them.

"What the hell happened to you two?" Cian asked the instant they stepped out of the trees at the edge of the clearing, near the Irishman's cabin. The Runner was sitting on the hood of his Land Rover, which was parked at the side of the cabin, smoking a cigarette, while silvery streams of smoke swirled over his head like a halo, though he was definitely no angel.

Sounding as exhausted as he felt, Wyatt said, "We ran into some trouble."

Cian exhaled another ethereal stream of smoke and smirked. "In that case, I hope the other guy looks worse."

"He looks like something out of a fucking horror flick," Jeremy muttered. "Got his goddamn head blown off."

Cian's brows lifted, and they explained about their run-in with the Whiteclaw Lycan and the surprising conversation with Sebastian Claymore that followed.

"Do you trust him?" Cian asked, taking another deep drag on his cigarette.

Jeremy shrugged. "I don't know. I want to, but this whole situation is messed up."

"Speaking of being messed up," Cian offered drily, "did I mention that you both look like shit?"

"You don't look so great yourself," Wyatt replied, surprised to realize that what he'd said was true and not just a snarky comeback. There were new lines of strain around the Runner's mouth and eyes, and one of his knees kept jiggling. Now that Wyatt thought about it, he realized Hennessey had been overly restless lately, not to mention chain-smoking to the point that it would have been hell on a human's lungs. "Seriously, man. You look rough."

"Yeah, but all I have to do is find a willing set of legs to crawl between, and I'll be good as gold," the Irishman drawled with a sharp smile. "What are *you* going to do?"

"Hell if I know." He grimaced, his injured shoulder hurting like a bitch.

"Well, I know what *I'm* doing," Jeremy murmured, heading toward his cabin, where Jillian had just opened their front door, her petite body backlit by a golden, welcoming glow of light.

"Can you let the others know what's happened?" Wyatt asked, casting an eager look toward his own cabin, where a soft, colorful light was shining in the living-room window, making him think Elise must still be up watching television.

"Yeah, I'll let them know."

"Thanks," he said, bringing his gaze back to Cian. From the look on Hennessey's face, it was clear that his fellow Runner had noticed how intently he'd been staring at his cabin. And that he knew why. But before his friend could give him any shit about it, the side door to Cian's cabin opened and a woman Wyatt recognized from Shadow Peak walked out. She was tall and busty, with minimal clothing and a well-used look that said she'd been screwed through the Irishman's mattress. She gave a little wave to Cian, then climbed into a small Toyota Wyatt hadn't noticed until then and headed out of the Alley. It didn't take a genius to figure out what had gone down between the two, and Wyatt lifted his brows. "Don't you normally go to the woman's place?"

Rolling his shoulder, Cian said, "Yeah, but I didn't want to leave the Alley. We need all the protection we can get."

Wyatt snorted. "Exactly how much use would you be to us while playing 'ride the pony' with your current fuck-buddy?"

The Runner gave a gritty laugh, a strange expression on his face that Wyatt had never seen before. "Not an issue. To be honest, despite what I said before about finding a pair of legs to crawl between, lately sex hasn't been quite as…*consuming* for me as it used to be." His tone was wry, with an unmistakable, underlying edge of something darker. "So there's no need to worry about my powers of concentration, Pall."

Wyatt grunted, no idea what he should say to that. He and Cian weren't exactly on "let's rip our hearts out and talk life" terms. Not that he had that kind of friendship with anyone. And that was for a good reason. He didn't ever know what to say when someone laid something heavy on the line like Hennessey had just done. *Buck up? Sorry?* Or the tried-and-true *Life's a bitch?*

Cian cut his hand through the air. "You know what? Just forget it. We never had this conversation."

"Er, right." Wyatt started to walk away, then stopped himself and turned around, saying what had just occurred to him before he could think better of it. "But the problem might not be sex, man. It might just be who you're having it with." He paused, then added, "Or who you aren't. You know. Sleeping with."

The tip of the cigarette gleamed like a demon's eye as Cian pulled in another long drag. Wyatt braced himself for a smart-ass comeback, but the Runner simply jerked his chin toward Wyatt's cabin and asked, "You gonna claim her?"

He damn near fell back on his ass. *"What?"*

"You gonna claim her?" Cian repeated, his deep voice for once devoid of its sarcastic edge as he slowly exhaled. "Because my advice would be to do it sooner rather than later."

"It's not that simple," he muttered, more than a little shocked that he was having this conversation with Cian, of all people. "If I care about her, then I've got to do what's best for her. Right?"

"Yeah, that's what I keep telling myself. But it doesn't make it any easier."

He blinked, cutting a sharp look toward the Irishman. What the hell? Everyone knew Hennessey was a man-whore, rolling from one bed to another. Christ, as far as Wyatt knew, the Runner had never slept with the same woman twice. The idea of him being hung up on one particular female was hard to take in—and yet, Wyatt recognized the shadows lurking in the Runner's silver eyes.

He'd seen them just that morning, when he'd looked in the mirror.

Chapter 12

At the sound of the front door opening, Elise slid her gaze from the sappy TV movie she'd been watching, hoping Wyatt wouldn't notice that she'd been crying. Then she got a good look at him and her eyes nearly flooded all over again.

"Oh, my God! What the hell happened?" she demanded in a breathless rush, surging to her feet and hurrying toward him. "Why are you bleeding?"

A flat smile twisted the corner of his mouth. "Jeremy and I had an interesting night. But I'm fine."

Fine? Was he joking?

"You don't look fine," she snapped, reaching out with her hands but unsure if she should touch him. His muscular torso was nothing but a soaked field of crimson. "You look like something out of *The Texas Chain Saw Massacre!*"

With a masculine snort, he shoved his hair back from his face and said, "Yeah, I think that's pretty much what Cian thought when he saw me. But most of it's not my blood."

"Well, that's a relief," she huffed, settling her hands on her hips. "If it's not yours, then who does it belong to?"

"We ran into a Whiteclaw soldier," he muttered, running his tongue over the front of his teeth.

Her eyes went wide. "Near the Alley? What was he doing all the way over here?"

"I only know what he told us, which was that he was trying to keep an eye on a woman for someone." His husky voice was tight with frustration and what was probably a lot of pain. "But before I could get any more out of him, Sebastian Claymore blew his fucking head off with a rifle."

"What was Sebastian Claymore doing on Bloodrunner land?" she asked, eyeing the angry claw marks in his shoulder, her stomach twisting at the thought of how badly the wound must be hurting him.

"That's the weird part," he rasped. "He claimed he made the shot to help us. That he's worried about the direction his uncle and brother are taking his pack. He also said that his brother especially has an issue with the Silvercrest, but wouldn't go into details."

She locked her gaze back on his. "Do you believe him?"

"I don't know," he muttered, watching her through the heavy weight of those long, incredible lashes. "I just know that I don't want you worrying about it."

Elise gave him what she was pretty sure was a slack-jawed look of disbelief. "Seriously, Wyatt? How can I not worry?"

He shook his head with a hard, curt movement, and she had to tilt her own head back as he closed the distance between them. "Because nothing's different than it was before I came home tonight. We still don't know anything for certain. Hell, Sebastian could be pissed at his brother for any number of reasons and be using us as a way to get rid of him. I don't know the guy well enough to trust him. All I know is that I will do whatever it takes to keep you safe. So promise me you're not going to obsess about this."

She wanted to tell him that it was a ridiculous request. Of course she was going to obsess about it. How could she not, when they were talking about one of the bastards who could very well be responsible for ruining her life? God, there was a part of her that just wanted to grab Wyatt's keys, run out and climb into his Jeep, and drive straight to the Whiteclaw's pack town of Hawkley. That wanted to confront this Harris Claymore face-to-face and hear exactly what he had to say for himself. Would she know if she saw him in the flesh that he was one of the ones? Would she be able to tell? Would more pieces of the puzzle start coming back to her?

"El?" Wyatt's deep voice jerked her from her troubled thoughts, and she blinked him back into focus.

"Sorry. I was just—"

"Don't," he grated, cutting her off. "Don't think about it."

She was surprised to feel her lips curving in a wry grin. "You're so damn bossy."

"I know," he said with a rough sigh, sounding exhausted. "And I'll grovel later. I promise. Right now, I'm rank and need to clean up."

She bit her lip, feeling awful for getting so wrapped up in her own drama, when he was standing there bleeding out right in front of her. "Do you need Jillian to look at your shoulder for you?"

"Naw. I can already feel it healing."

"Then come on," she said firmly, grabbing his uninjured arm and leading him through the cabin. "Let's go to the bathroom, where I can help you get sorted."

"You don't mind?"

She rolled her eyes. "Wyatt, you've been hurt. Of course I don't mind. I'm not that much of a bitch."

"You're not a bitch at all, El. I just wasn't sure how you were at dealing with shit like this and I didn't want to make you uncomfortable."

"Oh. Well, I'm not going to pass out on you or anything. Blood doesn't really bother me." Once she got him to the bathroom, she let go of his arm and asked him where he kept his first-aid kit, then pulled the plastic box out from the under the sink and started going through it for the things that she needed.

Clearing his throat, he said, "I'll just grab a quick shower, and then you can patch me up. Okay?"

She blinked as she swung her gaze toward him, her heart skipping a beat as she watched him undo the top button on his jeans. "Oh, uh, yeah, that's a good idea," she rambled. "I'll just, um, wait out…there."

"Suit yourself," he drawled with a crooked smile, as if he were perfectly comfortable stripping down with her standing right there, watching him.

Elise didn't bother shutting the bathroom door behind her as she fled, wanting to hear him in case he needed her. But she also didn't linger too closely, trying to sneak a peek. Instead, she paced the hallway as she listened to the water rattling in the pipes, trying to think about anything other than how the Runner's breathtaking body must look under the hot spray of water, all those hard, sculpted muscles sleek and wet, firm to the touch.

Trying not to think about him, huh? Yeah, great job I'm doing with that one.

"I'm decent now," he called out, snapping her out of her thoughts again.

She smoothed her hands over her tank top and jeans as she made her way back to the door, then nearly swallowed her tongue when she got a clear look at him standing on the bathroom rug. He was nude except for the white towel wrapped around his lean hips, droplets of water still clinging to his burnished skin as he lifted his arms, biceps bulging as he shoved his wet hair back from his face.

"Um, just sit on the side of the tub for me," she practically croaked, trying hard not to do anything embarrassing, like drool all over his sexy ass. Reaching for the antiseptic wipes she'd set out on the counter, Elise kept her focus firmly on his shoulder as she started to clean the wound, determined not to think about how big and beautiful and bare he was. Or how incredible his hard-muscled thighs looked as she stood between them.

"That should do it," she murmured a few minutes later, carefully covering the raw wounds with ointment and then adding a little to the cut on his cheek. None of the wounds were still bleeding, thanks to his rapid healing abilities, so she didn't bother covering them with bandages, knowing the fresh air would do them good. But they were probably going to scar.

When she said as much to Wyatt, he lifted one of his dark brows, no doubt thinking she was being ridiculous, seeing as how his muscular torso was littered with battle scars. "If they do, then they'll be in good company," he offered with a smirk.

"At least scars look good on a man," she murmured. "Not so much on a woman."

She watched the muscles in his gorgeous face tighten, his dark brows pulling together as he mulled over her words. "El, you—"

"I should get to bed," she blurted, interrupting him. If she didn't put some space between them now, she wouldn't be able to keep her hands off him...and it would only end in disaster. Nothing had changed since the last time he'd touched her. Not a single goddamn thing.

"What aren't you telling me?" Reaching out, Wyatt brought her face back toward him with a grasp on her chin. "Are you scarred from the rape? From what they did to you?"

She swallowed thickly and somehow managed a jerky nod, her face feeling as if it were on fire.

"It doesn't matter," he said in a gentle voice that was brimming with emotion. "They might have scarred you, sweetheart, but they sure as hell didn't break you. I think you're the—"

"Wyatt, just stop." The sharp laugh that came from her lips was brittle. "God, this is a such a bad id—"

He cut her off again. "There's no way you can doubt how much I want you," he argued, the gentle tone suddenly replaced by one that was rough and clipped as he moved back to his feet. "I hate the pain that caused them, but I don't give a shit about your scars, Elise. They're a part of you and I think you're fucking perfect." He drew in a ragged breath, pulling his hand down his face, then dropped it to his side. The stare he locked her in was deep and measuring, as if he were trying to see beneath her skin, burrowing his way into her secrets. Quietly, he asked, "But that's not what this is really about, is it? This isn't just about your scars. What else aren't you telling me?"

"Drop it, Wyatt."

"No." She watched the muscle that started to pulse in his jaw, mesmerized by its rhythm. "I'm sorry, but that's not an option, baby. I'm not backing down. Push me. Scream at me. Cut me down if you have to. But I'm not walking away this time."

Frustration sharpened her words, her voice caustic with fear. "I'm not one of those women who feels the need to pour all my bullshit out for everyone to listen to. Not even to my friends."

"*That's* bullshit." He vibrated with a raw, sexual frequency that pulled on her and was so damn hard to resist. "We're a hell of a lot more than friends, El."

She took a quick breath, reeling. "I...I don't let my lovers get this involved in my life, either."

His eyes narrowed. "You don't have lovers," he corrected her, the guttural words reeking of possession. "You have *me*."

"For what? An affair? You said you wanted to sleep with me. That you wanted us to fuck, Wyatt. That's it!"

The scowl that hardened his face would have made a weaker woman cower in fear. "Yeah, well, I've been known to say a lot of shit. You should ignore most of it."

"I think you're just prevaricating."

"Damn it, El. Don't you get it? It's not that I don't *want* to give you more. It's the goddamn irrefutable fact that you *deserve* more. You deserve a man who can give you *everything*."

"And that man isn't you?" she asked through trembling lips, feeling as if something were breaking apart inside her that couldn't ever be put back together.

He shook his head, his mouth a hard, flat line. "No, baby, it isn't. No matter how badly I wish that it was."

Her breath hitched, tears burning at the backs of her eyes. "Then what *are* you willing to offer me?"

"My body," he rasped, his deep voice stripped down to raw, blistering emotion. "Whatever you want from it. It's not enough, but it's yours."

Elise stared deep inside him, using every ounce of female intuition she possessed, and realized with a jolt that she wasn't the only one hiding things beneath the skin. Not just secrets, but an actual history that left you broken and raw. God, they were more alike than she'd realized. Not that she thought he'd suffered from the same kind of violation that she had. But there was something there. Something that had made him bleed emotion and left an internal scar. It shadowed the way he saw himself, just like her past shadowed her. Affected what he thought he could have. What he thought he deserved. She wanted to ask him what it was, but knew without any doubt that he wouldn't tell her, just like she wouldn't open her veins and spill her blood secrets to him.

"Wyatt," she whispered, just as her tear-drenched eyes went hot with longing. He groaned in response, pulling her close, the determined look in his own eyes stealing her breath. He ripped her shirt off over her head, tossing it to the floor while those dark, beautiful eyes stayed locked with her wide ones. Then he yanked her close again, crushing her against his chest, and his lips touched hers. Possessed them. He claimed her mouth with a kiss that was raw and hungry and flavored with lust, his body communicating its need through the feverish heat of his skin, making her burn. She loved it. Couldn't get enough of it. The lifesaving heat was staving off the cold that tried so hard to freeze her down as he unhooked the front clasp on her bra, his big, calloused hands shaking as he pushed aside the cups.

"Christ, you are so beautiful," he groaned, lowering his head. His breath was warm and damp as he nuzzled his face between her quivering breasts, then licked her, the seductive rasp of his tongue painting sensation across her scarred skin as he lapped his way to her nipple. He wasn't necessarily gentle as he took the tight tip between his lips and sucked, working it against the roof of his mouth, but she didn't want him to be. This, the way he was touching her, tasting her, was too perfect to want it to be anything other than the way that it was.

"You like that?" he asked, his soft lips moving against the silvery scars that marred her flesh.

"*Yes*. Do you?"

Breathing against her damp nipple, he rasped, "Oh, yeah. If I liked it any more, it would kill me, El."

"Mmm," she moaned, gasping as he pulled her back into the searing heat of his mouth. "I know the feeling."

Wyatt growled deep in his chest, wanting to fucking consume her. Her nipples, so sweet and swollen, were like little berries on his tongue. He couldn't get enough of the lush, intoxicating flavor. The soft, silken texture. But there were other places he needed to kiss and taste, so that she would know exactly how beautiful he found her. *Every* part of her.

With his hands under her ass, Wyatt lifted her against

the front of his body and carried her back to his bedroom, the pain in his shoulder nothing but a distant blur at the edge of his consciousness, crushed by his need. He wasn't anywhere near gentle as he tossed her back onto the bed and stripped off the rest of her clothes, until she was lying before him in nothing but skin.

Without giving her time to panic, he crawled onto the bed and spread her legs, crouching between them as he smoothed the pad of his thumb over the worst of the scars he could see. It was so close to her pink, beautiful sex, high on the tender flesh of her inner thigh, and he locked his jaw against the blistering burn of rage that seared through his veins like an acid. It was pure, gut-wrenching horror to realize how close he'd come to losing her before he'd ever even found her.

He knew, from his talk with Jeremy, that even though Elise could remember very little of the rape, she had been conscious of it happening, and he couldn't even begin to imagine how terrified she must have been. Tears of anger and grief burned at the backs of his eyes, his heart climbing into his throat as he tried to swallow down his fury. He had to shove the acidic thoughts away, knowing they were dangerous to his sanity. When he allowed himself to think about it, about what those bastards had done to her, the intensity of his hatred became such a violent, destructive force that it threatened to consume him. But it didn't belong here in this moment with them. No, this was meant to be about nothing but pleasure—*Elise's pleasure*—and Wyatt was going to use every goddamn ounce of experience he'd gained over the years to ensure that he blew her mind.

Breathing in rough, uneven bursts, he lowered his head and nuzzled his face against the velvety softness of her belly, just beneath her navel, the evocative scent of her arousal making his mouth water. He pressed his lips to her scars, one by one, touching the silvery lines with his tongue, while his heart beat out a hard, painful rhythm in his chest. Keeping his touch light, he drifted the fingers of one hand up the inside of her leg, then higher, until he was coasting them over her silken folds. His jaw clenched at the feel of her, so slippery and soft and delicate. She was melting into a hot, slick honey, and he could not bloody wait to get his mouth on her.

"I want to taste you, El. Make you come in my mouth. Do all the things I've told you about." She gasped, then moaned, her beautiful body twisting beneath him as she clutched at the bedding with her hands. "You okay with that, sweetheart?"

"Um…yes. No. I don't know, because I've never tried it. And you might not like it. I mean, with me," Elise whispered, more than a little shocked by how innocent she sounded. Or was *uncertain* the word she was searching for? She wanted to be bold and seductive for him so that this would be something he enjoyed and remembered. Something that rocked his world as strongly as it would impact hers. But she couldn't. It was too intimate. Too real. He was talking about putting that wicked mouth of his on the most private, sexual part of her body, and she—

"You're thinking too hard, baby. And there's no need." He took a deep breath, then pressed his lips to her hip bone. "You've got to trust me on this, El. I doubt there's anything in the world I'll have ever enjoyed more. Christ, if you taste even half as good as you smell, you might never get my head out from between your legs."

She giggled as her fears started to ease, then slapped

her hand over her mouth, embarrassed to have made such a girly sound.

Wyatt lifted his dark head and smirked. "Just trust me, okay?"

She nodded, still covering her mouth, which meant the cry she gave a moment later was muffled by her fingers. He'd leaned down and licked her, right over the opening of her body, where she was the slickest, and it had felt... *God,* she didn't have words. *Incredible* wasn't strong enough. Neither were *amazing, marvelous, outstanding* or any other freaking superlative meant to describe how mind-shatteringly awesome it felt to have the rugged, insanely gorgeous, sexy-as-sin Wyatt Pallaton going down on her.

Holding her open with his thumbs, he licked between her folds again, hungrily lapping as if he'd found something sweet that he needed more of, a visceral sound of pleasure rumbling deep in his chest. A moment later, he lifted his head a fraction and looked up at her, then licked her taste off his slick bottom lip. "You know what? I don't like it, El—I fucking *love* it," he rasped, and before she could respond, he'd lowered his head again, sucking on her swollen, softly pulsing clit in a way that was so damn wonderful it made her scream. Then he went a little lower and thrust his tongue deep inside her.

"God, Wyatt. It's so *good,*" she moaned, breathless and unable to stop from pushing her needy sex harder against his mouth, her fingers digging into his thick hair, holding him to her.

After that, anything slow and easy about the outrageously erotic act was over. He went at her like a man starved for the taste of her body, his hands shoving her thighs even wider apart as he moved his tongue in and out of her, eating at her with a purely raw, primitive hunger. He kept going until she was writhing and sobbing from shocking bursts of pleasure as a dark, explosive orgasm tore its way through her, devastating her from the top of her head down to her pointed toes. And even then he stayed with her, his damp mouth closing over her and greedily sucking, swallowing every drop of her release in the most carnal way she could have imagined.

"You are so damn addictive," he panted, suddenly looming over her, his face close to hers. She could see her moisture glistening on his mouth and chin, his sensual lips slightly parted for his ragged breaths. "And you taste so sweet, El."

His strong, muscular body was wedged between her legs now, the towel he'd been wearing no longer around his hips, and she could feel him against her thigh, brutally rigid and thick, burning with heat. She was breathing so fast she sounded like a percolator, but she wasn't ready to run. She wanted every part of him on her, *in her*. His long fingers. His clever tongue. And that hard, pulsing, magnificent cock.

Then he leaned down and touched his lips to hers, rubbing across them as they shared their breaths. She could taste herself on him and loved it, the explicit intimacy making her gasp. Needing to touch him, she rubbed her hands against the sinewy tension in his neck and shoulders, trying to draw him closer, climb inside him, wanting to immerse herself in him so completely she could read him like a book. Know his secrets and his history. Feel his pleasure. Hold his heart.

He was so damn tender with her it brought tears to her eyes. But his tenderness was underlined by something hot and rough and powerful. Elise could taste it in the deepening kiss, his breaths becoming jagged, the grip of his hands tightening as he fell to his side and locked her against him.

"More?" he asked when he pulled his head back to drag in air.

She nodded and bit her lip, needing a distraction from the dangerous path of her thoughts. And needing more of him. More of that erotic, bone-melting pleasure. She had a feeling that no matter how much he gave her, she would never get enough of it.

"More of my mouth?"

"Yes," she whispered, sifting her fingers through his silken hair. "I want everything."

He sucked in a sharp breath, then slowly exhaled as his eyes got darker, the primal hunger glittering in their depths becoming even sharper. "Trust me?"

Despite the predatory, almost possessive way he was staring at her, Elise didn't even have to think about her response. "Of course."

He fisted one hand in her hair as he kissed the hell out of her again, his tongue stroking and thrusting with skillful aggression while his other hand settled behind her knee, bringing it to his hip. When he finally pulled his mouth from hers, they were both breathing hard. "I won't hurt you, I swear. You want to stop, just say stop. Okay?"

Elise nodded, unable to get any words past her trembling lips. But she wasn't afraid. She was so freaking turned on she couldn't stand it.

Sliding his hand from her hip to the fiery curls on her mound, Wyatt slipped his hand lower, stroking her slick, petal-soft folds with his callused fingertips. Then he pushed two big fingers into her snug depths, hooking them so that he could hit that sweet spot deep inside her, and growled at the way her body clamped down on him, greedy for his touch. "I want in here, El. I want to be buried hard and thick and deep. Right *here*."

"Yes. God, yes."

He slowly pulled his hand from between her legs. "El?"

She moved onto her knees, the look in her eyes making his heart pound even harder—a deep, endless blue glowing with hunger, and beyond beautiful. Then she shocked the hell out of him by placing her hands against his stomach and pushing him to his back. Before he could ask her what she was doing, she leaned over him, her hot mouth covering the head of his cock, and he nearly died. Christ, he couldn't even remember his damn name. He was too long and thick for that perfect mouth of hers, but just like the night before, she somehow made it work. Somehow pulled him in deep into all that wet, luscious warmth, sucking and licking, and managed to reduce his higher brain functions into a grunting, gasping pile of primitive instinct.

"Fuck, El. You're gonna make me come."

"Good!" she breathed against his blunt tip as she stroked him with both hands, his body straining.

"Damn it, I want to come inside you," he growled.

He could just make out her sexy smile through the fiery veil of her hair. "Coming in my mouth *is* coming inside me, Wyatt."

"You know what I mean!"

She laughed as she sat up beside him, blue eyes bright and excited, that plush lower lip caught in her teeth, and there was something beyond breathtaking in her expression, thank God, that told him she was ready. That she wanted him. *All* of him. So out of his mind with need he was shaking, Wyatt quickly grabbed her and twisted her beneath him, his mouth hungrily latching on to a beautiful breast when someone started pounding the hell out of his front door.

"Ignore it," he muttered, wanting to kill whoever was out there as he dragged his mouth to her other breast, ravenously licking the sweet, puckered nipple.

"Open the hell up, Pallaton!"

"That was Eric!" she gasped, shoving against his shoulders with enough strength that it surprised him. Scrambling out from beneath him, she snatched up one of the pillows and held it against the front of her gorgeous body, as if she needed to shield her nudity from her brother.

Braced on his knees in the middle of the bed, Wyatt fisted his hands at his sides and fought for control. No one had seen Eric or his little wife for days—but then Wyatt could hardly blame the guy for spending his time with his new bride. What he blamed him for was the shittiest timing in the world.

He wanted to beg Elise to ignore Eric's pounding at the door but could see that it was already too late. She was searching in the tangled bedding for her discarded clothing, her cheeks burning with embarrassment. *Shit.*

"Wyatt! I know you're in there, so open the damn door!" Eric shouted. "We have an emergency!"

"Fuck," he snarled, rolling off the bed. He grabbed an old pair of jeans and yanked them on, hiking them over his hips as he headed toward the hallway. "I'll see what he wants," he said over his shoulder, forcing himself not to look at her. If he did, Wyatt knew he'd be on her again in a heartbeat, her brother be damned.

"What the hell is so important?" he growled as soon as he ripped his front door open.

Eric's dark gaze sliced over him with the sharpness of a blade, his nostrils flaring as he scented the lust still rolling off Wyatt's body. But the Runner didn't give him shit about it. Instead, he muttered, "We've got to go."

"Go where?"

Eric's guttural voice shook with rage. "I just got a call from Shadow Peak. Elise's house is burning to the ground."

Two hours later, Wyatt was finally pulling back into the Alley. What had undeniably been on its way to becoming the best damn night of his life had turned to shit. By the time he and Eric had made it up to Shadow Peak, Elise's house had been engulfed in flames...and Browning was presumed dead. From what they'd been able to piece together, her well-meaning neighbor had tried to save as many of her things as he could, only to get trapped inside the structure by the quickly spreading flames. They hadn't found the body yet, but Mason and Brody were still there, searching.

He dreaded telling Elise about the death, worried about how she would react. He knew she was going to blame herself, and he hated it. Hated that there was nothing he could do to make it right.

He and the others didn't have any doubt that the fire had been arson, and Wyatt wanted the bastards who were responsible so badly he could taste the violence of his need on his tongue. Wanted their damn blood on his hands. The only thing that had kept him from taking off like a madman to hunt them down was the fact that she was here, waiting for him. He'd left her with Carla for protection, and after helping out with the fire, Cian had come back down to join them.

With a harsh sigh, Wyatt parked the Jeep in front of his cabin, eager to get inside and just hold her, assuring himself that she was safe, even though he was going to have to tell her about Browning. But the instant that he and Eric climbed out of the Jeep, he knew something was wrong. Cian was coming down the front steps of his porch, looking grim-faced and pissed, and a thousand scenarios started running through Wyatt's head, none of them good.

"Before you try to kill me," the Irishman muttered, his hands braced on his hips, "I haven't called you because we only just realized a few minutes ago."

"Realized what?" he growled, slamming the Jeep's door. "Where's Elise? What's going on?"

Cian shook his head. "She's fucking gone, man."

"What? How the hell can she be *gone?*" he roared, while a sickening wave of fear cut through his insides, nearly bringing him to his knees. "Carla was meant to be watching her!"

Shoving his hair back from his face with a frustrated growl, Cian said, "I came over to check on them when I got back, and Carla and I were in the kitchen, putting some food together. I'd left my keys on your coffee table and Elise took them. I don't know how she did it, but she got the Land Rover out of the Alley without any of us noticing. We've tried calling her cell phone, but she's got the bloody thing turned off."

He swallowed, his throat too fucking tight to shout obscenities the way that he wanted to. But Eric wasn't having any trouble, cursing a streak so blue it was probably hanging over their heads like a toxic cloud, a deep scowl wedged between his dark brows as he snarled about needing to put a bloody wall around the Alley to keep people in. But Wyatt just stood there with his hands fisted at his sides, his chest rising and falling, while a muscle rapidly pulsed in his cheek.

"Pall, are you okay?" Carla asked, coming up beside him with Jillian just behind her.

He was only distantly aware of Cian's phone ringing as he cut a cold, narrow look in his partner's direction. "I asked you for one goddamn thing, Reyes."

She flinched, color leaching from her already pale face. "I know. I'm so sorry."

He clenched his jaw to keep from saying anything more, knowing his words would only hurt her. They weren't going to undo what had been done. He just had to focus on how to get Elise back. On figuring out where the hell she would run to. He knew damn well that she hadn't gone back up to Shadow Peak because they had scouts monitoring every road in and out of the town.

She'd definitely gone south, out of their territory, which meant anyone could get to her. The males who had broken into her house. The ones who had burned it down, most likely to draw her back to town and away from the Alley. Christ, she might have already fallen right into the bastards' hands, like a ripe piece of fruit slipping from a tree.

A thick, guttural sound scraped up the back of his throat, and Carla and Jillian both cast him worried looks, no doubt thinking he was about to lose his shit and go ballistic. He wasn't entirely sure that he wasn't, his wolf prowling beneath his surface, its visceral fury no doubt burning in his eyes, making them flash with gold.

"I don't believe it," Cian said with a gruff laugh,

drawing his attention. "It must be your lucky day, you son of a bitch. That was Max."

"And?" he snapped.

Cian shook his head wonderingly as he slipped his phone back into his pocket. "He and Elliot were down in Wesley tonight, following a few leads on the black-mail tapes. They passed Elise on the highway and were worried enough about her being on her own that they turned around and followed her. She just pulled into that cheap-ass motel on Highgate Road and has taken a room. My Land Rover is parked in front of it."

"Tell them not to leave until I get there," he called over his shoulder, already heading back to his Jeep.

Eric caught his arm, yanking him to a stop. "And when you get there?" he demanded. "What then?"

Wyatt met the Runner's worried gaze with one that was hard and steady. "Then I'll do whatever it takes to bring her back."

Eric's chest lifted as he pulled in a deep breath, and then he let go of Wyatt's arm, hitched his chin at him and said, "Good."

"You realize," Cian murmured a few minutes later, after he'd climbed into the Jeep with him and they were tearing down the road, "if Max and Elliot hadn't seen her, you might have never found her."

"Trust me, I know," he growled, pressing his foot down even harder on the accelerator. "And I'm never going to forget it."

Chapter 13

Lying on the ugly blanket that covered the motel-room bed, Elise stared up at the water-stained ceiling with her bleary eyes and tried not to feel. Or think. Or… anything. But it was impossible. All she could do was think. About what an idiot she was. What a miserable, pathetic coward.

In the end, she'd run, just like her mother.

Funny, how she'd never wanted to be anything like the woman, and now she was a spitting image. But at least Helen Drake had been trying to survive, in her own twisted way. Elise was just…

Well, hell. She didn't even know what she was. Empty? Draining away?

Stop the pathetic bullshit. You know you ran for more than one reason.

Yeah, well, at least there was that. The phone call

on her cell phone from Eddie's stepfather about the fire and his son's death had come just in time. If she hadn't run tonight when she did, she might have never gotten another chance. At least not before it was too late and more innocent people had paid with their lives because of her. The Runners and their loved ones had enough problems of their own. Last thing they needed was her bringing more doom and gloom down on their heads.

She was already deep in the process of working herself up for a freaking kick-ass pity party when someone started banging the hell out of her door. With a sense of déjà vu hitting her hard in the chest, she lurched up into a sitting position in the middle of the bed, staring at the door with wide eyes.

"I know you're in there, Elise. If you don't want the management calling the cops when I break this fucking door down, then you'll open it. Now!"

"Wyatt?" she whispered, her voice too soft for him to have heard.

"I'm giving you three seconds, Elise. Open the goddamn door!"

She scrambled off the bed and hurried across the room, her hands shaking as she twisted the lock, removed the chain and pulled the door open. Before she could get a single word out, Wyatt was gripping her shoulders, pushing her back so that he could enter. Then he let go of her, turned and slammed the door shut, and locked them both inside. Lifting his muscular arms, he braced his big hands against the door for a moment, head hanging forward, his breathing rough and heavy in the quiet stillness of the room.

"Do you have any idea how badly you scared me?"

His low voice vibrated with emotion, graveled and thick. "Any idea at all, Elise?"

A fresh wave of guilt twisted through her insides like a blade, making her feel even shittier than she already had. Which was really saying something. "Wyatt, I'm sorry," she whispered, licking her lips. "I…I didn't mean to worry you."

He let out a sharp, explosive breath, then pushed away from the door and turned to face her, his jaw clenched so hard it had to hurt. He wore his scuffed leather boots, jeans and a gray T-shirt, the seams on the sleeves stretched tight around his impressive biceps—the furious expression on his face just as equally impressive. His dark eyes burned with rage.

"You didn't *worry* me," he growled, his hands curling into fists at his sides. "You scared the holy living fuck out of me. Christ, Elise. Do you have any idea how lucky you are that it was *me* standing outside your door and not some asshole intent on ripping you to pieces?"

She swallowed and tried to respond, but her throat was locked too tightly.

His eyes narrowed to piercing slits of onyx, his burnished skin stretched tight over his cheekbones. "Answer me, damn it!"

"Yes, I know, and I'm sorry!" she blurted, panting, her face burning. "Did you… Are you here alone?"

He shook his head. "Max and Elliot are the ones who saw you come here, but I sent them back. Cian is still here, though, waiting in my Jeep in the parking lot across the street."

"And Eric?"

His jaw clenched even tighter. "Ready to put you over

his bloody knee for pulling this stunt. Be thankful as hell that he didn't come down with us."

She winced, hating that she'd upset Eric, as well. "I'm sorry to have caused so much trouble," she told him, her quiet voice not even close to steady, "but I'm trying to do the right thing. I… What are you even doing here, Wyatt?"

He stared back at her as if she'd grown a second head. "What am I doing here? What the hell, Elise? Did you think I was just going to let you run off like a child trying to get herself killed and not come after you? You might not give a flying shit about me, but I'll do whatever it takes to keep you alive." He came a step closer, forcing her to tilt her head back if she wanted to keep holding his blistering glare. "So why don't you tell me what *you're* doing here?"

"Isn't it obvious?" she mumbled. "I was running."

He looked stricken by her confession and so incredibly angry. "Why? Damn it, you told me you trusted me!"

"I do," she breathed out, wrapping her arms around herself.

"Then why did you run away?"

She gave a choked sob and sniffed, tears spilling from the corners of her eyes. But she didn't answer him.

"Did I hurt you?" he rasped, his thick voice cracking at the end. He stared over her head, as if he couldn't bring himself to look her in the eye when he asked the question. "Did I scare you?"

"No," she whispered, hating that she'd made him doubt himself, when he'd been so patient with her. When he'd done nothing but give of himself. When he'd made her feel such unbelievable pleasure. "It wasn't anything you did, Wyatt. It's *me*. I'm the problem, not you."

Feeling as if he'd been put through a goddamn emotional wringer, Wyatt shook his head. "Running isn't going to solve your problems, El."

She sniffed again, looking adorably defiant as she lifted her chin. "How the hell do you know?"

"Because I've tried it," he muttered, shoving an unsteady hand back through his hair, then dragging it down his face. "But problems have a way of following you. Trust me."

She shuddered, wrapping her arms even tighter around her middle.

"Now tell me why you ran."

"Because I don't want anything to happen to the people I care about!" she suddenly shouted, unable to keep the frantic, emotional words from pouring out of her. "Eddie's stepfather called my phone and told me what happened to him. Eddie had tried to call me today, but I ignored the call. I didn't want to think about what was happening up in Shadow Peak, which probably got him killed. If I'd told him to stay away from my house, he wouldn't have been inside!"

"That's bullshit, Elise! You know what he was like. I doubt he would have listened to you, no matter what you told him. For all you know the ones responsible for that fire forced him to call you, trying to draw you out."

"I still feel responsible," she snapped. "And I have other reasons, too."

"Yeah? Then let's hear them," he growled, still so angry he could feel his blood pounding through every cell of his body, hot and raging. His pulse was a deafening roar in his ears, his wolf so furious it wanted nothing more than to throw back its head and let out a bloodthirsty howl. Then it wanted to take her, claim her and make the primal, possessive bite that would bind them together for all eternity, body and soul. The bite that Wyatt knew, no matter what happened between them, she would never ask him to make.

And that he could *never,* no matter how badly he wanted it, ask her for himself.

"You want to know my reasons, Wyatt? I ran because my life is shit!" she screamed. "And because I want to have sex with you!"

He stared back at her, his eyes wide and unblinking, unable to believe she'd just said that. It was a moment before he trusted himself to respond, his voice little more than a hard, husky rasp. "Nothing is going to happen to the people you care about, El. The Alley is the safest place for your brother and Chelsea. And yeah, this sucks that it's happening to you, but running isn't going to solve a damn thing." He paused to pull in a deep breath, then slowly let it out. "And if you're finally ready to go to bed with me, then why the hell did you *leave* me?"

Her gaze slid away from his, darting to random places in the miserable little room. She ran her tongue over the lush, biteable curve of her bottom lip and whispered, "Because I want to, but I *can't.*"

"How many times do I have to say it? I will fucking wait until you're ready, woman. I'm not pushing you. I wouldn't— *Fuck!*" He rubbed a hand over his mouth, struggling to put his chaotic thoughts in order so that he could make her understand. Grasping her chin, he waited for her to bring that glistening, tear-drenched gaze back to his before he said, "I want *more* than just to get in your pants, Elise. That's not what this is about. Yes, I want you so badly I can barely think straight anymore. But there's more to it than that. A hell of a lot more."

"You won't feel like that for long, Wyatt. Because I can't sleep with you without telling you the truth," she said brokenly, swiping at her tears. "I wanted to earlier, because I lost my head. But I can't, because it wouldn't feel right. Not when there are things you need to know."

"Then tell me now."

"I will." Her breath shuddered out, her expression defeated. "I have to. But when I do, just… I want you to know that I won't hold you to what you've said. You're going to change your mind, and I…I understand."

His nostrils flared, jaw so tight he was surprised his teeth hadn't cracked. "You think I won't want you? What the fuck, baby?"

"Can we just get out of this place first?" she whispered. "I don't want to do this here."

Moving his hand from her chin to the side of her face, Wyatt rubbed his thumb against the quivering edge of her mouth, hating to see her so upset. "Putting it off isn't going to make it any easier, El."

"I know. I just… I don't feel safe here."

He closed his eyes, struggling for patience, then forced them back open and lowered his hand. "Come on, then."

It took only a few minutes to get El and the small bag she'd brought with her into Cian's Land Rover. Before they headed out, he called the Irishman to let him know they were heading back up to the Alley, telling him to go on ahead of them. Whatever was coming, Wyatt didn't want an audience for it. Hell, there was a good chance he wouldn't even be able to make it back to the Alley before needing to get his hands on her.

"You okay over there?" he asked, sliding a concerned

look over her flushed face as they headed out of the parking lot. "Want the AC on?"

Elise shook her head. "No, I'm fine," she murmured,
wondering if maybe there were a way out of this. A way
that she could actually have what she wanted, without it
all falling apart. Maybe even...

Oh, hell. Who was she trying to fool? She knew damn
well how dangerous *maybes* could be. When was she
going to learn? There was no magical *maybe* for her in
this scenario. Wyatt Pallaton was never going to give
her his heart, which meant he would never be able to
accept her the way she was now. Yeah, it sucked. But it
was a dose of reality she needed to grow up and swallow.

*Why? Why tell him anything? Why not just enjoy him?
Even if it's only for one night?*

God, she would have loved to. But she couldn't.
Maybe it was pride. Maybe she just couldn't stomach
having to pretend in the midst of their passion, since
there was always the chance he would notice that her
senses weren't quite...*right*. Whatever the reason, she
couldn't go through with it without telling him the truth.
But if she told him the truth, he wouldn't want her anymore, and she'd be right back where she started. Alone.
Starved for him.

Christ, catch-22's were such a freaking bitch!

Elise stayed silent until they reached the highway,
then finally forced herself to just get on with it and say
what needed to be said. "I'm not like I used to be," she
started to explain in a low but surprisingly steady voice.
"I've suppressed certain parts of myself for so long, I
don't connect with the wolf part of my nature anymore.
It's like it's not even there."

His expression became closed in a way that made her

wonder what he was hiding. "Then you don't even know if you feel it," he rumbled, taking one of his hands from the wheel to rub at the hard, shadowed edge of his jaw. "I'd wondered."

A tremor of awareness shivered up her spine. "Feel what?"

"Nothing," he muttered under his breath. Lifting the hand on his jaw, he pushed his long fingers back through the thick, dark strands of his hair, his gaze a little unfocused, as if he were lost somewhere in his thoughts.

"Wyatt, what are you talking about?"

He ran his tongue over the edge of his teeth, and it was so damn sexy she nearly gasped, only just stifling the sound. Then he flicked her a shuttered, burning look, before turning that molten gaze back on the road, taking a deep breath and saying, "I... You know I grew up mostly with my mother's family. I think more like a human than most of the Runners, but that doesn't mean I'm not a wolf at heart. I might not put it out there as much as the others, but the instincts are there, and they're strong."

Her heart was beating so hard that it hurt. "What are you saying?"

She watched his strong, corded throat work as he swallowed. Then he answered her question. "I'm saying that I recognized your scent the night of Max's *Novitiate's* ceremony."

Elise blinked, unable to believe what he'd just said. "Oh, my God, Wyatt."

The corner of his mouth twitched, and he shook his head. "Yeah, that was kind of how I felt about it, too. Damn near knocked me on my ass."

She had to reach out and steady herself with a hand on the dash, her head spinning. "You never said anything!"

He grunted as he rolled his shoulder. "What was I gonna say? You made it clear on the times I tried to talk to you that you wanted nothing to do with me." He slid her another shuttered, blazing look from the corner of his eye. "When I asked you to dance at the wedding, that was the first time you'd ever looked at me and seemed to really even *see* me."

"So then that's why you've been—"

"No!" The word seemed to punch from his chest with more force than he'd intended, making her flinch. He gave a harsh sigh and in a calmer tone said, "I wanted you the second I set eyes on you, El, before I'd gotten a single whiff of your scent. And even after I had, I didn't go slathering after you like a dog with a bone. Yeah, it affects me on a primitive level, but you affect me on *all* levels. That's just one of them."

"So even knowing my scent calls to you, you still don't want a permanent relationship with me?"

He worked his jaw, then muttered, "I told you that's about me. Not you."

She gave a short, bitter laugh, thinking that was about to change.

"Damn it, Elise." Wyatt shot her a sharp glare before returning his attention back to the road. "Whatever you have to say, it isn't going to make any difference to me. I'm still going to want you."

"I'm losing my Lycan senses!" she blurted.

"What?"

Swiping angrily at her tears, she said, "My senses. They're…gone."

"Jesus, El. Why?"

Her voice was low and strained, stripped down to raw, seething emotion. "I don't know. Maybe it's the trauma. Or maybe the fact that I no longer shift. I swear I don't know, Wyatt. All I know is that my senses are now little better than a human's. My sense of smell. My eyesight. My hearing."

"Are you sure?" he asked, reaching over and grabbing her hand, needing to hold it in his own. "Maybe you're just ill or something, sweetheart."

He didn't have to look at her to know that she was rolling those beautiful eyes at him, but he did. "Yes, I'm sure. It's been happening for a long time, getting steadily worse."

Christ, this explained so much, and he was pissed at himself for not seeing it. For not figuring it out on his own. He was also probably only seconds away from driving them into a bloody tree, considering he couldn't take his damn eyes off her. She looked so broken, so shattered, that it made his fucking chest ache. Needing to give her his full attention, he steered the Land Rover into a lay-by on the side of the highway, put it in Park and turned in his seat to face her, his left arm draped over the steering wheel, his right hand holding on to hers again.

"That's why you couldn't even sense those bastards in your house that night, isn't it?" he asked.

She bit her lip and nodded. "Yes."

"Why in God's name didn't you tell me? Have you told anyone?"

She shook her head, sending all that gorgeous hair tumbling over her shoulders. "I can't."

"Why the hell not?" he demanded.

The look she gave him was full of confusion. "Because I'm embarrassed, Wyatt. I'm a Dark Wolf. I'm meant to be powerful, not pathetic."

He could feel that muscle starting to pulse in his jaw again. "That is such a load of crap!"

"You don't know what you're talking about!" she shouted back at him, jerking her hand from his grip.

"Your friends. Your brothers. Losing your senses won't mean shit to them, Elise. You're just stuck in a bad loop, baby, letting your father's bullshit poison your thoughts. No one who cares about you is going to look at you any differently. And the only people who matter are the ones who care."

She covered her eyes with the heels of her hands. "Just stop, Wyatt."

"Hell, no, I'm not going to stop," he growled. *I'm only just getting started.*

Lowering her hands, she looked him right in the eye. "You don't have to pretend, okay? I know this means something."

He made a hard, thick sound in his throat and stared right back at her, unrelenting. "It doesn't mean shit to me, Elise."

"Of course it does!" she argued, slapping her hands against her thighs. "It must! You might have spent more time with humans than the rest of the Runners, but you're still an alpha wolf, Wyatt!"

"I don't care!"

She looked incredulous. "How could you not care?"

Reaching out, he caught her chin in his fingers and leaned forward, getting right in her face. "See, here's the thing. Your power isn't what makes you special to me, El. I couldn't care less if you ever change again or how fucking strong your senses are or they aren't. I'm drawn to you because of *you.* The woman. Not the wolf."

Elise blinked, unable to believe what she was hearing. "How can you say that?" she whispered, fresh tears spilling over her cheeks.

He shook his head, giving her a beautiful, exasperated grin. "Christ, El. How can I not say it?"

Making it sound like a sin, she said, "But I'm…I'm weak."

His grin slipped, his expression hardening into a fresh look of anger. "The fuck you are," he growled. "You're the only one who thinks you need to change. I want *you,* Elise. Not some version that doesn't exist. And I sure as hell don't want to change you into something you're not. I just want you however the hell I can get you."

Before she could throw another argument back in his face, he curled his hand around the back of her neck, dragging her forward, and his mouth came down over hers, hungry and rough, just the way she liked it. Or at least the way she liked to be kissed by Wyatt. She didn't know what ghosts in his past haunted him, but it didn't change how she felt about him. All she knew was that she needed him. Needed this man more than she needed water and air and sunlight. She needed him over her, covering her, holding her down. Needed the strength of his powerful arms and the heavy press of his incredible, muscular body. She needed *him,* and she was taking him. *Now.*

Breaking her mouth from his, she moaned his name.

"Yeah?" he whispered, burying his face in her hair and pressing a soft, provocative kiss against the sensitive spot beneath her ear.

"Take me home. To your cabin."

He pulled his head back, locking that smoldering gaze with hers. "Then what?" he rasped, the delicious huskiness of his voice making her shiver.

Elise smiled through her tears. "Then it's time you finally took me to your bed…and kept me there."

Chapter 14

Wyatt's hands were shaking so badly he could barely get his damn key in the lock, and Elise couldn't help but grin. Muttering a guttural string of curses under his breath, he had to try several times before he managed to unlock his front door, and then they were finally inside. He slammed the door behind them, quickly setting the lock, then grabbed her, jerking her against his body so hard and fast that she gasped. She reached for the hem of his T-shirt, ripping it over his head, needing the touch of his sleek bronzed skin against her palms, loving that she'd made him sweat. His chest was fever-hot, chasing away her chills, while excitement continued to feed them. She was caught in a never-ending loop of sensation, coming undone but intoxicated by every moment of it.

And she was free to enjoy herself, without any guilty secrets weighing her down.

In an amazing turn of events, she'd told Wyatt the truth, and he hadn't turned away from her. And even better, he'd received a call from Jeremy just before they reached the Alley telling him that Eddie had been found alive! It turned out that his parents had been mistaken about him being in her house while it burned down, because Mason and Brody had stumbled across his unconscious body as they'd been searching the woods behind her house. He'd taken a serious hit on the head and was still feeling groggy, so the details of what had happened to him were unclear, but the Runners believed he'd tried to go after whoever had set fire to her home. She could only be thankful that whoever was responsible had knocked him out instead of killing him. According to Jeremy, Jillian was working with Eddie and would have his recent injury healed in no time, leaving him in the care of his parents.

All of which meant that she was free to lose herself in this moment…and the man who had finally managed to drag her out of the darkness of her past and back into the light. She wanted so badly to enjoy this time with him. To lose herself to the feel of his body. But even more than that, she wanted Wyatt to enjoy *her*.

"I can't wait," she groaned, burying her face against his mouthwatering chest. She drew in a deep breath, loving the scent of his skin. She didn't need her heightened Lycan senses to know that he smelled delicious. Hot and male and a little salty. Before the night was over, she wanted to run her mouth over every incredible inch of him. But there was something else she needed even more, and as he shoved his hands into her hair and tilted her head back, lowering his face over hers, she said, "I want you inside me, Wyatt. Now!"

"Not yet," he growled against her mouth, breathing hard. "I need to cool the fuck down first."

Before she could argue, he started herding her toward his bedroom as he stripped them both down, ripping her clothes from her body. Literally. It was the sexiest, most erotic thing Elise had ever experienced, and the way he looked at her, as if he wanted to eat her alive, made it possible for her to simply enjoy herself, without worrying about her scars. If they didn't bother Wyatt, then she sure as hell wasn't going to let them bother her.

Everything had happened so fast tonight, and she didn't have a clue where their relationship was headed, beyond sex. Had no idea how it was going to play out in the end or if they even had something that could be called a "relationship." But she wasn't going to let that stop her. She'd finally accepted that she'd fallen in love with the sexy, complicated Runner. Had completely and utterly given him her heart, with no hope of ever getting it back, and so she was going to be greedy and take as much of him as she could. Be thankful for each and every moment they had, for as long as they had them.

And she was going to start tonight. God only knew Wyatt made it easy for her to enjoy herself. Just the feel of his deliciously hard, breathtaking body pressed against hers was enough to make her light-headed with pleasure. And the feel of his hot, wet mouth covering her breast as he took them both down to his bed nearly made her scream. He sucked hard on one nipple and then the other, his tongue deliberate and intent, as if he were feeding on her reactions. As if he were addicted to the taste and heat of her skin. She writhed, running her hands over the bunched muscles in his broad shoulders as sharp cries crawled up the back of her throat. Cries that were lusty and hoarse, telling him exactly how much she craved what he was doing to her.

Then he rolled her pliant body to her front, moving her as if she weighed no more than a feather, when she was hardly a little wisp of a woman. As his warm lips pressed a tender kiss between her shoulder blades, and he flicked his tongue against her skin, pleasure spiraled through her in a burst of searing sparks of heat. *Wow!* She hadn't even known that her back was an erogenous zone, but she quivered from the touch of his mouth and his tongue as he worked his way down her spine, until he was literally kissing her ass. Then his mouth was gone, and the next thing she knew he was straddling her legs as he kneaded her bottom with his big hands.

"Christ," he growled. "You have such a sweet ass, El."

She pressed her smiling face against the sheets and laughed. "I'm glad you like it."

"I don't like it. I fucking *love* it." He trailed his fingers along the sensitive crease, going lower, until he was squeezing his hand between her thighs, stroking the swollen, slippery folds of her sex. He worked one of those long fingers inside her, then added another, his breath hissing between his teeth as she tightened around him, sticking her bottom in the air. "Damn, woman. You're driving me crazy."

"I think that's my line," she gasped, her breath hitching as he replaced his fingers with his thumb, then started rubbing those two slick fingers against her softly pulsing clit. She came in a violent, blinding rush, stunned by how quickly the orgasm hit her, her throat raw from the force of her screams by the time her body had finally started to ease back down. Then he pulled his thumb free, shoving those long fingers back inside her clutching tissues. He leaned over her and set his teeth in her shoulder just as he hooked those wicked digits at the perfect angle, hitting that sweet spot deep inside her that made her go wild, a second orgasm slamming into her hard on the heels of the first.

Elise thought he might let her catch her breath then, but he just kept pushing…and pushing…his rough voice at her ear, telling her exactly how much he liked making her shiver and burn and melt for him. He was diabolical in his intent to blow her mind, steeping her in sharp-edged ecstasy until she was no longer made of bone and blood and tissue. She was nothing but lush, decadent, pulsing currents of heat and need and sensation, lost in a timeless sea of passion, utterly at his mercy.

By the time he rolled her onto her back again, she could only breathe in sharp, desperate gasps, every individual cell of her body craving his possession. He pressed his hot, hard body against hers, bracing himself on his elbows as he touched his lips to her damp temple and nuzzled her skin, tasting her with the tip of his tongue.

A slow, evocative smile curled her mouth. "Are you licking me?"

His chest shook with a husky laugh. "Busted."

She turned her head to the side, giving him better access as he worked his way down the side of her throat, licking and nipping. "Why?"

"Because you taste so damn sweet." *Lick.* "And addictive." *Nip.* "And insanely delicious."

"Mmm…I love the way you taste, too."

He froze at her words with his head buried between

her breasts, his body locked hard and tight with tension as a raw, primitive sound rumbled up from deep in his chest. "Wyatt?" she whispered, stroking his hair with her hand, sensing that he was struggling with his control. "Shh, it's okay. I trust you, remember?"

"Jesus, El. I can't wait," he growled, his hot breath puffing against her damp skin. Then he suddenly lurched to the side, reaching for the top drawer in his bedside table, and she knew he was going for a condom.

"You don't need it," she murmured, reaching out and grasping his wrist.

Blinking the salty sting of sweat from his eyes, Wyatt cut his burning gaze back to Elise, his heart giving a little kick when he found her smiling up at him. "You sure?" he rasped, the idea of sinking into her in the raw damn near killing him.

"I'm on the Pill. Have been for a long time. So if you want—"

"Hell, yes, I want!" he practically shouted, cutting her off. He knew he owed her a sweet, tender seduction, but he just couldn't do it. He'd needed her for too damn long, and now he was helpless to do anything but feed his craving. Shoving her thighs wide, Wyatt kneeled between them and gripped her behind her knees, holding her open as he stared down at the flushed, glistening folds of her sex. For a moment, he almost forgot how to breathe, she was *that* stunning. So fucking beautiful it blew his mind.

Bracing himself over her on a straight arm, Wyatt reached down and positioned himself at her delicate entrance, his chest working like a frigging bellows. He could feel the burning heat of her stare as he pressed forward, sinking into her a few inches, and the pleasure immediately rolled up his spine, spreading through his body like a hot, molten heat. His eyelids quivered as his nostrils flared, throat working as he gave a hard swallow, damn near choking on emotion. Then he gave her a little more, working against her body's tight resistance, and it was even better.

Christ, what the hell is happening to me?

It was true that he'd always liked sex and fully enjoyed it, but now he realized that was only because he'd never grasped what he was missing. Hadn't understood. But he got it now. God, did he get it. It was like living with a lifetime of vanilla and then suddenly finding yourself immersed in a flavor so amazing it actually had the power to change you. To shift and twist and torque you into something new. Something better. Something that...belonged.

Feels fucking incredible, his wolf rumbled, its guttural voice thick with pleasure. *Need more...*

Yeah, he did, too. But as she gripped his biceps in her soft hands, Wyatt knew he had to be careful. He was built too damn big for her snug sheath, his thick shaft dragging at the plush, silken walls of her sex. He had to work in careful nudges to make her take a little more of him, the soft, voluptuous flesh slippery and slick. But she was so tight it was unreal, and he felt like a complete bastard for loving it so much when he knew she had to be uncomfortable.

"Sorry," he gasped, closing his eyes as he concentrated on going slow. After what felt like an effing eternity, he was finally lodged against the mouth of her womb, her tender sheath pulsing around him in an exquisitely hot, possessive hold. His lips pulled back from his teeth, and sweat rolled from his temples, stinging the corners of his eyes. "You're so damn tight, El, and it feels incredible. But I'm terrified I'm gonna hurt you."

"You won't," she breathed out, running her soft hands over his shoulders.

"I'll be careful," he groaned, shaking as he fought for control. He pulled back, then carefully worked himself back into her slippery heaven, his jaw clenched so hard his teeth hurt. All he could keep thinking was that this was his woman, and he finally had her, and she felt more perfect than anything he could have ever imagined. Perfect, hot and drenched…and tighter than a goddamn fist.

"Wyatt, look at me," she whispered. *"Please."*

He lifted his spiked lashes, trying to conceal how hard this was for him as he finally locked his burning gaze with hers.

"Don't you dare hold back on me," she said in a low, fervent voice, squeezing his shoulders. "I want *all* of you. Everything. All that you've got, Wyatt. It won't scare me. I promise."

"Christ, El. You think I don't want that? But I have to take care of you. I don't want to hurt you."

"Everything," she snapped stubbornly. "Right now. Or walk away. I don't need to be coddled like a baby."

"I'm not coddling you!" he growled, pulling back his hips and then pushing in even deeper. "And no way in hell am I leaving you!"

Cupping the hot side of his face in her palm, she said, "Then stop worrying about how I'm going to react to what you want and just take it."

"You don't know what you're asking for." His voice was rough, his muscles twitching as he fought to hold still inside her.

She lifted her hand, pushing his hair back from his

brow, and gave him a playfully crooked smile. "Trust me, Wyatt. I just might surprise you."

That's my girl, tossing those challenging words right back at me.

A choked, gritty laugh punched up from his chest, and he came down over her, bracing his weight on his elbows as he pressed his forehead against hers. "Okay, we'll do it your way, El." He lifted his head and gave her a hard stare. "But you have to promise to tell me if it's too much."

"I promise," Elise whispered, loving the way his eyes got even darker when she bit her lip. She could feel his need and his power locked up tight inside him, but it didn't frighten her. It just made her feel needed and powerful herself. Made her feel wanted...and necessary. An amazing feeling, when she'd never been necessary to anyone before. Her brothers loved her, but they didn't *need* her.

Wyatt *did*.

True to his word, he pulled back his hips and then squeezed himself back inside, working against her tight resistance. Then he did it again and again, each grinding lunge making her gasp as he nearly went beyond her limit, hitting the end of her, her nails digging deeper into the slick indentations of muscle on his back. And somewhere in the midst of it all, her body stopped resisting. She was still tight, clenching down on him with every mind-shattering stroke. But the pleasure was outweighing the discomfort, making her desperate for every incredible thing he could make her feel. She'd been so starved for so long, and now she couldn't get enough.

"Harder," she moaned, craving the feel of him letting go. *"Faster!"*

He gave her exactly what she'd asked for, using every part of his magnificent body to immerse her in a pleasure that was so deep it threatened to consume her. Their bodies heated and trembled, skin sliding against skin as he moved and thrust in an ever-increasing rhythm, shoving himself into her. His hips hammered against hers as he gripped the backs of her knees again, spreading her even wider, a savage, visceral growl on his lips as he somehow rode her even harder. He found her lips, his wicked mouth working over hers with hungry aggression, kissing the holy living hell out of her, until they had to break apart for air. Sharp, breathless cries repeatedly spilled from her lips as he took her…and took her, the bed slamming into the wall so violently she was surprised they hadn't busted through it.

And, boy, would that be a fun one to explain to my brother, she thought with a mischievous smile, running her open mouth up the strong, corded length of Wyatt's throat, loving the salty taste of his skin. Almost as much as she loved the wickedly sexy sounds he made when she did it.

"Fuck, El. I'm going over," he growled, burying his face in the curve of her shoulder, his breathing hard and ragged. Then he suddenly reared back, taking her with him as he sat on his heels, her legs straddling his powerful thighs, his strong hands clamping her to him as he rammed his massive shaft deeper. He shoved into her with two hard, thick thrusts, the blistering heat of his release surging inside her, again and again, making her scream as it triggered her own powerful, heart-stopping climax. His body shuddered as dark energy roared through him with savage force, feral and wild, and for the first time since they'd shared their first kiss, Elise felt the press of his fangs sliding against her skin. He didn't break the surface, just skimmed them over her damp flesh, letting her know they were there. It was the loveliest compliment, telling her that she'd not just satisfied the man, but his beast, as well.

"You okay?" he whispered, sounding out of breath, while her body continued to pulse around him in little vibrating aftershocks of pleasure that made them both twitch and groan.

She licked her lips, searching for her voice, and finally managed to find it. "I can honestly say that I've never been better. There isn't even a close second, Wyatt."

He lifted his head and smiled at her, slow and sweet and heartbreakingly beautiful. "Me, too."

"You liked it?" she whispered, sounding shy, which just made her laugh, considering she'd been a freaking wild woman.

"I loved it," Wyatt rumbled, and it was so damn true. Christ, he'd come so hard—so *much*—and for a moment there he'd wondered if it were ever going to stop. "You've ruined me for life." *And you've sure as hell ruined me for other women.*

She smiled, the glowing expression on her beautiful face telling him how much she liked what he'd said, and she lowered her head, pressing those plump, tender lips to his healing shoulder. "I hope you didn't hurt yourself," she murmured, her husky voice soft with exhaustion and concern and what he sure as hell hoped was happiness. Raw, blinding "I'll never be able to get enough of this man" happiness.

Oh, yeah, she'd ruined the hell out of him.

He didn't know how it was possible, but he was still hard as a rock inside her, his body craving the feel of her. The warmth and the sweetness. He'd never felt like this in his life and it should have been scaring the shit out of him, but he was too damn gone to care.

Keeping them connected, Wyatt laid down with her in his arms and forced himself to carefully pull out of her body, not wanting to make her any more tender and sore than she was probably already feeling. He might be in a world of hurt, already needing more of her, but he could suck it up and control himself when he knew it was what *she* needed.

"Tell me something," he whispered into the moonlit darkness after reaching over and turning out the light, thinking he could get closer to her in other ways, instead of just the physical. "Something that nobody else knows about you, El."

"Why?" she asked, sliding her leg over his hip.

He held her a little tighter, loving the press of her soft, feminine body cushioned against his hard planes and hair-roughened limbs. "Because you're mine and I want to feel close to you."

He could feel her smile against his chest. "Okay, but you had better not laugh at me."

"I wouldn't dare," he murmured, grinning as he pressed a kiss to the top of her head.

"Well, you know the book you read to me the other night?" she asked a little breathlessly, her voice shaking with nerves.

"Yeah."

She took a deep breath, her delicate fingers clenching against his side, then slowly exhaled. "Um, well, I'm writing one of my own."

A broad smile spread across Wyatt's face. He didn't

know what he'd been expecting, but it hadn't been that. "Are you serious?"

Nodding, she said, "Yep."

"That's so incredible," he told her, unable to resist hugging her even tighter. He was probably crushing her, but she wasn't complaining.

"Well, I haven't done anything with it yet," she murmured shyly. "It's just a dream of mine, really."

"But you're putting the work in and doing it, El. I'm so proud of you."

"Thanks," she whispered, and he could tell by her voice that there was a wide, beautiful smile on her lips as she pressed a kiss to the center of his chest, right over the heavy beat of his heart. Their bodies were still heat-glazed and slick, the air thick with the scents of raw desire. His was earthy and male, hers so mouthwatering he just wanted to lick her from head to toe, lingering over all the sweet spots in between. He was still hard and aching, but she was falling asleep against him, and that was, in its own way, just as sweet. God knew he craved her more than he could have ever imagined craving a woman—but he craved these moments, as well. The trust it took for her to snuggle against him, surrendering to sleep. He'd have given his right arm for the ability to stay there, beside her, wrapped around her like a friggin' octopus. Arms and legs tangled together, heads sharing the same pillow. Her beautiful face the first thing he saw when he opened his eyes in the morning. *Every* morning.

Yes-s-s, his wolf hissed inside his mind, but he knew he had no business listening to it.

Wyatt waited until she slept peacefully, then carefully moved from the bed. Standing at the side of the mattress, he shoved his fingers back through his hair, wishing like hell that he could just crawl back onto the rumpled bedding and cuddle up against her. Drape himself in her womanly curves, her mouthwatering scent filling his head, while need simmered through his veins in an intoxicating rush.

He thought about the conversation they'd just had about her writing, and smiled. Who would have guessed the little badass redhead was such a romantic at heart? He loved knowing her secret. Loved that she'd trusted him with it. And now he wanted to know them all. Wanted to be intimately acquainted with every facet of her personality, of her very soul, and claim them for his own.

Damn it, he didn't want to leave. What he wanted was to *stay.* He wanted to hold her in his arms, letting her sleep for a while, and then wake her up by kissing his way down her beautiful body, spreading her legs, and lashing her clit with his hungry tongue until she was moaning and begging him to come into her again. To take her. Make her come in another one of those blinding, mind-shattering climaxes that damn near stopped his heart. His wolf prowled beneath his skin, restless and possessive, wanting it every bit as badly as the man. But they couldn't have it, because he didn't trust himself.

Hating his past and the mistakes he'd made more deeply than he ever had before, Wyatt stalked quietly from the room, forcing himself to leave behind the only thing in the world he'd ever wanted for his own…and knowing damn well that he didn't deserve to keep it.

Chapter 15

As she opened her eyes to the watery morning sunlight, it took Elise all of two seconds to realize that she was the only person lying in Wyatt's sex-rumpled bed. Running her hand over the far side of the mattress, the sheets were achingly cold, and she knew that she'd spent the night alone. He'd left her instead of sleeping beside her, and a spark of anger slowly started to build beneath her lingering happiness.

The coward. She'd taken a chance and given him everything last night, but he hadn't done the same. No, he'd cut and run, and she felt she deserved an explanation.

It didn't take her long to brush her teeth and hair, then dress in a flowing white sundress that was flirty but casual, which she'd thankfully had in the small bag he must have brought in from Cian's Land Rover sometime during the night. Struggling to control her temper, she padded out of his bedroom on her bare feet and went in search of him.

"You left me," she said with a soft note of accusation the moment she found him sitting behind his desk in the small room he used as an office. "You didn't sleep beside me last night."

A lock of hair fell over his brow as he looked up from his laptop, a guarded expression on his gorgeous face that made her heart give a painful little jolt.

"I trusted you," she told him, coming into the room. He was bare-chested and breathtaking, and even though she was upset, she couldn't take her eyes off him. "Can't you trust me, too, Wyatt?"

Drawing an unsteady breath, he said, "It's not the same, sweetheart."

"Why?"

He sat back in his leather desk chair and rubbed a hand over his mouth, watching her with a look that was equal parts wariness, fear and need. Finally, he scraped out a stilted reply. "Most nights I have…nightmares, El. Violent ones."

She tilted her head a bit to the side as she studied him. "I'm sorry. But why does that mean that you have to—"

"Because I don't want to hurt you!" he choked out, surging to his feet so quickly the chair he'd been sitting in crashed against the wall behind him. Fisting his hands at his sides, he said, "Don't you get it? I don't trust what I might do if I slept beside you. If I struck out and hit you by accident, I wouldn't be able to live with myself."

Understanding started to filter through her frustration, and she walked over to him, putting her hands on his powerful shoulders, begging him with her eyes to open up to her and tell her about his demons. Because she knew they were the driving force behind more than just his refusal to sleep beside her. They were what kept him from thinking she would want him for more than a hot, blistering affair. What kept him from following his primal instincts and demanding she give him everything, every part of her, forever.

His dark gaze was locked tight with hers, his hands clutching her waist as his lips parted, and she prayed to every god she'd ever heard of that this was it—that he was going to open up to her *now.* But all he ended up saying was "I'm sorry, El. After last night, the last thing I wanted was to upset you." He lowered his head, burying his face in her hair, his lips moving against the sensitive shell of her ear. "Forgive me?"

"I guess," she murmured, unable to stay irritated when he was melting her down with the sensual touch of his mouth at the side of her throat.

His hands started to slide up her back, and she could feel his heat through the thin cotton of her dress. "Please, baby. I'm begging you."

She gave in with a soft sigh of surrender. "Well, when you say it like that, yes. I forgive you."

"Thank you," he said huskily, slanting his mouth over hers with a ferocity that made her breath catch. The devastating kiss was deep and hungry, their tongues rubbing and tasting, his hands in her hair, tilting her head until he had her right where he wanted, the angle letting him plunge into her mouth again and again. When their lungs were aching for air, they finally broke apart to draw in desperate breaths—and then their lips were fusing together again, as if drawn by a magnetic force. She lost herself in the warm silk of his mouth, intoxicated by his taste and the way he touched her.

"I want you," he growled, gently nipping the side of her mouth as he cupped her jaw.

"Mmm," she moaned, while he pressed tender kisses across her flushed cheek. "You can have me, Mr. Pallaton."

His low voice rumbled in her ear, and she could tell he was smiling. "I'm holding you to that later, Miss Drake."

Confusion creased her brow. "Not now?"

"Don't tempt me," he breathed against her lips, before lifting his head. Electric sparks of heat skittered in the air between them as their gazes locked, and she knew he'd felt it, too, his hands tightening in her hair. His rugged face was tense with lust, and there was a grittier edge to his words as he said, "I'd have you on your back, legs spread, with every inch of my dick buried deep before you could even blink, sweetheart. But your brother wants to talk to you. He's already stopped by twice. I told him you were still sleeping."

"Oh. Does he, um, know that we slept together?"

"Would you care if he did?" he asked a little too carefully, a vulnerable edge to his words that she knew he didn't want her to hear.

"No." She gave him a soft smile. "I don't want to hide what happened between us."

His lips curved into a crooked grin that was stunningly beautiful, the wicked heat in his dark eyes melting her, making her even wetter than she already was. "Good. Because I'm pretty sure anyone who sees us together is going to know I'm thinking about getting you naked again. I can try, but I doubt I'll be very good at hiding it."

Elise was still smiling as she lifted up onto her tiptoes and kissed him again, her hands finding their way into the silky mass of his hair as if it were the most natural place in the world for them to be. He made a deliciously thick, aroused sound in the back of his throat, his powerful arms wrapping around her, holding her close as he lifted her off her feet, taking her mouth as if he wanted to own her, and she laughed into the kiss, happier in that moment than she could ever remember being. It was every birthday and Christmas and special occasion that she had longed for as a child, all rolled into one bone-melting, heart-stopping kiss.

"Jesus, you are so damn dangerous," he growled against her lips, before setting her back on her feet.

Elise touched her fingers to her tingling lips as she grinned, loving that he let her see how badly he wanted her. It was written like a neon sign flashing in his smoldering eyes, carved into the tight bunch of his muscles beneath his dark skin. "I guess I'll just go and, um, finish getting ready, then."

She started to turn to leave, but he gripped her waist and said, "No."

Her pulse raced as she lifted her brows. "No?"

"Eric can bloody well wait," he muttered, slowly bunching the skirt of her dress in his fist, inching the fabric up her thighs. "I can't."

A breathless laugh rushed up from her chest. "Finally! I was hoping you'd say that!"

He smiled as he gave her a quick, hard kiss. Then he lifted his head, and Elise gasped as she saw the sharp, visceral hunger etched into the masculine angles of his face. Keeping his dark gaze locked with hers, he trailed a rough hand up the back of her thigh until he was touching her between her legs, his strong fingers playing skillfully over the drenched satin panel of her bikini-cut underwear—and then he tore them off of her. "You have no idea what you do to me, do you, El?"

With his heart beating out a hard, hammering rhythm, Wyatt watched as Elise shook her head, thinking she was the most gorgeous woman he'd ever known or seen or imagined. Unable to wait, he lifted her with his hands under her sweet ass and moved her to his desk, shoving his laptop aside so that he could sit her on the top. Her mouthwatering scent filled his head as he ripped the sexy sundress he figured she'd worn just to drive him insane over her head, then tossed it to the floor, too desperate to get to her soft, womanly curves to be careful.

"I meant what I said, El. I can't wait," he growled, spreading her legs and stepping between them, his heavy gaze focused in sharp and tight on the pink, glistening folds of her sex. His hand shook as he ripped open his fly, only lowering his jeans enough that his cock could spring free.

She gasped as she glanced down at him, blue eyes bright with need. "Me, neither," she moaned, leaning back and bracing herself on her elbows, giving him a breathtaking view of her flushed face, lush breasts and smooth belly. "Hurry, Wyatt!"

Gritting his teeth, he reached down and positioned himself, then watched with burning eyes as his thick shaft stretched open the puffy, delicate entrance. The clasp of her inner cushiony walls as he worked himself into her was so slick and tight and sweet, it nearly made his eyes roll back in his head. The woman was so hot she was going to burn him to a crisp.

Nearly a minute later, they were both breathing hard, and Wyatt was still only about halfway in. He wanted to thrust and shove and work his way deeper, but she was so goddamn snug. "I swear you feel even tighter this morning. How the hell is that possible?"

"Sorry," she whispered. "I think I'm, um, swollen. You know…from last night."

"Never be sorry," he groaned, leaning down and pressing his forehead against hers. "What you are is perfect, El. Every sexy little inch of you."

"You, too."

He snorted, shaking his head. "Hardly. But I love that you think so." Knowing he was going to lose it, he wrapped his arms around her slender form, picked her up, then sat back in his leather desk chair, putting her on top of him. "Seriously, El. Don't ever be sorry for being so tight for me. Or for getting even tighter after I've ridden you hard," he said with a quiet growl, squeezing her ass. "Because I love how snug you are. I'm just worried about hurting you. It would make me feel like such a bastard."

Straddling his lap, she stared down at him with a teasing gleam in her beautiful eyes and laughed. "It's not your fault you're built so over-the-top, Wyatt."

With his hands firmly gripping her backside, he slowly pulsed his hips, pushing in another inch. His breath left his lungs on a low growl, his hands shaking. "But this is the first time in my life I actually wish I was smaller."

She giggled, and he gasped as he felt the sweet sound vibrating around his dick. "You know, I'm pretty sure no man has ever uttered those particular words before."

"Yeah, well, if I screw this up," he groaned, breathless, "you won't ever let me touch you again. And *I'm* pretty sure that would kill me."

She wiggled her hips, taking another inch, and he

cursed, his legs parting wider as he braced his bare feet on the floor. "Jesus, El."

"Sorry this is taking so long."

Panting, he gasped, "'S'okay. Take your time, baby."

She lifted her hand and touched his face. "Wyatt, I want you to enjoy this."

"I am," he choked out, gripping her hips so hard he knew she would probably be bruised.

"Liar," she whispered. "You look like you're in pain."

"I'm not." He squeezed his eyes shut, using everything he had to keep it together. "*Christ.* You feel so good, El. I just don't want to—"

"You won't," she murmured, cutting him off. "Wyatt, look at me. *Please.*" She waited until he'd lifted his lashes, then stared deep into his eyes. "If you lose control, I'm not going to freak out on you. Okay?"

A rough, animal-like sound ripped up from his chest, and the next thing he knew he was yanking her down as he thrust up inside her, shoving himself deep. She cried out, her head falling back as he withdrew and then slammed back into her, the feel of her tight little sex clamping around him so hungrily driving him mad with need, instead of slaking it. The more he had of her, damn it, the more he wanted. The more he *craved.*

Surging to his feet again, he laid her back on the desk and drove into her even deeper. The air filled with their hitching breaths, serrated moans and the wet, slapping sounds of raw, aggressive sex. He used every muscle in his body to grind into her, his biceps bulging as he gripped her shoulders, holding her in place for the deep thrusts being powered by his ass, abs and thighs.

"Come on me," he forced out through his gritted teeth. Reaching down, he ran the callused pad of his thumb over the pulsing heat of her clit, working it in firm circles, and his breath hissed through his teeth as her inner muscles tightened and started to convulse, sucking at him like a throat. "Now, baby. I need you to come for me now!"

She arched beneath him, a throaty, breathless cry on her lips as she went over, clenching him hard, drenching him in liquid heat, and he came with her, ejaculating with so much force his eyes turned wet with tears. Squeezing them shut, Wyatt buried his face in the curve of her shoulder, biting back the words he so desperately wanted to say...but couldn't. And despite the violence of his release, he was still hungry for more. Christ, there was no stopping point with her. He could have stayed hard all damn day, buried deep in her tight little body, and taken her until they were half-dead.

Loving the feel of her hands stroking down the sides of his spine, he pressed his lips to the top of her head. "I always tell myself I'm going to be gentle with you, but it doesn't happen."

"Well, you won't hear me complaining." Though her reply was playful, there was a quiet undercurrent to the husky words that let him know she was speaking with complete honesty. "I trust you," she added. "Which means that I can enjoy myself when things get wild between us. Actually, when it comes to you, the wilder the better."

"Thank God," he groaned. "Just...please don't run from me again, El."

"Wyatt."

His arms tightened around her. "Promise me."

"All right, I promise," she whispered, stroking his hair. "But will you do something for me?"

Lifting his head, he said, "Anything, babe. What is it?"

Elise shivered from the burning intensity in his dark eyes, nearly forgetting what she wanted to ask. "I was, um, hoping you could take me up to Shadow Peak this morning. I need to check on my house and see if there's anything that can be salvaged."

With a frown on his lips, he carefully pulled himself from her body, then shook his head. "That's not gonna happen."

She blinked up at him. "Wh-what? Why?"

Pulling her up into a sitting position, he placed his hands on her hips as he said, "Because it's being taken care of. Brody is overseeing the salvage operation today with Max and Elliot. They're boxing up anything they find worth keeping and then we'll have it all brought down to the Alley."

"But I don't live here in the Alley," she argued, feeling as if she'd been bulldozed. She didn't care for the feeling, or for the way he was dictating to her, as if she couldn't make her own damn decisions. And while she wasn't particularly sentimental about things, like a lot of women she knew, it broke her heart that the beautiful new furniture he'd picked out for her was gone. She couldn't help but hope there might be something worth saving that the others would just carelessly throw away.

As if he could sense her growing frustration, he caught her chin in his fingers and lowered his face over hers. "I'm sorry," he rasped. "I'm not trying to be a dick, El. But there's no reason for you to be there. It's just going to cause you pain to see your home destroyed. I'm not putting you through that."

"Wyatt, at the very least I need to check on Eddie."

"Browning's fine. Trust me, Elise. The best thing

you can do is stay here, where we know you're safe. There's no need to go and put yourself in danger. And after what happened last time, I'm not going to let you take another risk."

She exhaled in a huff, conflicted and irritated but touched at the concern she could see on his face. "You're being unreasonable," she muttered, but her voice was soft, letting him know she was giving in.

A tight smile twisted the corner of his beautiful mouth. "I know. But it's only because I want to do what's right for you." When she opened her mouth to argue again, he pressed his lips to hers, silencing her with a soft, sweet kiss. "I also know that you're a smart, amazing, independent woman who can make her own damn decisions," he said against her lips. "But I just want to keep you safe. I swear to God I'm not trying to control you."

Hearing the genuine sincerity in his husky words, she gave in with another sigh, flicking her tongue against his lips to let him know she was done with the argument. A low groan vibrated in his chest as his tongue swept into her mouth, taking possession. It was a deep, ravaging kiss that left them both a little breathless, his eyes glittering when he finally lifted his head. Golden beams of sunlight caught the dark sheen of his hair as he gave another slow shake of his head, a crooked grin on his lips. "You'd better go," he murmured, his tone wry as he stepped back, "or I'm liable to keep you on this desk the entire day."

She smirked as she hopped back down onto her feet, snatched up her dress and pulled it over her head. Smoothing it into place, Elise was almost afraid of how happy she felt inside as she gave him another quick kiss, then headed to the bathroom for a long, hot shower. She wanted to ask Wyatt to join her but knew she needed a bit of time to herself to get her thoughts sorted. Above all, she had to remember to stay in the moment and not get carried away with thoughts of the future. Had to enjoy what she had and try to find a way not to worry about where it was all heading.

Not the easiest thing she'd ever tried to do, but Elise was determined not to put any pressure on him. He was already putting his life on the line to protect her, not to mention being caught up in the preparations for what looked to be a coming war. If ever there were a time to cut a guy some slack, it was now.

Once she'd cleaned up and gotten dressed again, this time in a pair of khaki shorts and slouchy blue sweater, she left Wyatt working in his office and walked over to Eric and Chelsea's cabin. After Eric spent a good long while griping at her for leaving the Alley on her own the night before, they talked about Eli, who had yet to respond to any of the messages Eric had left at the last number they had for him. Of course, they also talked about her house. When she'd started to complain about Wyatt's refusal to take her up to Shadow Peak, Eric had surprised her by taking the Runner's side. It made her wonder what had been said between the two when she wasn't around. Heck, she'd have thought Eric would side with her just to cause trouble for Wyatt, since he clearly hadn't been happy about her staying with him. But that didn't seem to be the case. Then her brother surprised her even more by inviting Wyatt over for lunch with them.

If she'd been a bit shocked by the way Eric had taken Wyatt's side in the whole "seeing her house" argument, she was nothing short of amazed by how civil her brother treated the man he had to suspect was sleeping with her. Considering how strong Eric's Lycan senses were, he could probably scent Wyatt on her skin despite the fact that she'd showered, which made his behavior even more unexpected. But then, she knew Eric had a lot of respect for Wyatt, which helped. And she was sure that Chelsea had been working on her stubborn brother as well, which meant that Elise owed the human a hell of a thank-you the next time they were alone. It would be fun if she could put together some kind of girls' night out for all the females in the Alley, and she made a mental note to talk to Jillian about it the next time she saw her.

Once she and Wyatt had helped clear up from lunch, they headed back to his cabin, wanting to give Eric and Chelsea some privacy. Wyatt put on a pot of coffee, and as they sat in the kitchen at the table, he finally persuaded her to show him the romance novel she'd been working on. They talked about the story, and she even explained why she was so drawn to romance, telling him how it had started out as a therapeutic experience to write about emotions and feelings that she'd worried she would never again be able to feel on a personal level. She even confessed that she found the biggest challenge to be the happily-ever-after ending that readers wanted, but enjoyed escaping into the fantasy that so few people managed to find in real life. He gave a quiet laugh, pointing out that storybook endings seemed to be pretty prevalent in the Alley, and she blushed as she agreed, hoping he didn't think she'd been trying to make a roundabout point with him, since she knew damn well that wasn't going to happen for them. But despite her embarrassment, it was clear that he thought it was wonderful that she was doing something she loved, and she couldn't help but melt a little inside at how proud he seemed of her.

A little later in the afternoon, they visited with some of the other Runners and their mates, and she even managed to apologize to Cian for taking his Land Rover. But then Torrance left with Michaela, and Jillian had to take Sayre down to Covington for some shopping, so Jeremy went with them, and even Eric and Chelsea decided to tag along. Cian had just gone to check out something on the south border of the pack's territory, when Carla got an urgent call from Milly, the employee at the alarm company Carla had asked to look into things. They'd known it might take a while for Milly to access the information they wanted, since it required her to sneak into the main computer system. But she was finally calling with what they'd been waiting for. Carla spoke with her for less than a minute, then ended the call and told them what she'd learned. According to Milly, on the night of the wedding, when Elise's home had been broken into, Glenn Farrow had used his personal computer to hack into her account earlier that day, allowing him to create a secondary code that would bypass her system. Neither of the males who had broken into her house that night had been Farrow, which meant he'd obviously given the bypass code to someone else.

Wyatt was furious, ready to go for Farrow's blood, which was why Mason insisted he stay behind, while he and his father went up to the mountaintop town to look for the Lycan and bring him in for questioning. Seeing as how Wyatt wasn't about to leave her alone and Carla couldn't go on patrol by herself, Mason had called in several of the scouts who worked for the Runners to temporarily patrol the Alley's borders.

It was obvious that Wyatt wasn't happy about not getting to go after Farrow himself, but Elise knew he was trying to hide it. Though he hadn't come out with any stunning declarations about his feelings after their incredible night—and morning—of passion, he was going out of his way to put her at ease and make her smile. And although he hadn't tried to get her back into bed yet, she knew it wasn't from a lack of desire. There was a constant, smoldering hunger in his dark eyes every time he looked at her, and he'd kissed her whenever she got within two feet of him, the sexy, greedy thrusts of his tongue telling her exactly how much he wanted back inside her.

"That's probably Carla," he said, when someone started knocking on the front door. "She mentioned coming over to talk about Farrow." But when he pulled the door open, Elise instantly felt the shift in him. Within the blink of an eye, he went from relaxed to on edge, and as she peeked around his shoulder, she saw why. Instead of his Bloodrunning partner, a male she recognized from the photos Wyatt had shown her as Sebastian Claymore stood on the porch.

"How the hell did you get here?" Wyatt demanded in a low, deadly voice.

Speaking in an agitated rush, Sebastian said, "I'm afraid it was easier to slip past the scouts who are patrolling the Alley's borders at the moment than it was to explain to them why I needed to talk to you."

While Elise stood off to the side, sick with dread, she listened as the Whiteclaw Lycan claimed to need Wyatt's help in stopping his brother before he could launch an unsanctioned hit on the Alley, the purpose of which was supposedly Elise's own kidnapping and torture. Sebastian then claimed that he'd uncovered some shocking facts about his brother's so-called obsession with her—things he believed could shed some light on events that had happened three years ago. She silently prayed that Wyatt would refuse, but the instant she saw the raw fury on his face when he turned toward her, she knew he'd decided to go.

"I'll be back as soon as I can," he told her, heading toward a cabinet that stood against the wall just behind her, after asking Sebastian to wait for him outside. She watched him take out a handgun and check the clip, then tuck the weapon into the back of his jeans. "I'll stop by Carla's on my way out and tell her to head over here. She'll be in charge of your protection while I'm gone."

"Wyatt," she murmured, stepping closer and putting her hand on his arm, "I have a bad feeling about this. There's something about that man that makes me uneasy. *Please,* don't go."

He closed his eyes for a moment, exhaling a ragged breath, then slid her a dark, shuttered look. "Damn it, don't do that," he rasped, keeping his voice low. "You know I don't have any choice. If Seb is right about his brother, I can't throw away the opportunity to stop him before he causes us more trouble. I'm not letting that bastard anywhere near you."

"And if he's not?" she whispered. "What if he's not right? What if it's something else?"

Reaching behind her neck, he pulled her toward him and pressed a quick kiss to her trembling lips. "I know how to take care of myself, El. You don't need to worry about me." Then he let her go and started heading toward the door.

Panic made her voice shrill, her breaths coming in sharp gasps. "Why are you doing this? Putting yourself in danger because of me? I'm not your woman, Wyatt. We haven't bonded. Haven't made any promises. This isn't your responsibility!"

He didn't bother turning around as he said, "There might not be any promises between us, but you're fucking blind if you think you don't mean anything to me."

With those stunning words dropping like a massive weight between them, he went outside to join Sebastian, slamming the front door behind him.

Minutes turned into a half hour...and then another... the passage of time slowly killing her. Elise knew something was wrong, but there was no one besides Carla to complain to, and the Runner agreed with her. Unfortunately, there wasn't anything Carla could do until the others made it back. She refused to leave Elise alone, which meant she couldn't go after Wyatt. And he wasn't answering his phone.

As the minutes rolled by, her tension increased, making her shaky and ill. She about jumped out of her skin when someone started pounding on the cabin's front door, hoping like crazy it would be Wyatt. But as she wrenched it open, Elise found a haggard-looking Sebastian Claymore standing on the porch. And he was alone.

"Where's Wyatt?" she demanded. "What the hell did you do to him?"

Claymore struggled for the breath to explain as he stumbled past her into the house, bracing himself with one hand against the interior wall. "We were attacked."

"Attacked? By who? You just *left* him?" she growled, amazed when she felt her beast begin to stir deep inside, from a place she had never thought it would break free from. Clenching her jaw, she smashed the feeling back down, unable to deal with it when she was in pure, blinding freak-out mode over Wyatt. "Where *is* he?"

"We got separated," the Lycan panted, "and I couldn't get back to him. But he'd told me to come here if anything happened and make sure you were okay."

"No," she said in a low voice, something about him making her feel incredibly anxious. He made her freaking skin crawl! "You're lying."

He looked confused. "Elise, why would I lie? What have I ever done to make you distrust me?"

"I don't know you," she forced out through her gritted teeth.

"I was a friend of your father's," he offered, still struggling to catch his breath.

Huh. If he'd thought that was going to win him any points in her book, he was sadly mistaken. And she was done wasting time on the idiot. Turning to Carla, she asked, "Do we have weapons we can take with us? We need to go out and look for Wyatt."

"Yeah," the Runner murmured, casting an uneasy look at Sebastian. "But I don't think you should go, El. Wyatt will kill me if anything happens to you."

"We don't have a choice! Everyone else is too far away. It's up to us to go find him!"

Sebastian took a step toward her, shaking his head. "I'm afraid I can't let you do that, cherry. I told him I'd keep you safe."

Oh…*God*. She couldn't explain how—she just knew. In that moment, Elise knew *exactly* who had been in her house the night of her brother's wedding. Who had whispered in her ear all those years ago, when he'd been tearing her body apart. And then she realized what the Lycan had just called her. *Cherry. Cherry girl...*

"You sick bastard! Why me?" she whispered, the words feeling strange on her prickling lips. Her heart was racing, skin cold, clammy. She blinked, data crunching in her head too quickly to keep up with all the details. He'd known her father, but she'd never met him before today. So why *her?* What had she done to deserve what had happened?

"Why you? What do you mean?" he asked with a phony look of confusion, acting as if he didn't understand what she was talking about.

Wishing like hell that she could release her claws and rip him to shreds, she said, "You know exactly what I mean, you son of a bitch!"

"Elise?" Carla asked sharply, moving closer to her side.

For a moment, she thought he was going to keep denying it. Then he shook his head and gave a low laugh, a sly smile kicking up the corner of his mouth. "What can I say?" he drawled, his dark eyes glittering behind the thick lenses of his glasses. "You were my first real taste of power and I loved it. It *stuck.*"

"What the hell is he talk—" *Thunk.* From the corner of her eye, Elise watched as Carla's body slumped to the floor. A man she didn't recognize was crouched behind the petite blonde, holding a square of white cloth over her nose and mouth.

Shit!

Elise sucked in a quick breath, ready to scream, when

she felt someone behind her, a strong arm suddenly shoving something against her face.

Then everything went black.

Chapter 16

Wyatt had never known anything as viciously savage as the emotion that tore through him when he realized what he'd done. That he'd allowed himself to be tricked by a lying little bastard because of his thirst for revenge and, in doing so, had put Elise in danger.

Christ, I am such a goddamn idiot!

One second he and Sebastian had been making their way through the forest, deep in conversation, and in the next Wyatt had found himself surrounded by a group of Whiteclaw soldiers. A group of males who had obviously taken the "super soldier" drug. He knew he'd been set up, and in that moment he'd been consumed by every dark, deadly, visceral emotion that he'd ever seen or experienced in others. His mind had filled with visions of him ripping the Lycans to pieces, and both he and his wolf had relished the mental images. But a bloodbath wasn't something he'd had the time to execute, even if he'd been strong enough. Not if he wanted to save Elise. Save her not only from Sebastian Claymore and his psychotic family, but also from her own demons. Because he knew what she would do if she found herself facing that nightmare for a second time. She might be beautifully strong and a romantic at heart, but there was no way she would let them have that kind of control over her ever again.

Knowing he had little time, Wyatt had used his knowledge of the woods and successfully evaded the soldiers, but they'd blocked his way back to the Alley. Thankfully, he'd heard them talking about how Sebastian would be taking "the Drake bitch" back to Hawkley, and so he'd used every ounce of speed he possessed to make it to the Whiteclaw's pack town as quickly as he could. It wasn't difficult to evade the scouts patrolling the pack's borders, but finding the house where Elise had been taken wasn't nearly so easy. He thought he was done for when a soldier called out an alarm after spotting him, but then a disturbance at the edge of town drew everyone's attention. Hiding between two buildings, he heard one of the Whiteclaw males tell another one to get more guards for the house where "Sebastian's bitch" was being kept, and thanks to the light drizzle that was covering his scent, Wyatt was able to follow the Lycan to a dilapidated building at the end of the street. Despite the rain, he caught a whiff of Elise's scent the second he came around the back of the house, the guards still getting themselves organized in front. Hoisting his body up through an open window, Wyatt found himself in a shadowy hallway with a series of locked doors down either side.

Pulling in a deep breath, he followed Elise's scent to the second door on his right and unlatched the locks as quietly as he could, not wanting to alert the chattering guards who were gathered out front. The instant he stepped into the dim room, he spotted Elise hunched down in the far corner. She was almost in the same position she'd been in after the Lycan had attacked her in her bedroom the night of the wedding—arms wrapped tight around her knees, body swaying forward then back— and his heart damn near shattered.

"Oh, Christ, El." Quietly shutting the door, Wyatt hurried toward her and dropped to his knees, wanting to yank her into his arms but terrified to touch her. She was still dressed in her clothes, but her hair was a wild, tangled mess, smears of blood and dirt on her pale face, arms and legs. And there was a damn manacle wrapped around her left ankle with a metal chain that was attached to the wall, a broken manacle lying off to the side. "Are you okay, baby? Did they hurt you?"

She'd flinched at the first raw sound of his voice, and now she wet her lips, blinking up at him like a person suddenly being drowned in light after days of darkness, her voice little more than a whisper. "Y-you came."

"God, baby. I was so scared that you'd been hurt." His voice cracked, and he had to clear his throat before he could go on. "Terrified that you would do something… that you would—"

"I wanted to," she confessed, cutting off his rambling. She bit her lip, then said, "When Sebastian told me what they're planning for me tonight… *Oh, God, Wyatt.* I wanted to. But I couldn't. I kept thinking that if I killed myself then I would never get to see you again."

"You're so damn strong," he groaned, unable to wait

a second longer to take her into his arms. "And you're never getting rid of me," he growled, crushing her against his chest as he pressed his lips to her forehead.

Burrowing closer to him, she spoke in a broken, breathless rush. "Sebastian told me that I was their t-test run. His and his brother's. That they used the first compound of the drug on me to see how it would w-work."

He cursed rough and low under his breath, his teeth clenched. Wanting her out of that damn manacle, he reached down and cracked it apart with his bare hands, careful not to hurt her. Then he started to pull her back into his arms, when he spotted the broken manacles lying on the floor on the other side of the room. Blood drained from his face as he finally caught a lingering, familiar scent on the air. He'd assumed his partner had gotten away during the kidnapping, but that obviously hadn't happened, because she'd been in this room with Elise. "Sweetheart," he croaked, bringing his worried gaze back to hers. "Where's Reyes?"

Tears streamed down her face. "She'd gotten free of her chains and had started to work on mine, but then she heard the guards outside the door talking about how you'd just been spotted in town. I tried to stop her, but she said you would never make it to us with all of them after you. So she…she tricked them into opening the door and then got past them and I could hear them all going after her. I think she tried to sacrifice herself or s-something so that you could reach me."

He swallowed against the rise of bile in his throat, his head pounding as he tried to come to terms with what she'd done.

"Do you think she got away?" Elise whispered.

"I hope to God she did," he said with a choked growl. "And when we find her, I'm kicking her crazy little ass."

"Me, too." She hiccuped.

Taking her tearstained face in his hands, Wyatt took a deep breath and said, "Elise, you have to shift. The instant the moon rises, I need you to change. Okay?"

"Wh-what?" she croaked.

"You heard me, sweetheart. No arguments. I need you to do this for me."

Panic twisted her pale, beautiful face. "I can't!"

"You can," he growled, determined to fight her on this to the bitter end. "You *have* to, because I love you and I'm not going to lose you."

"Nooo," she sobbed, shaking her head. "I can't! I *won't!"*

Wyatt gripped her shoulders and gave her a firm shake, making her lift those tear-drenched eyes back to his. "Listen to me, El. Either we leave here together or we're going to die here together. You understand? If we're going to fight our way out, you've got to shift, sweetheart."

Clutching his arms, she cried, "Please, Wyatt. Don't do this. If you can't get us both out, then go. Leave me here. Don't you dare stay here and die with me!"

"I mean it, Elise. You want me to live, then you had better help me get your ass out of here. Because I refuse to leave the woman I love behind!"

She blinked, looking stunned, as if she'd only just realized what he'd been telling her. "You love me?"

He held her face in his hands and lowered his forehead to hers. "I do. I have for a long time now. And I'm a fucking idiot for not telling you before."

Her lips parted, but before she could say anything

in response, Whiteclaw soldiers burst into the room. Shoving Elise behind him, Wyatt immediately released his claws and fangs, fighting with everything that he had, but it wasn't enough. Blood sprayed as he slashed, jabbed, kicked and torqued with a savagery he could only imagine was scaring the hell out of her, but there were too many of them. Once they'd overpowered him, they took the gun he had on him and dragged him from the room still fighting and shouting, and carried him out to the street. He was so goddamn terrified for Elise that he couldn't think straight, his rage obliterating his reason.

The biggest of the Lycans threw him to the ground, and two others grabbed his arms, jerking him to his knees. Knowing damn well they were all powered-up on the Whiteclaw's "super drug" even though they were still in their human forms, Wyatt jerked his gaze up to clash with Harris Claymore's narrowed brown eyes. The bastard stood only a few feet away from him, looking older than the last time Wyatt had seen him, the years away from his pack obviously spent doing some hard living. As he studied the Lycan, taking in the size and shape of his body, Wyatt realized it was Harris he'd fought in Elise's living room the night of the wedding.

But he suspected that it was really Sebastian who had a sadistic obsession with Elise. Harris, he had a feeling, was just his younger sibling's lapdog.

"Where's your brother?" he growled, wondering where the son of a bitch was hiding.

Harris laughed, then jerked his chin toward the Lycan who was stalking from the trees off to Wyatt's left. Not only was the male massive, his normally slight build bulked with muscle and several inches taller than his actual height, but his change was also further along than it should have been, considering the sun was still sitting low in the sky. His face was still human, but with a short snout distorting his nose and mouth, his ears pointed and tipped back.

What the hell?

At the look of shock on Wyatt's face, Sebastian's chest shook with a gritty laugh. "If there was a pill that could make Alice bigger, I thought why not me?"

"You're not just bigger," Wyatt growled.

"True," the Lycan murmured, rubbing his snout as he came closer. "And soon I'll even have a pill that allows me to completely day-shift. I won't need all that archaic lore that ol' Drake had to use. A little pill under my tongue—" he snapped his claw-tipped fingers "—and poof, I'll be able to do whatever I want. You think your bickering pack will be able to fight us then? You think anyone in the region will back you when they know what they're going up against?"

"You really think this shit is going to go your way?" he snarled, struggling against his captors.

"Everything goes my way!" Sebastian sneered. "I get everything I want." A slow, sickening smile tilted the corner of his distorted mouth, and his voice dropped. "You should know that better than anyone."

Wyatt fought even harder to get free, knowing damn well the son of a bitch was talking about Elise.

"Would you like to know where this came from?" Seb asked him, pulling a scrap of pink fabric from the front pocket of his jeans. "Think of it as a war trophy, the way some of your ancestors were known to take a scalp. This is how Eli managed to track down… Well, you know the story, right?"

"What the fuck is that?" he forced out through his clenched teeth, his chest heaving.

"A piece of the Drake bitch's pretty little panties." Sebastian lifted the fabric to his nose to take a deep sniff, then grinned. "The drug we gave her was an early sample. Screwed with her memory but didn't manage to make her want us. She fought us the entire time, which is why these still smell like sex and blood and pain."

"You motherfucker!" Wyatt roared, fighting harder to get free, his fangs shooting longer than they'd ever been, desperate for the bastard's throat.

A husky laugh slipped past Sebastian's dark lips, and he rubbed the scrap of fabric against the side of his face. "That was how Eli found our friend Danny. Danny and I split this little trophy. I hid mine in a safe place, but Danny went off with his portion in his front pocket, after drenching it in her blood. Idiot wasn't thinking. When your brother ran across him, he knew the instant he caught the scent of her blood that he'd found one of us."

Wyatt swallowed, shaking, wishing like hell that he'd been there with Eli that night. That he'd been able to take the asshole's life with his own hands.

"It was so funny to save your life in the woods the other night, knowing I'd fucked your woman. And you never had a clue," Seb murmured, enjoying the show he was putting on. Tucking the fabric back into his pocket, he cocked his head a bit to the side, and there was a maniacal light in his eyes as he came a little closer. "That's the problem with you alphas. You never suspect the betas. But we'll be the ones to take over the world."

"Not today you won't, you little shit."

Every head turned sharply toward the front steps of the house, where Elise stood, her claw-tipped hands dripping with crimson blood. *Holy shit!* Had she killed the guards who'd been told to stay outside her room? She must have, and Wyatt could only stare in complete and total wonder, his damn eyes wet with tears.

She'd released her claws and fangs, her dark blue gaze burning with rage, glowing in the pale beauty of her face, the fading sunset setting the auburn strands of her hair on fire. She looked so fucking hot he felt his jaw drop and, God, that was a sure sign of how deeply she affected him. Here they were, trapped in this life-and-death situation, surrounded by the enemy, and she was overwhelming him with lust and emotion.

Unfortunately, he wasn't the only one overcome by the sight of her.

"Hmm. I didn't think it was possible for you to be any sexier than you were that night, broken and bleeding in the mud. But this look suits you," Sebastian drawled, his body showing the clear signs of his interest with his bulging jeans. "My old man was always telling me that I shouldn't fuck my enemies. That it makes things too messy. But you're an exception, aren't you? A little snatch like you—you were just made to be fucked."

"You're a monster!" she snarled, the graveled words nearly drowned out by Wyatt's earsplitting roar of fury. The guttural sound was only choked off when one of the Whiteclaw soldiers came up behind him, wrapping his arm around Wyatt's throat as he struggled.

Stepping closer to the steps where she stood, Sebastian's shoulders shook as he cackled. "Are you really in a position to cast stones, Miss Drake? After the things your own father did? His blood flows through your veins. Doesn't that make you a monster, too?"

She watched him through narrow, burning eyes, the

blue so bright it was almost blinding. "Yeah, I have his blood," she rasped. "And I'll use it to rip you to bloody pieces."

He laughed even harder. "You couldn't change then, and you can't completely change now. And I know why." He grinned as he moved forward another step, closing the distance between them. "You're weak and pathetic. A sniveling little bitch who was so easy to break, it was a joke. You should have heard the things Daddy Drake used to say about you. How ashamed he was. No one has ever loved you. No one even cares if you live or die. They just put up with you out of pity."

Wyatt struggled harder against the bastards holding him, willing her with his eyes not to believe it. Her breathing quickened, and he could see the pounding of her pulse at the base of her throat.

"We never told him we were the ones who used you that night," Sebastian murmured, his next step bringing him to within a foot of where she stood. "But knowing how your father felt about you, I can't help but think he would have approved. If we had explained that you were a means to an end, he would have understood. He didn't think you were any better than a lab rat. If not for your brothers, he probably would have handed you right over, grateful to us for taking you off his hands."

Rage erupted from her in the form of her hand cracking across Claymore's muzzled face. But in his hybrid Lycan form, his head barely moved from the blow.

As the sun dipped a little deeper on the horizon, Wyatt's wolf seethed within his body, desperate to escape and fight for the woman they loved. But there wasn't going to be enough time. She needed to deal with the bastard *now*, before it was too late.

"Goddamn it, Elise! Fight him!" Wyatt managed to shout, just as the Lycan behind him shifted his hold.

Her chest shuddered as she breathed in violent gusts, tears streaming over her pale cheeks. Then Sebastian motioned for the soldiers to move in on her, and she froze. "You don't get to touch me," she told them, the low words thick with fury. "And you sure as hell don't get to touch him," she said with more force, cutting her brilliant gaze in Wyatt's direction. Their gazes locked, a thousand messages and emotions flying across the crackling connection.

And then she went into motion.

From one instant to the next, her eyes bled from blue to a scorching golden-amber, and she became the most perfect killing machine he'd ever seen. He knew, in that moment, that her Dark Wolf had finally risen inside her, determined to protect her from these monsters.

His eyes burned as he watched her take out the White-claw soldiers closest to her, while the others panicked and tried to flee into the forest, seeking an escape from the brutal carnage. She moved so quickly, Wyatt could only see her in a blur of colors. Peaches-and-cream skin, flaming red hair, blood-soaked claws. His mouth gaped with shock when she took out the two behemoths who had been holding his arms, as well as the one who'd held his throat from behind.

He was distantly aware of his friends arriving in the midst of the chaos. Every Runner, with the exception of Carla, was spreading out behind him, along with others. Moving to his feet, he cast a quick glance over the blood-ied group, who had obviously had to fight their way into the town, surprised to see Elliot and Max were among them, as well as Mason's father, Robert. There were even a few pack members who had recently made it clear that they were tired of the divide between the Alley and the town.

Wyatt had called Cian on his way to Hawkley, telling him he was going after Elise. The Runner had promised they wouldn't be far behind him, but he hadn't expected them to be able to mobilize so quickly when they'd been scattered in so many different directions.

They were all watching the scene with wide, shocked eyes, same as he was, not knowing what to do…or how to help. Not that she needed any. His woman was kicking ass unlike anything he had ever seen, and Wyatt was so damn proud of her he was nearly choking on it. And then she was suddenly standing before him, no more than a few feet away. She was in her completely human form again—but she was still incredibly strong. Strong enough to trap Sebastian Claymore's shuddering body in her arms, his back to her front, and her claws held tight against his throat.

Sensing that she needed some time to figure out what she wanted to do with the Lycan, Wyatt gave her a moment as he turned his attention to the others. Brody tossed him a gun, which he tucked into the front of his jeans before looking at Mason. "Did you find Farrow?"

Mason shook his head, his expression grim. "He's gone missing."

With a muttered curse on his lips, Wyatt cut his gaze toward Cian, who was holding a struggling Harris Claymore against the front of his body, the Lycan's arms twisted behind his back, much like Elise was holding Sebastian.

"Found this one trying to run away," the Irishman murmured, his gray eyes glowing with a cold, deadly fire. "I have a vested interest in ridding the world of slime. Do you mind?"

"Not at all."

Cian's fangs flashed as he released his hold on Harris, blocking the blow the Lycan immediately aimed at his face. With a sibilant hiss of sound, Cian freed the claws on his right hand and drew his arm back. Then he swung, slashing his claws through the air, nearly severing the Lycan's head from his shoulders. As Harris's bulky body fell to the ground, Cian lifted his arm and licked the blood from the inside of his wrist, a feral gleam in his glowing eyes. Wyatt cast a quick look over their group, gauging the fresh surge of shock on their faces. They knew Hennessey was an incredible fighter, but they had never seen anything like that. Even Brody, Cian's partner, looked as if he were struggling to understand how the Irishman had taken his opponent down so easily.

"El?" Wyatt rasped, finally bringing his gaze back to hers. He let her know with his eyes that whatever happened next, it was her call.

She dropped Sebastian's body at his feet, then stepped back. At his questioning look, she shook her head, her slender throat working as she swallowed. "Can't. Don't want to touch him."

"You sure?" he asked, kneeling down. Satisfaction burned through his veins as he sunk his claws into Sebastian's groin, the Lycan's startled hiss of pain nearly making him smile.

She nodded, then dropped to her knees, swaying, her clothes hanging off her pale form in tatters. Cian for once didn't make a snide comment. He simply shrugged out of his gray flannel shirt and gently placed it around her shoulders. Then Eric came forward and reached for his sister, crushing her against his chest. Seeing that she was safe and surrounded by his friends, Wyatt turned his attention back to the whimpering man he literally had by the balls. Sebastian's hybrid form had bled back into the fragile shape of the man, his pale skin dotted with sweat. But the look in his eyes was still defiant. Gloating and evil.

"Did you kill Farrow, after he did your dirty work?" Wyatt asked, his voice low and deadly. "Or are you letting him hide behind your skirts? Was he one of the ones who attacked Elise three years ago? I want names, you bastard. All of them."

"I don't know anything about Farrow!"

He let his claws sink a little deeper. "I'll ask you once more, Claymore. You answer truthfully, and I'll give you a quick death. You fucking lie to me, and I give you my word that we'll be here all night. Hell, if I have Jillian keep you alive, we could go on for days."

Sebastian curled his lip and laughed. "You're not a sadistic torturer."

Wyatt leaned right into the Lycan's face. "I love her, you piece of shit. She's *mine*. Mine to protect. Mine to avenge. I will do whatever needs to be done for her. Without guilt. Without remorse. Without a second thought." He twisted his claws even deeper, hitting bone. "Still think I won't deliver on my threat?"

The cockiness in Sebastian's gaze finally bled away, replaced by a sickening look of fear. "It was me and Harris. And his idiot friend Danny, who was the one who first started cooking up our drugs. He's the one your brother killed." He swallowed thickly, closing his eyes. "And then there was my uncle."

Wyatt snarled. "Roy?"

Seb nodded, then lifted his lashes. Bitterness thickened his words. "We were his first blackmail tape, though he called it insurance for Danny's benefit. He didn't fuck her until she'd lost consciousness. But he worked her over rougher than the rest of us. Said she was the sweetest little piece of ass he'd ever had."

In a violent burst of rage, Wyatt grabbed Sebastian's head and gave it a violent twist, severing his spinal column and instantly ending his life. "Where's Roy?" he rasped, looking around at the Whiteclaw soldiers who had started to edge closer to their group as he moved to his full height, leaving Sebastian's lifeless body lying on the ground. When no one answered him, he roared, "Where the fuck is he?"

"I'm right here." Flanked by two guards, Roy Claymore walked around the edge of the house where they'd been keeping Elise and made his way into the street. He was a tall, brawny male, with thick black hair, a crooked nose and the moral code of a rat. "Once again, it looks like the Silvercrest Runners are taking care of the trash for me. First Curtis Donovan, and now my nephews," he muttered, flicking a disgusted look over Harris's and Sebastian's bodies.

"I thought Seb and Harris were your golden boys," Wyatt growled.

"They were, before they went into heat over the bitch. I never wanted them to leave. That was my brother. He learned what we'd done after her brother killed Danny, and feared it would lead to war. Once the story of what had happened to her began circulating the mountains, we knew the fool hadn't given her enough of the drug to blank her mind completely. Me, I was ready to test our strength against the Silvercrest. But not my brother. He worried for days that she would remember something that would bring your pack knocking on our door. And in the end he sent his own flesh and blood away, fearing what else they might do to cause trouble. At the time, I thought he was wrong. Now," he muttered, rubbing his jaw, "well, I begin to see there was some truth in his fear. When I brought them back, I told them to forget her. She'd served her purpose, but there were more important things for us to focus on. But the little idiots just wouldn't listen," he ended with a sneer.

"Why did you even want them back in the first place?" Cian asked from Wyatt's side.

"Because a good leader always invites his soldiers home in time for war."

"A soldier fights for what's right," Wyatt growled. "You and your nephews are nothing more than butchers."

"Butchers. Monsters. Soldiers." Roy looked at Elise and smiled. "Rapists. Whatever you want to call us, this *is* a war."

He could have wasted time arguing with the bastard. Making threats. Venting for all the vile shit this son of a bitch had done. Hell, he would have gone ahead and just killed him then and there, but he didn't want to risk another fight when Elise needed to be taken somewhere safe. And with Roy's guards, it would definitely be a fight. That being the case, Wyatt simply lifted the Glock Brody had given him and fired, shooting the Lycan right between the eyes. The wolves at Roy's sides snarled with outrage, but neither moved to attack, protecting the fallen body of their leader. Wyatt knew that Roy would likely survive the shot, but the healing process was going to hurt like a bitch. And when they next met on the battlefield, he would get his revenge.

"We have to get out of here—*now,*" Cian muttered at his side as they caught sight of more Whiteclaw soldiers coming down the road. Wyatt's teeth were clenched together too hard for him to speak, so he simply responded with a jerky nod, took Elise from Eric's arms and headed into the forest with the others.

Minutes later, they were sitting in the back of Mason's truck while Wyatt held Elise on his lap, his lips at her ear as he told her how proud he was of her. And how incredibly sorry he was that he'd let her down. She didn't say much in response, but kept her arms wrapped tight around his middle, as if she were exactly where she wanted to be. There were so many things he wanted to say to her about how he felt, but didn't know how. Until he had all the crazy shit going through his head sorted out, he knew it was best to just keep apologizing. God only knew he owed her at least a thousand apologies, if not more.

And he sure as hell owed her for saving his life.

Without any doubt, Wyatt knew that what he and the others had witnessed had been some form of the powerful Dark Wolf bloodline that flowed through her veins coming to the fore, which left him with so many questions. It was said that a Dark Wolf could only truly awaken when he or she had found their life mate, but without her Lycan senses, there was no way to know for certain if Elise's wolf had recognized him as its other half. He wanted it so badly—that certainty and the bond. But the fact that she might *never* recognize him on an instinctual level didn't change how he felt about her or make him want her any less, because there was nothing he would change about her. *Nothing.* The woman was more perfect than anything he could have ever dreamed, and he hoped to God she would decide someday that she needed him as badly as he needed her.

Even though he knew damn well that he didn't deserve her.

The moment they hit the Alley, everything erupted in a flurry of chaos and activity. They were in the process of organizing a search for Carla, loading up on weapons at Mason and Torrance's cabin, when Torrance's cell phone rang. She was standing close to Wyatt, and he noticed her look at the number on the phone's screen with an odd expression on her face before quickly answering the call. "Carla?"

The petite redhead listened for a moment, then looked at Wyatt and handed the phone over to him. He went into one of the other rooms to talk, where it wasn't as noisy, since not everyone there had realized he was taking a call. He argued with his partner for a full minute, until she finally hung up on him. Knowing he must look shell-shocked when he came back into the living room, he tried to explain, but all he managed to mutter was a rough "She's doing it."

"Doing what?" several of the Runners asked at the same time.

"Carla stole a car and now she's…" He broke off, looking at Eric and Elise. "I don't know what's going on, but Carla said she knows how to find Eli. She's gone to bring him back home."

They all looked as confused as he felt. As far as they knew, Carla Reyes and Eli Drake had never even met. Why had she taken off to find him? What had happened to her at that compound? What did she know that they didn't?

And why in the hell did his partner think Eli Drake was the answer?

Chapter 17

Whoever had said that guilt was a bitch didn't know the half of it. An hour after the call from Carla, Wyatt had left Elise at Torrance and Mason's, where she was still busy helping to patch everyone up. When he'd snuck out of the cabin, Sayre had been trying to aid Cian with a particularly deep cut on his shoulder, and the Irishman had been adamantly refusing. Whatever was going on with those two, he had a feeling it was going to cause a hell of a shit storm when it finally hit.

But at the moment, he had his own colossal fuckup to deal with.

Or not, his wolf snarled. *Seeing as how you're running like a coward.*

He wasn't running, damn it. He just needed some time to get himself under control, because every single fucking moment that went by was testing him. Pushing him to his breaking point. The longer he'd stayed near her tonight, the stronger the need had become. His control had been shot to hell, and he knew there wasn't any getting it back. Not until he'd gotten what he needed. Which was her. Or more specifically, him claiming her sweet little ass and making her *his*...forever.

Unfortunately, that was the last damn thing that Elise needed right now. Christ, after what he'd done, and after she learned the truth about him, he wasn't sure she would *ever* want it. Which just made him want to howl from the pain and frustration cutting through him like a knife, making his emotions bleed.

He was in the middle of tossing things into the duffel bag he'd set on his bed when Elise came into his bedroom wearing a borrowed shirt and jeans, her blue eyes narrowing as she frowned at him. "Wyatt? You snuck away from there without me. What's going on?"

"Nothing," he murmured, tightening his jaw. "I just need to get away for a while."

"Get away?" she echoed, the quiet words rough with worry. "I don't understand."

He swallowed thickly and tried not to look at her as he pulled a few pairs of jeans out of a drawer in his dresser. "I'll be back," he scraped out, turning back toward the bed. "I just... I can't stay here. Not right now."

"Why? Because of me? What the hell, Wyatt? Is this... Are you dumping me?" Her voice was getting louder, rising with her anger. "You screwed me and now you're done? Is that how this works?"

He made a hard, thick sound at the back of his throat and shoved both hands back through his hair. "No, damn it! You think I want this? I don't want to go. It's the last fucking thing that I want! But you deserve a hell of a lot better than a bastard who constantly screws up losing his control with you!"

"Screws up what?" she asked, the words shivering with emotion. "What are you talking about? You haven't screwed up. You saved me! Don't you see that?"

He slanted her a narrow, burning look. "Was I saving you when I let Seb lead me away from you today?"

"Don't," she croaked. "Don't do that, damn it. That was *not* your fault. You were doing what you thought was right."

He cursed something foul under his breath, then grabbed another handful of clothes and shoved them into the bag. "Feel free to use the cabin while I'm gone. No one will bother you."

She made a choked sound, and he watched from the corner of his eye as she pressed the back of her hand to her mouth. "So you're just going to run? You can't stay with me while sorting out whatever is going on in that thick head of yours?"

He couldn't stop his stupid hands from shaking, so he clenched them into fists at his sides. He needed a bloody straitjacket to keep himself in line around her, his body physically aching with the need to grab hold and yank her close. Keeping her there. Forever. "I'm trying to do what's right."

"By leaving me?" she asked, swiping at the tears spilling over her cheeks.

The tears were killing him.

Unable to remain still, he turned and took a step toward her, ready to shake some sense into her so that she could finally open her eyes and see the big picture. Finally see that she was too fine and good and beautiful for someone like him, even though it was the last thing in the world he *wanted* her to realize. But guilt was ripping him up, and he heard himself shouting, "I almost got you killed!"

Her chin shot up, those sky-blue eyes blazing fire. "The hell you did. This was not your fault! How many freaking times do I have to say it?"

"You don't understand," he argued, cutting his hand through the air in frustration, wanting to knock the shitty reality of this situation right out of the goddamn room, so that he could just do what he wanted. "You don't— *Shit, Elise!* You don't even know what you're talking about."

"Then explain it," she snapped, throwing her arms out at her sides, blocking the doorway. Elise figured she had to look like an idiot, but she didn't care. At that moment, nothing mattered but getting through to him.

A muscle pulsed in his jaw as he turned his head to the side, his bare-chested body rigid with tension, muscles cut beneath his dark skin as if they'd been carved by a blade.

Breathing in rough, jagged bursts, he growled, "This isn't the first time I've fucked up, Elise. When I was younger, I...lost someone."

Oh! Her insides twisted with unease. "Was she your girlfriend?"

He lowered his head, squeezing his eyes shut. "No. But she was my friend. Her name was Robbie. I wasn't in love with her, but I loved her like a sister. Like my family."

"What happened?" she whispered, dreading what he would tell her.

"We, uh, had planned to meet out by the lake on the reservation at midnight to go for a swim. She'd been having a crappy time with her boyfriend and was feel-

ing down. So I'd told her we'd spend the night out at the
lake, just goofing off. But I didn't go. Not when I was
meant to." A bitter laugh slipped from his lips, thick
with self-loathing. "I got a call from another girl. So I
met up with her instead. Thought there'd be plenty of
time to satisfy my own needs, before I kept my word
to Robbie." He lifted his head, looking her right in the
eye. "Robbie went early, and some asshole followed her.
Then he attacked her. And I wasn't there. I was too busy
getting laid while my friend was being repeatedly raped
and nearly beaten to death by some monster. How's that
for heroic?"

"Oh, God, Wyatt. I'm so sorry."

He scrubbed his hands over his face, and "Yeah"
seemed to be all he could get out.

"What happened?" she asked again.

Pacing away from her, he braced his hands on the
sides of the window that faced the woods. "I showed up
at the lake just as he was leaving her. She looked…" His
voice cracked, and he had to swallow before he could go
on. "She looked at me and grabbed the knife he'd left on
the ground beside her, then slit her own throat."

"Jesus," she whispered.

He made a thick sound and shook his head again, as
if it could force the grim image out of his mind.

"And the man?" she asked. "You killed him?"

"Yeah," he grunted. "I gutted the son of a bitch with
my claws. Just not in time to help her."

As heart-wrenching a story as it was, Elise was glad
that he'd told her, because she understood so much now.
Why he didn't think he was worthy of a relationship, no
doubt letting his guilt fester in his soul until it'd completely colored the way he saw himself. And then there

were the nightmares that most likely played the girl's death out before his eyes over…and over. Her heart broke for Robbie, and her heart broke for Wyatt, too. For the pain he'd carried with him all this time, blaming himself for something that was never his fault to begin with.

He flinched when he felt the soft touch of her hand against his shoulder. "So because of what happened, you think the answer is to walk away from me?"

His hands balled into fists against the window frame. "Damn it, you think this is what I want? I'm trying to do what's right for you."

"Well, this isn't right. This sucks! So just stop it!" She was suddenly screeching like a madwoman, but there was no help for it. She felt mad. On edge. Desperate and impassioned.

"I made a promise to you," he argued hoarsely, pressing his forehead against the glass. "One that I broke by leaving you here, instead of staying to protect you."

"Yeah, because of the fact that you care about me and wanted to make that Claymore bastard pay for what he did."

His shoulders lifted as he drew in a deep breath, then slowly let it out. "You don't need me anymore, El. I always knew you were strong. You're whole now."

"That's such bullshit. How can I be whole without you? Call me crazy, Wyatt, but I'd rather not go through my life only half-alive."

"You're not—"

"Stop!" she shouted, jerking him around to face her. "Wyatt, you believed in me when nobody else did. Not even myself. How could I not love you, you big beautiful idiot?"

He gave her a hard, pained smile. "Gratitude is not love, El."

Staring deep into his dark, tortured eyes, she said, "You're right. But you'd better sit your ass down on that bed and get comfortable if you want me to list all the reasons why I *do* love you. It's gonna take a while."

"But I almost got you killed," he growled, repeating himself. "Don't you get that? I swore that I would die to protect you, and then I made the biggest mistake of my life. As much guilt as I carry for what happened to Robbie, this is even worse. Because it was *you*."

"Honestly, Wyatt. I know you're not stupid, so stop being such a dumb-ass. You are not God. You are not invincible. The past was not your fault and neither was this!"

He clenched his jaw but didn't argue, and she blanched as a horrible thought suddenly shoved its way into her head. "Oh, God. Wait a minute." She stumbled back a step, one hand pressed to her forehead as her thoughts reeled. "Are you even being honest with me? Are you sure this isn't because I can't… I mean, just because I managed that partial shift tonight doesn't mean I'll be able to do it again. Not unless your life is in danger."

He looked stunned. "*My* life?"

"I didn't change to save myself," she told him, wishing he would just grab hold of her and never let her go. "If that were the case, it would have happened the moment they took me. I changed to save *you,* because of what you mean to me, just like Eric did when Chelsea's life was in danger." She licked her lips and said, "That's what being a Dark Wolf means, I guess. Doing whatever it takes of you to save the person you love."

"Christ, El."

She lifted her chin. "But as far as shape-shifting goes, there's a good chance that was it. So maybe that's what this is really about. Maybe it's about *me*."

"I couldn't care less if you ever shift again," he growled with fury, his voice continuing to rise with each hard, guttural word. "That's not why I love you. Yeah, that little demonstration you gave us of that Dark Wolf blood inside you was even more bad-ass than Cian—and that's really saying something. But it does not matter," he forced out through his clenched teeth. "I don't give a shit if I ever see it again, El. I don't care. I want you for you. I love you because you're perfect exactly the way you are!"

Her heart was beating like mad with happiness, but her voice was still thick with exasperation. "And I could say the exact same thing about you." Tears streamed down her face as she stepped closer, pressing her hands against his broad chest. "I love you," she said brokenly, her voice shaking. "I am *in* love with you. With every part of you. I'm not perfect, and I don't expect you to be perfect, either. I just need you to be mine."

"El."

"Don't you get it, Wyatt? You blaming yourself for the things that have happened is like me blaming myself for the rape."

Raw fury darkened his face, his corded throat working as he swallowed. "Like hell it is. You did nothing wrong."

"And neither did you. You didn't hurt Robbie. You didn't make her go early to meet you, and you didn't make her kill herself. You were a young man who got caught in the middle of an awful situation, but it was *not* your fault. It wasn't your sin. But this, what you're doing to us, it will be. If you let it control you now, if you walk away from me, that's on you, Wyatt. Can you really live with that?"

"But I let people down, Elise. I've let you—"

She got right in his face, pounding her fists against his chest. "That's bullshit! You've saved me, Wyatt. Put your life on the line for me, pulled me out of the pit and made me start living again. You've taken my heart and made me love you. And if you even try to walk out that door, you should know that you won't get away. I will follow your ass to the ends of the earth if I have to. You had to go and be all wonderful and sexy and incredible, blowing my mind, claiming my heart, and now you can goddamn deal with the consequences!"

She was sobbing by the time she was through, sounding hysterical, and he made a low, fractured sound deep in his throat, suddenly crushing her against him as he buried his face in her hair. "I *want* you. I *love* you, damn it. So much that it's killing me. But I want what's best for you, El. You deserve the best. *Only* the best."

"Wyatt, you're not only the best, you're the only one," she cried. "There is no one else. There never will be anyone else. Please don't pull me back and then just leave me here. Just…don't. I'm begging you."

Dropping to his knees before her, he caught her hands in his and brought them to his lips, kissing her knuckles as he stared up at her shocked face with eyes that were damp with tears. "Okay," he told her, choking the word out. "I know I screwed up and I'm so sorry. But I can't do it—I can't let you go. I love you too damn much. Need you too much. You're… Like I said before, you've completely *ruined* me, woman."

"Then that's only fair," she whispered, sniffing, "because you've ruined me, too." Her eyes narrowed with warning. "And no more pussying out like that hero in the book you read to me. Because it's time to man up, Wyatt."

He laughed and pulled her closer, crushing her in his fierce embrace. "I get it," he groaned, nuzzling his face against her middle, where butterflies were dancing in a frenzy. "Hell, it's not like I'd have gotten far anyway." Pulling his head back, he stared up at her with a wry, dazzling smile. "Five minutes and I'd have been back here on my knees, just like this, crawling right back to you."

"I need you, Wyatt. So much," she told him, burying her hands in his silky hair. "Now. *Forever.* Please stay with me."

"I will," he vowed, holding her tight. "I love you. More than I know how to explain with a bunch of words. But if you'll give me the chance, I'll spend the rest of my life showing you exactly how much you mean to me, El. You will *not* doubt it. I swear. Not even for a second."

"Oh, wow. That was so beautiful. I knew you could be romantic, but I didn't know—"

"I can be anything I need to be for you," he said in a low voice, his tone almost reverent. "*Anything,* El."

"I just need *you,* Wyatt. That's all. Just be yourself and we'll be golden."

His mouth twisted with another wry smile. "You sure, baby? Because the real me would toss you over my shoulder, carry you over to that big bed we're going to share and spend the next twenty hours fucking your gorgeous little brains out."

She ripped off the shirt she'd borrowed earlier from Torrance, and let it drop to the floor. She couldn't help but give a soft laugh when his hot gaze dropped to her breasts just as quickly. "I'm waiting," she told him, loving the way he made her feel so beautiful, scars and all. "Come on. And don't hold back. Not for a single second."

His nostrils flared as he sucked in a sharp breath, his dark eyes smoldering with something that was possessive and hot and deliciously primal as he slowly brought that heavy-lidded gaze back to her face. "As much as I want to do exactly that," he told her, his fingers clenching against her hips, "you need time, El. Time to think long and hard about what you want. Because the next time I touch you, I'm going to mark you."

She shivered at the stunning burst of emotion those husky words made her feel. "I don't, Wyatt. I don't need time."

"I take you to bed," he growled slowly, "then my fangs are in your throat."

"Good."

"Good?"

"It's about damn time," she said boldly. "Don't you think?"

With a rough growl, he surged to his feet and brought her close, crushing her naked torso against his chest, the heat of his skin making her gasp. "You're staying here with me, in the Alley, forever."

"You bet your sexy ass I'm staying."

He smiled against her lips. "I wasn't giving you a choice, sweetheart. You'll have to kill me to get rid of me now."

"Never," she groaned, pushing her fingers into his hair. Their lips brushed once, twice, and then he took control. With one hand gripping the back of her neck and the other kneading her ass, he kissed her like a man who'd been starved for her taste, his tongue wet and wicked and wild in her mouth, making her breathless. "You know, considering where this is headed," she gasped, "I should probably tell you that I need to go up to town tomorrow to get my Pill prescription refilled."

He lifted his head, his chest jerking with his ragged breaths, and his dark gaze locked hard on hers. "Maybe."

"Maybe?" she repeated with a soft laugh, shivering as he stroked a big hand up her spine. "Um, you don't want to get me pregnant, Wyatt."

His brows slowly started to draw together. "Like hell I don't," he growled.

Elise froze, her eyes shot wide with shock. "You want kids?"

Lowering his head, he got right in her face. "As many as you want to give me, when you're ready. I'll love them all."

She swallowed against the fresh wave of tears burning at the back of her throat and struggled to whisper, "But they could be like *me*."

He suddenly looked as if he wanted to kiss her and throttle her at the same time. "You mean perfect?"

She could only shake her head in response.

"I'm serious about this, El."

"You really want babies?" she asked in complete awe. "You want to start a family? Our own family?"

"I want everything with you, sweetheart." As if to prove just how much he meant those incredible words, Elise could suddenly see the sharp points of his fangs gleaming beneath the sensual curve of his upper lip. But she wasn't afraid. How could she be afraid when she was so damn happy?

With her heart melting in her chest, she blinked back

her tears and smiled up at him. "I want everything with you, too."

"That's my girl," Wyatt whispered, relieved as hell when he saw the perfect trifecta—*trust, belief and love*—glowing in her beautiful blue eyes, a part of him still in shock that this was happening. That he'd told her everything, and she'd stayed. *She'd stayed.*

Yeah, it'd been scary, opening himself up like that. Making himself vulnerable. Giving her the ultimate power over him. But it was already hers, and he couldn't go on alone. He needed to be with her, to be at her side. Needed everything she had to give…and then he needed her to dig deep and give him even more. Because he was more than ready to give her everything that he was. Every part of him.

They belonged to her. Every. Single. One.

This, right here, was where he belonged. Yeah, he didn't deserve her. But he was going to do everything in his power to be a man who did and worship the ground she walked on. Before the night was over, he *would* make the bite that would bind them together forever. For all eternity. Put his heart in her hands and trust her to keep it safe, because that was exactly where it belonged. *With El.*

And when he did, it was going to be the best goddamn moment of Wyatt's life.

Birdsong. Sunlight. Warm, sex-rumpled sheets. Mmm. It was *almost* perfect. The only thing missing was the feel of that deliciously hard, hot male body that had held her through the long hours of the night. Elise might be in Wyatt's big ol' bed all alone now, but he'd slept with her.

And that wasn't all they'd done. Last night had been…
Wow, there weren't even words.

She'd been so wrong when she'd thought there was
nothing that could heal her. Nothing that could stop the
pain. All she'd needed was Wyatt. Not just his body,
though she enjoyed the hell out of it. But what she'd really needed was his heart.

They'd both bared themselves to the other. She'd
shown him her external scars. He'd finally shown her
his internal ones. And it had brought them closer. As
close as two people could ever possibly get.

Stretching, she felt a smile curve her kiss-swollen
lips, their surface hot and sensitive, as if she'd been permanently marked by him. And that wasn't the only way
that he'd marked her.

It hadn't taken long before his control shattered and
he'd bitten the hell out of her, making the blood bond that
meant they could never be torn apart. Then she'd bitten
him back. After that, she was surprised they hadn't broken the bed, their mating had become so…*wild.* Maybe
even a little savage and violent, but she'd realized that
when drenched in love, that kind of sex could be incredibly emotional. It took trust, on both sides, and they'd
been so overwhelmed that when they came they'd damn
near lost consciousness. They'd laughed at their antics
when they'd finally found the strength to drag their heat-
glazed bodies to the shower, so happy they'd practically
glowed.

She still felt that way. Felt…changed, in a good way,
as if everything in life was better and brighter, full of
hope and possibility, even with the trouble they knew
was coming. She wasn't going to be weighted down by

fear for a moment longer, because she knew that she could face anything, so long as Wyatt was beside her.

Somehow, she had finally found her place. Her *home*. It wasn't every day that a person got lucky enough to find their own happily-ever-after—and she readily admitted that she'd been a skeptical fool not to truly believe, because there was nothing more real than what she'd found with her sexy Runner. And whether she ever managed to completely shift or not, she would fight to the death to protect it. To protect Wyatt.

After their shower, they'd spent the night in bed, lost in each other. They'd made love and talked for hours, dragging their naked bodies to the kitchen for sustenance, before falling back into bed for more breathtaking passion…and those long, soulful talks that were bringing them so much closer together, the bond a miracle they were both lost in. They knew that rough times were ahead, but no matter what life threw at them, they would have each other. And that made *anything* seem surmountable.

Wondering where he'd wandered off to, Elise finally tossed back the covers, ready to climb out of bed and track him down, when a warm, mouthwatering scent suddenly reached her nose. Sitting up in bed, she was about to go explore, seeking the source, when the man who completely held her heart walked into the bedroom, smiling his wicked grin at her, the look in his dark eyes impossibly happy. She started to smile back at him, when her breath caught, her eyes going huge, both hands pressed against the center of her chest, where her heart was beating so hard that it hurt.

Oh, my God…oh, my God…oh, my God!

Wyatt rushed toward her. "Jesus, El. What's wrong, baby?"

"Nothing," she whispered, blinking up at him as he sat beside her on the bed. "Nothing's wrong. It's just that...*God,* Wyatt. You smell so good."

A look of confusion creased his brow. "Huh?"

"Do you...do you know what you smell like?" she asked, feeling the tears start to gather at the backs of her eyes.

Slowly, he shook his head.

Mouth trembling, she said, "You smell like *mine*."

"Yours?" He blinked as his jaw dropped. "Elise? Are you...? Did you...?"

She nodded, grinning at him like a fool, but too freaking happy to care.

He made a hard, thick sound and dragged her into his arms for a ravenous kiss. When he finally lifted his head, she was gasping for breath, and the smile curling his lips was slow and sexy, his dark eyes glittering with love that she could feel moving through her, a part of her. "I told you that I just might surprise you, baby."

She laughed as he lowered his head, nuzzling the side of her throat, so happy she didn't think she would ever stop smiling. "You most certainly did."

"Can you scent the others?" he whispered. "I was coming in here to wake you up because nearly everyone has shown up and they brought breakfast with them. They're all waiting in the kitchen."

She shook her head. "I had no idea. I can't smell them at all."

His low, husky rumble of laughter filled her ear. "It probably makes me sound like a caveman, but I think it's incredibly hot that I'm the only one."

"It wouldn't matter, you know." She ran her fingers through his glossy hair as he lifted his head, staring deep in her eyes. "You're mine no matter what, Wyatt. But I can't say that the way you smell doesn't make me want to devour every inch of you."

"Now you know how I feel," he murmured, rubbing his nose against hers. "But I'd love you no matter what, El. You know that, right?"

"I know," she whispered, kissing the side of his beautiful mouth. "You loved me when I was broken, and because of that, you helped make me whole again."

"Damn it, that's it. I need to fuck you, baby. Right now," he growled, kissing the side of her throat, his tongue flicking against the marks he'd made in her tender skin when he'd bitten her.

"I want that, too," she said with a breathless laugh, tilting her head back for him. "But you said the others are waiting for us."

Lifting his head again, he gave her a warm, wicked smile that curled her toes. "Let them wait," he rasped. "I'll cook for you later."

"I'll hold you to that," she teased.

"You can hold me to anything, sweetheart. Just so long as you always hold me."

Blissful tears filled her eyes as she smiled and placed her hands on the back of his neck, pulling him down for another kiss. A kiss that started out sweet, but quickly built into something hot and explicit, and she couldn't get enough. Knowing this perfect moment was the first of many to come, Elise surrendered completely to the man who would forever hold her heart and her trust, knowing she would never run again…unless it was into Wyatt's arms. Where she belonged.

And where she always wanted to be.

Epilogue

One week later...

The day after Wyatt had made the bite that would bind him and Elise together for the rest of their lives, he'd proposed. He gave her his mother's ring, a simple white-gold band with three sparkling diamonds, and she cried so hard he'd had to wait several minutes before she was finally able to give him a husky, beautiful *yes*. Eager to make her his wife, he wanted the wedding to take place as soon as possible, but they were going to do their best to wait until they had Carla back in the Alley, and hopefully Eli, as well. Personally, Wyatt didn't know if he could wait that long. He and Elise had made the blood bond, but he wanted it all. His name after hers and his ring on her finger. Wanted the human marks of a couple as desperately as he'd wanted the Lycan ones. And he knew, without any doubt, that she would be the most beautiful bride the world had ever seen.

Eric was happy to walk Elise down the aisle, but Wyatt knew she was hoping that Eli might come home to do the honors. And the Runners were still hoping the renowned mercenary would come back to help them fight the war.

Two days after the events in Hawkley, they received word that Roy Claymore had recovered from the bullet Wyatt had put in his brain and that he was currently in talks with the Youngblood pack to the west of them, who had yet to decide where their loyalties would lie. The smaller pack had to know that if the Silvercrest fell, they would be next. But their decision depended on how much they feared Roy and the rest of the Whiteclaw... and how much influence Roy held with them through his blackmailing efforts.

As for the Greywolf to the north of their territory, they had chosen to cover their own asses instead of coming to the Silvercrest's aid. In the last meeting Mason had with their Elders, he was told that the pack would most likely make their own move against the Silvercrest's northern land to ensure that their borders were protected in the event Shadow Peak fell to the Whiteclaw.

Which meant they were on their own. But they weren't going down without a fight.

As for Glenn Farrow, they were still searching for the Lycan, but had been unable to locate him. If he was in Hawkley with the Whiteclaw, the Runners knew the bastard could give their enemy valuable information about the pack's security—and so they were being even more vigilant than usual. Robert had been great at helping to recruit more help within Shadow Peak, and the training sessions Mason had wanted to set up would be starting within the next few days.

There was a storm coming, they had no doubt. But they were willing to do whatever it took to be ready. Eric had called for a special meeting up in Shadow Peak, and they would all be attending later that night. The newest Runner was going to announce their plan to move the pack's youngest and eldest members down to the Alley in the coming weeks for protection. Any women who wanted to fight would be allowed to do so, though Wyatt secretly hoped they would choose to stay and provide help in caring for the others. He knew it probably made him sound like a chauvinistic ass, but the idea of a woman being hurt in combat made his gut ache.

Still, he doubted there was a chance in hell he would be able to convince Elise not to fight. The night after they'd made the blood bond, she'd asked him to come out to the woods with her, wanting to see if she could take the complete shape of her beast. Though he loved her no matter what, he'd been beyond proud when she'd fully shifted. He'd joined her in his Lycan form, and together they'd gone hunting, running wild through the forest, their beasts connecting on a level that had affected them both. When they'd finally made their way back to the cabin and retaken their human shapes, they'd fallen into the shower together and damn near killed each other with the ferocity of their lovemaking. But he had no doubt that she'd loved it, the gorgeous smile on her lips when they'd finally stumbled into bed all the assurance he had needed.

Elise had opened his eyes to what it meant to need another person more than he needed to eat or breathe or sleep—which meant he was both incredibly protective *and* possessive of her. But he was also proud as hell of her strength, both inside and out, and if she wanted to fight at his side, she would have his support. As well as his promise to protect her with his dying breath.

Somehow, after all the crap they'd been through, they'd found each other. Found that place where they could put the past and its baggage behind them, and live a little freer, knowing that no matter what came their way, they would face it together. Even war.

As they climbed the front steps of their cabin, coming back from dinner with Mason and Torrance, Wyatt was confident that whatever the future held, the Runners would triumph in the end, for one simple reason: they weren't fighting for power or money or glory. They were fighting for love.

Pulling his mate into his arms, he lowered his head and whispered into her ear, telling her how thankful he was that she'd come into his life. How much he loved her. How much he needed her.

And that he always, *always* would.

On the other side of the Alley, Cian looked at Jillian as they sat on his front porch, and slanted her a grim smile. "If I ever turn into such a lovesick jackass like Pall over there, please do me a favor and put me out of my misery."

Lightly, she said, "You won't get off that easily, Hennessey."

"I won't become like that poor bastard, either," he rasped, taking a deep drag on the cigarette he held between his thumb and forefinger.

Laughing softly under her breath, she said, "Keep

going through women faster than a gigolo, but you know your day is coming."

His dark brows lifted. "Oh, yeah? You know something I don't, lass?"

"I know you can't run from fate." She shook her head, and her voice got softer. "Even one that scares the hell out of you."

"I'm not scared of anything," he muttered, blowing out a sharp stream of smoke.

Her cryptic smile made chills race across his skin. "Well, boyo," she whispered, mimicking his lilting accent. "You should be."

* * * * *

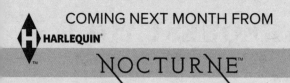
#175 THE VAMPIRE HUNTER

In the Company of Vampires

Michele Hauf

Kaspar Rothstein is determined to find the witch responsible for manufacturing Magic Dust, a substance that can drive vampires insane. When Kaspar rescues a witch from a vampire attack, he instantly falls in love with her bright blue eyes and quirky strength. Until he realizes she may be the very witch he has been searching for....

#176 MOON RISING

Lori Devoti

The vampire-werewolf war has been over for sixty years, but now someone wants to stir it back up. Marc Delacroix, a vampire, and CeCe Parks, a werewolf, must forget their differences and work together to find a lost treasure and solve multiple murders. Along the way, they discover much more about the werewolves, the vampires...and the rebellious longings of their hearts than they ever thought possible.

HNCNM1213

REQUEST YOUR FREE BOOKS!

2 FREE NOVELS FROM THE PARANORMAL ROMANCE COLLECTION PLUS 2 FREE GIFTS!

YES! Please send me 2 FREE novels from the Paranormal Romance Collection and my 2 FREE gifts (gifts are worth about $10). After receiving them, if I don't wish to receive any more books, I can return the shipping statement marked "cancel." If I don't cancel, I will receive 4 brand-new novels every month and be billed just $22.76 in the U.S. or $23.96 in Canada. That's a savings of at least 17% off the cover price of all 4 books. It's quite a bargain! Shipping and handling is just 50¢ per book in the U.S. and 75¢ per book in Canada.* I understand that accepting the 2 free books and gifts places me under no obligation to buy anything. I can always return a shipment and cancel at any time. Even if I never buy another book, the two free books and gifts are mine to keep forever.

237/337 HDN F4YC

Name	(PLEASE PRINT)
Address	Apt. #
City	State/Prov.	Zip/Postal Code

Signature (if under 18, a parent or guardian must sign)

Mail to the **Harlequin® Reader Service:**
IN U.S.A.: P.O. Box 1867, Buffalo, NY 14240-1867
IN CANADA: P.O. Box 609, Fort Erie, Ontario L2A 5X3

Want to try two free books from another line?
Call 1-800-873-8635 or visit www.ReaderService.com.

* Terms and prices subject to change without notice. Prices do not include applicable taxes. Sales tax applicable in N.Y. Canadian residents will be charged applicable taxes. Offer not valid in Quebec. This offer is limited to one order per household. Not valid for current subscribers to Paranormal Romance Collection or Harlequin® Nocturne™ books. All orders subject to credit approval. Credit or debit balances in a customer's account(s) may be offset by any other outstanding balance owed by or to the customer. Please allow 4 to 6 weeks for delivery. Offer available while quantities last.

Your Privacy—The Harlequin® Reader Service is committed to protecting your privacy. Our Privacy Policy is available online at www.ReaderService.com or upon request from the Harlequin Reader Service.

We make a portion of our mailing list available to reputable third parties that offer products we believe may interest you. If you prefer that we not exchange your name with third parties, or if you wish to clarify or modify your communication preferences, please visit us at www.ReaderService.com/consumerchoice or write to us at Harlequin Reader Service Preference Service, P.O. Box 9062, Buffalo, NY 14269. Include your complete name and address.

PARA13R

THE VAMPIRE HUNTER
by Michele Hauf

"Go!" Kaz shouted at the woman who had stumbled upon his
fight against four vampires.

"Impressive." Strangely, she clapped, giving him due reward.
"Like a knight who fights for his mistress's favor."

Kaz arched a brow. Why hadn't she screamed and run? That
was the normal MO for unknowing humans who stumbled
onto a slaying.

Something is wrong with this chick.

As he looked her over, he dashed out his tongue, taking a long
stroll over her black hair, streaked on one side with white. Her
heart-shaped face was shadowed by the night. And that mouth.
All pink and partly open and—he swallowed—kissable.

"Generally," she said, unaware of his distraction, "when the
knight defeats the bad guys, his mistress grants him a favor,
such as a ribbon for him to proudly display."

He rubbed his jaw and chuckled softly. "I'm not much for
ribbons. Guess that means I'll have to take something more
fitting."

Kaz wrapped his hand about her neck and curved his fingers
against her silken hair as he bent to kiss her distracting mouth.

About them, the vampires showed no sign of coming to, yet he remained aware.

Their lips crushed, compelled to one another. Soft and wanting. The burn of her mouth against his flamed his tongue with the sweetest fire. Made him feel alive.

He'd never kissed a woman who felt quite so…right.

When he pulled from the kiss to dart a look back and forth between her blue eyes, he suddenly *knew*. Destined? People didn't just stumble into another's person's life randomly.

Everything happened for a reason.

"Once more?" he asked on an aching tone.

This time when she tilted up her face to meet him, she moaned into the kiss and wrapped both hands about his waist. This woman fit him, as no other woman had fit before. Felt right. Felt different.

Felt dangerous.

"I…" she began. A sweet smile struggled with uncertainty. She shrugged her fingers through her loose sweep of hair. "Suddenly don't know how to walk away from you."

He'd like to wrap her in his arms and take her home with him and leave the world behind. Unfortunately, the real world had begun to groan near his feet.

"What's your name?" she asked.

"Kaspar Rothstein. Kaz to friends and those I tend to kiss. And you?"

"Zoë. Uh, Zoë to friends and those who tend to kiss me."

At that moment, he fell, right into her stunning blue eyes and lush pink smile.

**Don't miss the dramatic conclusion to
THE VAMPIRE HUNTER by Michele Hauf.
Available January 2014,
only from Harlequin® Nocturne™.**

HNEXP1213

HARLEQUIN®
NOCTURNE™

Will it be love or loyalty?

The discovery of lost treasure imperils the fragile peace between the vampire and werewolf populations— especially when werewolf Cece Parks and vampire Marc Delacroix arrive at the remote site with the same agenda—to claim the loot. But when suspicious deaths begin occurring, the enemies must band together.

The truth proves far more complicated than either group can imagine—particularly when Marc finds himself inexplicably drawn to Cece. Now loyalty to his race and his forbidden desire are about to collide….

MOON RISING

by

LORI DEVOTI

**Available January 2014,
only from Harlequin® Nocturne™.**

www.Harlequin.com

HN88588

Love the Harlequin book you just read?

Your opinion matters.

Review this book on your favorite
book site, review site, blog or your own
social media properties and share
your opinion with other readers!